The
spra
yard
drau
even the house. All the water was pumped in the yard and was heated in coppers and carried up and down stairs and passages.

One never arrived at Foxholes to a blank shut door and a pealing bell; visitors, heralded by the squeak of the gate, were always greeted on the weedy drive before the front door. And here they all were, Sue with her curls flying, Grandmother with a rare smile, Father waving his hat, and her mother, so small and white, holding a mass of starched frills and shawls which was the new brother.

Marinda jumped down. She did not know whom to kiss first, and she stood still for a moment looking with choosing eyes at the welcoming faces.

'I can read,' she said.

Also in Hamlyn Paperbacks
by Margaret Maddocks

DANCE BAREFOOT

THE OPEN DOOR

MARGARET MADDOCKS

'Fair shines the day on the house with the open door'
Robert Louis Stevenson

Hamlyn Paperbacks

THE OPEN DOOR

ISBN 0 600 33735 9

First published in Great Britain 1952
by Hurst & Blackett Ltd

Hamlyn Paperbacks edition 1980

Hamlyn Paperbacks are published by
The Hamlyn Publishing Group Ltd,
Astronaut House,
Feltham, Middlesex, England

(Paperback Division: Hamlyn Paperbacks,
Banda House, Cambridge Grove,
Hammersmith, London W6 0LE)

Printed and bound in Great Britain by
©ollins, Glasgow

For Joyce and Jack

CONTENTS

Book One

Book Two

Book Three

Book Four

Book One

Chapter 1 — THE NEW BOOK

Three important things happened to Marinda Fairfield when she was six years old. She learnt to read, her brother Andrew was born, and Queen Victoria died. She always thought of these events in that order of importance and in after years it seemed to her that they all happened at once. With one of those blinding flashes of first memory, she could always see herself as she was in 1901, a fair child, with a look of delicacy which prevented her from being pretty, but gave her a fragile attraction. She was not, however, as delicate as she looked, in spite of the fact that the two brothers and one sister born between her elder sister Sue and herself had died. Rather, her pallor was the result of the inherent fineness of her skin and the over-anxiousness of a mother who had lost three babies in six years.

'Marinda,' called her aunt's voice from the dark well of the stairs, 'Marinda, child, where are you?'

Marinda slid off the wooden chest on the landing where she had been sitting, pretending that she could read the new book which Edward Stonebridge, one of her uncle's apprentices, had bought her.

'Oh, there you are,' said her aunt, putting her finger along the ridge of her corsets as if to give herself a little space. 'Well, child, your poor mother has had a little baby – a boy – only six pounds, but quite strong.'

Marinda was only vaguely conscious of a noise below in the street because she was filled with great joy, not so much about the baby, but because she wanted to go home again to Foxholes, to the noisy warmth of the nursery, the bristly cheek of her father when she kissed him in the morning, to the smell of Bessie's ironing and her mother's baking. She even wanted to hear, because it was familiar, the stern voice of her grandmother.

She said, with the tactless honesty of childhood: 'Oh, please! May I go home – at once – now?'

Her Aunt Emma loved children with the passion of the

childless. She had offered to have her sister's younger girl 'when the time came' and had given herself endless pains to make the child's stay pleasant, altering her rigid routine, icing cakes and dressing dolls. Marinda's words ran through her heart like a sword and gave sharpness to her voice. 'Of course you can't go home yet. No one can do with you at home just now. The new baby makes a lot of work.'

'Sue is at home,' argued Marinda mulishly. For all her air of fragility there was a rocklike determination about her which made her in later years a woman of character, but which was at six years old considered to be obstinacy.

'Sue is older and can make herself useful,' said her aunt. 'And don't read any more until I have lit the lamps. You will try your eyes.'

Marinda dropped the book on the chest and prepared to wait in the half light for the darkness before which her aunt thought it was extravagant to light the lamps. The new gas lamps in the shop were already lit, for Marinda could see the reflection warming the pavement below as the door opened and shut. Her aunt turned to go, defeated by the sudden docility of her niece. From the stairs leading to the ground floor of store-rooms and shop came a confusion of voices, and then her husband appeared at the bottom with the *Marchampton Evening Journal* in his hand.

'Oh, George,' called his wife, 'Belle has had a son. Mr Frisby drove in and left a message.'

But her husband had news of his own and he hardly listened to her.

'The old Queen is dead,' he said, waving the black-bordered paper.

His wife still thought her tidings were more important, and she went on: 'Six pounds. Belle is very tired, but she is all right, poor girl. I shall go over with the carrier on Saturday.'

Her husband shouted up the stairs almost at the same time: 'She was over eighty. So now we have a king. She was on the throne when I was born. So Belle has a son. Well, she wanted a boy.'

He turned and walked back down the long, dark passage

to the shop, muttering to himself, 'It will be queer to say "God save the King" – very queer.'

To Marinda, sitting back on the chest with her legs dangling, the birth of her brother seemed inextricably mixed with the death of the Queen, and she knew nothing of the mysteries of birth and death. Her grandmother's dog had died and babies were often born. She pondered for a moment on what it might mean. Her aunt, in a fit of absentmindedness, caused by two great events, had lit the lamp half an hour before time. Eagerly Marinda picked up her book and spelled out the words under the pictures. *'Rose loved her cat very much.'* Suddenly, in a flash of comprehension which almost blinded her, she realized that she could read – not just words like 'cat' and 'mat', for she had been able to do that for a long time, but whole lines. A world of nothing but books and reading seemed miraculously before her. She read on, turning the pages with a feeling of power and wisdom until her aunt came to fetch her for bed.

'I can read,' she said. 'Isn't it wonderful? Oh, Aunt, isn't it lovely? I can read properly.'

'Bless the child! There's no need to get so excited. There's nothing so clever in reading and it's a great waste of time.'

She undressed the excited child and made her say her prayers, with an appendix for the new brother, before she sank into the enfolding billows of the second-best feather bed. A candle was generally left flickering on the dressing-table, for the bedroom was a long way from the parlour and Emma South did not want the child to be frightened.

'May I read for a little while?' asked Marinda.

'Indeed, no,' answered her aunt, folding up a flannel petticoat, a cotton petticoat, a chemise and a pair of drawers and laying them neatly on a chair. 'You go to sleep and dream about your dear little brother.'

But Marinda did not want to think of her baby brother. He was all mixed up with the Queen who was dead like Granny's dog. She wanted to read, and as soon as her aunt's footsteps died away she jumped out of bed and fetched her book from the chest of drawers, but she found she could not see and she dared not move the candle from the dressing-table, with its fringed mats and painted china trays and ring stands. So, with her book under her pillow, she lay watching the shadows on the ceiling, thinking how clever she was and longing for the morning.

The chemist's shop of George South was on the corner of West Gate and Castle Street and from its doors one could see almost all that went on in Marchampton except the discreetly separate life which was screened from the vulgar vigour of the town by the walls of the Cathedral Precincts and King Henry's School. The town beyond the Market Cross was out of bounds for the boys, whose speckled straw hats were only seen on the occasions when their parents brought them to Brush's Tea Rooms for enormous teas, and the clergy seldom strayed beyond the West Gate. Many secrets of these secluded haunts were known to George South as soon as Dr Grieg wrote the prescriptions which Edward Stonebridge and James Keith, the apprentices, had such difficulty in deciphering in the dark cubby-hole labelled 'Dispensary'. Every pill was pounded in the pestle and coated with sugar by Edward Stonebridge – every cachet was measured with frowns by George South himself. He knew that the Archdeacon's wife was costive, when old Lord Marchampton's gout was troubling him again, and that young Mrs Sheldwich was expecting.

At the same time George South kept himself slightly aloof from the other tradesmen in the town. In the rigid strata of a small town in the late nineteenth century he and his father had occupied a niche which set them apart, or so they thought, from people like Tom Cox, the butcher, and Jeremiah Daventry, the cornchandler. People said George South was 'a character' because he had a passion for old china and read the New Testament in its original Greek. He often prescribed himself with reckless assurance to people too poor to pay Dr Grieg's fees. He knew that he was better educated, largely through his own inner stirrings, than his fellow tradesmen in Marchampton, but this filled him not so much with a feeling of superiority as with a sense of difference.

His wife made herself a cheerful circle of people such as Mrs Tom Cox and Jeremiah Daventry's sister Margaret, who kept house for him, and the young Lintotts, who had taken over the drapery stores in Market Street. Disappointment over her childlessness and the uncongenial tastes of her husband had sharpened her tongue, but she was sentimental and kind-hearted and in great demand at missionary sales and Band of Hope teas.

It was this unexpected softness which led her to show such kindness to Edward Stonebridge. The younger apprentice, James Keith, lived in Marchampton with his parents, and the few hours when he was not pounding pills or polishing bottles in the shop he spent at his home. But Edward came from a far-away village on the Welsh borders and his widowed mother had lately died, so that when Emma South offered him the comfort of the parlour for his free time she was doing more than she need have done for an apprentice who 'lived in'. He was a thin, awkward youth of nineteen who ate enormously of the good food which Emma and Jinny, the general maid, cooked for them in the dark kitchen by the store-rooms.

To Marinda, used to the light rooms at Foxholes with their low windows reaching to the ground and the front door open except in very bad weather, the darkness of her aunt's home made her afraid. She hated, almost without knowing that she did so, the menacing walls of the neighbouring buildings and thought longingly of the wide lawn in front of the morning-room at home with nothing but a row of poplars at the end of the field to come between them and the blue humps of the Marchampton Hills ten miles away. She was not old enough to realize that this view was one of the most beautiful in all England. To her, at six years old, it meant, as it was always to mean, her home.

When her brother was two weeks old she lay propped up on her elbows reading by the light of the fire, waiting for Jinny to arrive with the silver teapot, for it was Sunday, and tea was laid on the round table in the parlour. The best Rockingham tea service, a seed cake, a plum cake, two sorts of jam with spoons laid at a coy distance from their glass dishes, and acres of thin bread-and-butter, white, brown and currant-spotted. Edward Stonebridge came down from his room with his finger in a book, glorious in a high collar and button boots. George South was called from the dining-room, where he had been sleeping off the effects of roast duck, and his wife came up from the kitchen where she had been unlocking the jam for the feast. She had found some with signs of mould and the vexation of it did not leave her. She felt defied by the mould and she talked almost to herself about it while she tied Marinda's pinafore and poured out the tea.

Marinda slipped into her place by the side of Edward and kept her book upon her knee.

'Marinda,' called her aunt sharply, 'put that book away at once.'

'Mr Stonebridge has a book. I saw it,' argued Marinda with a tilt of her chin.

Emma prayed silently that the child might not defy her, and Edward put his hand over the pocket where his book lay and his pale face blushed with guilt.

'Don't argue,' said Emma. 'It's a very ugly habit in a little girl. Put the book away at once.'

George South picked up his plate and looked lovingly at its colourings. It was a service which he had bought years ago at a sale and using it always gave him pleasure. He adjusted his steel-rimmed spectacles and ran his fingers over the gilt edge, appreciating the warmth of the glaze, completely cut off by his thoughts from the dramatic atmosphere of Marinda's defiance. For the child's fingers were tightly pressed on the binding of the book and there was a dangerous blaze in her aunt's eyes, which was somehow incongruous with her air of inexperienced helplessness.

'Look, Marinda,' said Edward, 'your book can stay with my book until after tea.'

He took it gently from her, and as her small fingers uncurled from her treasure her mouth melted back into its childish softness. Her aunt sighed deeply and her uncle said, as he had done almost every Sunday for the past ten years, 'That tea service was a bargain.'

The bread-and-butter circulated and Mr Stonebridge said he would prefer quince jelly to strawberry jam. The air had cleared.

Since Marinda had learnt to read she had spent every

spare minute with, as Jinny put it, 'her nose in a book'. When she ran out of the few children's books in the house she started on other forms of literature. For one whole day she had driven everyone mad by dragging the Family Bible round the house, pretending she was the parson by reading it aloud. As her uncle opened the daily paper she stood by his side and spelt out the headlines in such deadly earnest that no one dared to correct her mispronunciations.

'Cat-as-trophy in mine.'

'Akcident to doctor's niece.'

'Seducked girl's suikide.' She read slowly, demanding to know the meaning of every word until her uncle was forced to fold up the paper and wait until she had gone to bed before he could read it himself.

It was then that Jinny, who had witnessed her new accomplishment, bought her *Brave Nelly, or Weak Hands and a Willing Heart,* a touching story, alleged to be fit for a child's gentle mind, of a poor ragged girl with a gin-sodden father, whom she converted in the last chapter but one, by reciting texts, and refusing to fetch the gin, before dying in the final chapter. It was this masterpiece which Edward now took back and placed in the pocket of his best blue suit.

'What are they going to call the baby brother?' he asked, changing the subject, while Emma looked at him gratefully.

'Andrew George,' answered Marinda. 'When I go home he is to be christened. Aunt Emma, when do I go home?'

The child made it so plain that she was only in Marchampton on sufferance, and all the blackcurrant pastilles from her uncle's tin in the shop and the treats which her aunt tried to arrange could never comfort her for the absence of her mother and father and Sue and Bessie and the dogs, and even her grandmother.

Her mother had not recovered from this baby very quickly and there had been moments of anxiety which had been concealed from Marinda, but the air of mystery only frightened her and she was now convinced that everything at home would stay safe only so long as she was there.

'Henry says he could take her back next market day if Belle is well enough, or send Jeff Oldham,' announced

Mrs South, trying not to care that Marinda's eyes were shining with excitement. 'If I had children of my own, it would not be so,' she thought bitterly, dreaming of the perfections of her unborn family.

'How many days is it until market day?' asked Marinda.

'If you have finished, Marinda,' said her aunt, ignoring her question, 'you may have your book back. Say your grace first.'

Marinda piously folded her hands and said an incantation which she knew had to come at the end of a meal before she could leave the table. Edward took the book out of his pocket and promised to come and play Ludo as soon as he had drunk his second cup.

'Do have another piece of cake, Mr Stonebridge, you are so thin,' wailed Emma, who felt that the apprentice's knobby elbows and thin wrists were a reflection on her catering.

Edward refused, as was only polite, but, upon the inevitable pressure, he quickly changed his mind. He was very fond of Mrs South's plum cake.

Two market days went by before Jeff Oldham came to fetch Marinda. The drawn-out days of childhood had dragged by, rain-spattered and wintry, before Marinda sat in the governess car with its speckled cushions, looking at Prince's shining black rump moving up and down with delightful rhythm, and watching, with her usual half-fearful interest, the reins wound round the hook which was Jeff's left hand. She wished her father had come to meet her. He would have let her drive Prince part of the way and not make her walk up Grassy Hill. But then he would also not have driven so fast down the other side, which brought them to the valley where the low roofs of Foxholes lay comfortably in its pastures with the river running down, swiftly at first from the March Hills, and then more placidly in and out of the meadows, until it joined the Severn above Marchampton.

Ahead of them, for the last six miles, lay the familiar outline of the March Hills, rising suddenly from the plain and dropping as suddenly again the other side, and looking for all the world like some monstrous animal crouching there. As soon as Marinda saw the familiar outline her heart lifted and she felt as if the front door of her home had opened to welcome her. All her life the sight of these hills seen on end from the train, as it rounded the curve into Marchampton, or emerging gradually out of the mist of distance on the road from London, was to affect her with this curious feeling of welcome and safety.

She thought of Mr Stonebridge and the book he had given her. She had been jumping about in the passage waiting for Jeff to drive into the yard of the Castle Inn opposite, when Edward came out quickly from the shop, looking over his shoulder anxiously as if he were a schoolboy playing truant.

'I have brought you a present, Marinda,' he said. 'I think perhaps soon you will be able to read it.'

'I can read now,' said Marinda importantly, peering past his legs so that she should not miss the sight of Jeff's arrival.

'And, Marinda,' said Mr Stonebridge in a voice that was half a whisper, 'when you leave your aunt, say that you are a little bit sorry.'

'But I am not sorry. I am as glad as glad. I want to go home. It is much nicer there.'

She looked up at him with her bright truthful eyes and he could not find words to explain that he knew her childish callousness hurt her aunt's feelings. He did not even know how he was aware of this.

'Your Aunt Emma is a good, kind aunt and she has no little girl of her own,' he said, adding, 'try not to hurt her feelings.'

She did not know what he meant at first and then, with a burst of comprehension, she knew that she must be sorry for Aunt Emma. She was sorry for the monkey which came down Castle Street with the barrel-organ. She had cried most of one day when Buttercup's calf had been taken away last year. Her father had said she had made more fuss over it than Buttercup – and there was pig-killing. Somehow Aunt Emma did not belong to these things, but she wanted to please Mr Stonebridge because he had given her something to read.

Her aunt had come down to stow her away in the

governess car with her little wicker basket and a bottle of physic for her mother and a new doll. They had all come out from the shop. Her uncle, the two apprentices, and a skinny child who was always known as 'The Boy'. Jinny, too, was standing by, taking a peek at Jeff. She was not frightened by his hook. It was surprising, she giggled, what he could do with it.

Marinda was sitting up in the corner opposite Jeff.

'I am sorry to be going, Aunt Emma,' she said.

Edward Stonebridge had smiled at her, thinking uneasily that he had taught a naturally truthful person to lie. Her aunt had hugged her delightedly, saying: 'Are you, darling? We shall miss you. Shan't we miss her, George?' And suddenly Marinda had found that she really was sorry to be going.

'I am sorry, I am sorry,' she kept saying as Jeff pulled and jerked the reins and clicked his tongue and the car moved jerkily across the cobbles and Prince edged gingerly into the traffic.

'Bless the little dear,' said Jinny, her eyes on Jeff.

They were all standing on the pavement, waving until Marinda's red bonnet disappeared through the West Gate and George South discovered to his horror that Canon Lane had been waiting unattended in the shop for nearly five minutes.

Marinda opened the book when she was waiting outside Farley Post Office and General Stores while Jeff went in to fetch the paraffin, and when Miss Finch came out to speak to her and to give her a humbug she was happily stroking the bright blue covers of *The Wide, Wide World*.

She took a humbug and said 'Thank you', as she had been taught, and then, anchoring the sweet with difficulty on one side of her small mouth, she said, 'I can read now, Miss Finch.'

'Eh, can you now?' said Miss Finch. 'Then you'll soon be knowing everything.'

'Yes,' agreed Marinda happily.

'Well, that's very clever, I'm sure.'

Jeff jerked the reins and Marinda felt suddenly as if she loved Miss Finch very much. She loved Miss Finch and Farley and everything she saw, as they turned down the steep lane by the church to Foxholes. Most of all she loved coming home. Everything about her felt soft with joy.

Foxholes Farm was the last morsel of a small estate which had belonged to Henry Fairfield's forebears. The big house, Fairfield Manor, and the other farm across the river had been sold in his father's day to pay his debts. Henry could never quite forget that his ancestors had sat in the squire's pew at Farley Church and that the North transept was furnished with long descriptions of the virtues of the Fairfields cut through the centuries on their memorial tablets – Jane Fairfield and her seven daughters; Mary Belinda Fairfield, wife of Henry and their infant daughter; Anne, wife of William of the parish of Upton St George – they were all there to remind him on Sundays of past glories.

He had farmed Foxholes since his father's death and had married a farmer's daughter; her father had been one of his father's tenants, but he never quite considered that he himself was a farmer pure and simple, which was one of the reasons why he made so little money. He hunted twice a week in the winter, held shooting parties in the autumn and fished in the swift brown water of the Brene. On Sundays he walked with pride round his fields. But too much at Foxholes, said his neighbours, was left to Jeff Oldham.

The farmhouse was not big, but it lay sprawling across the garden and foldyard with the two rooms added in 1820 by William, father of fourteen children, and a bow window added by Henry's father, who wished to improve his drawing-room and so succeeded in spoiling the south-east front. Except for these additions the façade was the black and white of Marchshire. In 1901 no one considered it to be architecturally interesting or even beautiful. It was a homely but inconvenient farmhouse, draughty, ill-lit, with no bathroom or even a tap inside the house. Primitive sanitation was hidden in shrubby corners. All the water was pumped in the yard and was heated in coppers and carried up and down stairs and passages.

If the Fairfields were blind to its architectural charms, which were in a later era to cause people to exclaim at its crisp black and white beams half covered with wisteria and honeysuckle, so were they blind, or used, to its deficiencies. As Jeff opened the wrought-iron gate while Marinda held the reins, the squeak it gave, which was the sign at Foxholes of an approaching visitor, brought the whole family spilling eagerly from the house. One never arrived at Foxholes to a blank shut door and a pealing bell; visitors, heralded by its squeak, were always greeted on the weedy drive before the front door. And here they all were, Sue with her curls flying, Grandmother with a rare smile, Father from the field, waving his hat, Bessie with her floury hands and a backward glance to her baking, Jim and Frank from the yard, leaning on pitchforks, and her mother, so small and white, holding a mass of starched frills and shawls which was the new brother.

Marinda jumped down. The dogs sprang up and licked her face as she held her book high above their leaping bodies. She felt so happy and excited, something inside her seemed to be bursting. All round her were the people she loved, who made her world and kept her safe. She did not know whom to kiss first, and she stood still for a moment looking with choosing eyes at the welcoming faces.

'I can read,' she said.

Chapter 2 — THE CHRISTENING

Andrew George did not receive his names officially until August. In spite of the fact that he was a lusty though small baby, he was treated by everyone as if he might splinter at a fierce glance, and it was not until August that his mother and grandmother considered the air had warmed sufficiently for him to be dowsed with water at the font of Farley church. By August he could and did spring about in everyone's arms like a fish in a net.

'You must have him christened before he can walk, Belle,' said old Mrs Fairfield, 'or there will be no peace for anyone.'

Belle remembered quickly that James and Henry, the twins, and Jessie Ann had all been christened correctly at six weeks and had shortly afterwards been hidden by sad little mounds in the churchyard. She could hardly believe her eyes when she looked at Andrew, fat and imperious, keeping the whole household in a continual state of activity on his behalf.

'Marinda, see if Andrew is asleep.'

'Sue, tell Bessie I want some hot water.'

'Henry, I think Buttercup's milk is better than Glory's. Will you see that Jim brings it in for Andrew?'

'Mother, do you think you could do the embroidery for Andrew's pelisse? You do it so much better than I do.'

He was all the more precious because Belle had been told that she must have no more children. She had told no one about this. It had not even been mentioned between herself and her husband, though old Dr Brickett had promised her he would 'talk to him'. She felt a little puzzled and ashamed as to how this might be achieved, but she had had six children in twelve years and was relieved that it was to end.

With Fate's usual injustice, Andrew was much more beautiful than either of the girls. His hair was as fair as Marinda's, but already it curled in entrancing rolls, while hers hung like skeins of fine silk, straight and unmanageable. Sue had curls, tight ringlets, which never seemed to grow any longer, but her hair was a nondescript colour and her turned-up button of a nose and small bright eyes, which gave her in later years the pert attraction of a kitten, were considered hideous when one compared them with Andrew's blue eyes and perfect features.

'He is exactly like his Grandfather Fairfield,' said old Mrs Fairfield proudly.

'His eyes,' said Belle defiantly, 'are like my family's. No Fairfield that I ever met had blue eyes.'

'Blue eyes reproduce themselves very easily,' asserted her mother-in-law. 'If there are blue eyes in a family it's impossible to keep them out.' She dismissed 'blue eyes' as if they were Andrew's only bad feature. 'The shape of his head, his hair, his curls are pure Fairfield.'

Belle put her hand to the fringe net which kept her usually straight hair in the kinks and coils induced by a night in curlers, and could not but agree.

'It's a pity,' said Mrs Fairfield, 'that Marinda has your hair.'

Marinda, lying on the lawn with her long hair tangled from a game of hide-and-seek, wished suddenly she could cut her hair off so that it would not have to be jerked and combed by Lucy until the tears ran down her face. She tickled Andrew's nose with a pigeon's feather which she had found. At first he smiled, a great toothless smile. She was delighted and let the feather explore his ears and the back of his neck. Then the feather accidentally whipped the corner of his eye and his mouth became a square and he began to roar. Marinda could not bear to see him cry. She hugged him and he pulled at a handful of her hair so that she, too, screamed. There was sudden pandemonium. Sue and his mother and grandmother rushed to comfort the baby. After a time he condescended to calm down and Marinda, hiccuping faintly, was fetched by Lucy and sent to bed half an hour early, while Andrew rode a cock-horse on his grandmother's knee.

From the day he was born he was outrageously spoilt. Everyone in the house fought for his favours and he had only to lift his voice to have his own way. His sisters were convinced that no baby was as beautiful or as wonderful as their brother, and Marinda became jealous, not of him, according to later textbooks of psychology, but of Sue, who, being twelve, was allowed to dress him and push the pram, and even on occasions to bath him. He was to them the perfect substitute for a doll.

Belle's cousin, Fan Trent, who had come from London for the christening and was to be his godmother, was not so impressed.

'He's a perfect little tyrant,' she exclaimed when she found it was impossible to keep her cousin's attention for more than three minutes unless Andrew also approved. 'I should just let him yell.'

'Don't be barbarous,' retorted Belle. 'He might have a pain.'

'Not he, bless him,' said Fan acidly. 'Now tell me about my co-godparents. I hope they are both eligible bachelors.'

'I'm sure I don't know what you want with eligible

bachelors. I thought you were really engaged properly this time.'

'I was engaged properly last time and the time before that. There's nothing improper about my engagements, I assure you.' She paused and laughed. 'Except, of course, that they are rather numerous.'

'That's what I mean,' said Belle anxiously. 'Sue darling, run off and help Lucy get the things ready for Andrew's bath. You'd like to see him bathed, wouldn't you?'

'I should love it,' answered Fan, with an amount of emphasis which took the sincerity out of her words. 'I expect the little darling will splash me all over. You've not told me yet who his godparents are.'

Belle was still pondering on Fan's last words. She could not imagine that anyone could forgo the delight of seeing Andrew in his bath. It was the great moment of the day and yet there was a touch of scorn in Fan's voice.

'Oh! The godparents? I'm afraid, except for you, they are rather dull. We used up all the good ones on the others. The new vicar, Mr Lorimer, is one.'

Fan looked interested.

'He is married,' said Belle hastily, 'and has two children. And the other one is young Mr Stonebridge. He is George's apprentice and George has taken a great fancy to him. He has just passed his exams and has done very well, got honours or something. Anyhow, George was very pleased and now he is going into the business. His mother died last year and left him a little money. Didn't Emma tell you about him?'

'Perhaps she did. I don't remember. We don't write very often. It's my fault. I never was one for letters. What sort of a young man is he besides being very worthy?'

'He is nineteen,' said Belle decidedly, as if being nineteen prevented him from having any other qualities.

Fan laughed. 'And I am twenty-eight. Well, even at nineteen –' And then she laughed again at Belle's shocked face.

Marinda, who had been lying on a rug under the cedar tree reading *The Swiss Family Robinson,* flung away the grass she had been chewing and followed her mother and her aunt into the house. She found her aunt exciting and that whenever she was there the grown-ups' conversation became mysterious, with nods and winks and sentences in what passed in the Fairfield household for French.

Grandmother made remarks about little pitchers and Sue and Marinda were always being sent off on errands just as the topic became absorbing. Bessie said 'Miss Fan was a gay one', and that's what she was, thought Marinda, who was beginning to think of words and consider them and their meaning. 'Gay' meant Aunt Fan's charm bracelet jingling as she played *The Blue Danube,* and her skirts swishing as she ran up the stairs, and her voice calling from her bedroom, 'Come along, poppets, and see the new frocks I have brought for you.' It also meant the laughter that floated up from the garden after the children were in bed and Aunt Fan singing duets with Mr Lorimer in spite of his wife and two children and Edward Stonebridge, who was only nineteen.

'I think I must be very unnatural,' said Fan after the ceremony of the bath was over and the imperious Andrew was being sung to sleep by Sue, it being her turn for this much valued duty. 'Of course, I know Andrew is a lovely baby, but I don't really feel about him the way you all do.'

Fan saw in her mind's eyes Andrew, king-like in his bath in the nursery, watched by an admiring audience of everyone in the house. Even Bessie took a moment off from her preparations for the christening feast to worship quickly at the shrine. But Fan had balanced herself on the fireguard, giving little jumps to be out of the way of Andrew's splashes. Now that he was in bed at last she experienced a sense of release. He took the stage which she was used to occupying.

She pulled Marinda towards her.

'Now at this age,' said Fan, 'I do like them. They are beginning to be interesting.'

'Oh, of course,' agreed Belle. She did not dare to say that she had loved all her children most when they were small and helpless and the ones who had died remained perfections of love and loveliness in her memory.

Marinda's hair was caught back with a band of bone, so that she looked a little like the illustrations to *Alice in*

Wonderland. Her mother took it off gently and began to brush her hair. A hundred strokes every night it had to be, but tonight no one counted, for both Belle and Marinda were listening to Aunt Fan, as one always did. Somehow Fan had the talent of making her own views and adventures sound as important to others as they were to herself.

'Oh, I shall marry in good time,' she was saying. 'Though I don't know that I even want to be married at all.'

Belle was shocked. Fan as a permanent spinster was unthinkable – even dangerous.

'All the men I meet are so dull,' complained Fan. 'I need someone who will make me laugh most of the time and beat me if I annoy him. They're all so meek and silly – pining away and being sorry and letting me walk over them.'

'Even Guy?'

'Most of all Guy,' said Fan decidedly, and Belle did not dare to ask when Fan and Guy Hale were going to be married, because she feared the answer. She went on brushing Marinda's hair, letting its silky strands run through her fingers, thinking that she wanted nothing more wonderful than her own life at Foxholes. She was so content with an unreasoning and unquestioning happiness since Andrew's birth, that she wished everyone to share it.

Marinda was soothed, too, by the rhythmic strokes of the brush. Through the open door she could hear Lucy putting away the bath and Sue's voice singing bravely through her repertoire, from *There's a friend for little children* to *Nelly Bly*. It was a moment of the day when everything seemed tidy and cosy.

'Why don't you give the child a fringe?' suggested Fan. 'Her forehead's much too high. Look . . .'

She pulled back Marinda's hair, and the child, jolted out of another peaceful world, edged away.

'Come here, I am going to make you look much prettier,' coaxed Aunt Fan. She bunched Marinda's hair across her wide high brow. 'Now she doesn't look so hideously clever. Give me the scissors, Belle.'

'I don't know . . .' began Belle, looking from Fan to

Marinda with dubious fascination, but she produced the scissors and in five minutes Marinda had a fringe.

'Let me look,' said Marinda. 'I want to look.'

'Wait a moment,' said Aunt Fan, brushing the fringe so that it looked like a pale gold cap.

'There – you look quite pretty.'

Marinda went to the mirror and tiptoed so that she could see herself. She looked so strange that she felt she was probably another person. She turned round and smiled at her mother and her aunt, feeling that she was now so good and pretty that she would never be in trouble again.

'It is an improvement,' admitted her mother. 'You do have smart ideas, Fan. I suppose it is living in London. Come and say "Good night" to Grandma, child.'

Marinda was so happy because she was now really pretty that she hopped all the way down the passage to her grandmother's sitting-room. Aunt Fan followed her, snapping the scissors, anxious for praise from the old lady, with whom she was often out of favour.

'Fan has given Marinda a fringe,' said Belle, as Marinda ran in to give her grandmother a kiss.

Old Mrs Fairfield held the kiss at bay by holding Marinda at arm's length to inspect her face. She looked severely at Fan.

'You've made the child even plainer than before,' she said with the heartlessness of old age, as if Marinda were deaf and feelingless. 'She never was a beauty,' went on the relentless old voice, 'and now she looks vulgar. You would have done better to have left well alone, Fan. Good night, child.'

But Marinda could not speak. It was as if she could not think of enough words to tell them how she hated them.

'Say good night, Marinda.'

Marinda glowered at her grandmother from under the offending fringe. She opened her mouth, but all that came out was a long scream and then tears.

'I hate you!' she yelled. 'You are ugly yourself, old and ugly.'

'Good gracious!' bristled Mrs Fairfield. 'Well . . .' She drew in a long breath with surprise, while Marinda continued to scream. 'I had a sweet for a good little girl, but now I shall give it to Sue. You want a good whipping.'

She had meant no harm, and if she had thought she had dealt Marinda's self-confidence a lasting blow she would have been hurt and amazed. At Foxholes in 1901 child psychology was not studied.

'Never mind,' said Aunt Fan, as Belle led the sobbing child to her bed. 'I think the fringe is very nice.'

She laid the scissors sorrowfully on the chest of drawers while Marinda continued to scream. Sue ran in from the nursery and said that Andrew simply couldn't go to sleep if Marinda made all that noise, and Belle and Lucy hurried off to Andrew, leaving Marinda with her breath caught with sobs.

Fan was nonplussed. Although a great favourite with children she did not like them once they became a bother. As she drew the curtains and closed the door softly behind her, Andrew's roars could be heard from the nursery.

Marinda turned over when the door closed and she had no longer an audience for her sorrow. Her eyes fell on the scissors lying on the low chest of drawers. She was not allowed to play with scissors, she knew, except the blunt ones kept for wet-day games in the nursery cupboard. But she felt so out of favour that she was given further courage for naughtiness. If she cut the fringe off, she thought she would be the old Marinda again. The scissors were hard on her small thumbs, but they were sharp, and soon a lump of the trouble-bringing fringe had gone. The point of the scissors made a small nick in her cheek from which a trickle of blood began to ooze, but Marinda was fascinated by the feel of the blades on her hair. She took, experimentally, a handful from the side and gave a snap to the scissors. The hair fell off on to the floor, leaving stray strands on her night-gown. As she was about to cut the other side Sue came in to fetch her new work-box. It would be another hour before anyone as old as Sue had to go to bed, and Andrew was at last asleep.

With the curtains drawn the light in the room was dim and Sue did not at first recognize the enormity of her sister's behaviour. She was a child who found it easy to be good and was a particular favourite with her grandmother. This and her twelve years separated her from Marinda, to whom she appeared to live over the boundary of that country where grown-ups had special unaccountable privileges.

Bessie said she was 'that old-fashioned', and Aunt Fan told Belle that her elder daughter would turn into a little prig if she didn't look out.

'What are you doing out of bed?' asked Sue severely.

Marinda dropped the scissors with a guilty jump and then Sue saw the appalling wreckage she had made. She ran out of the room and up the passage, calling, 'Mother, come, just look at Marinda!'

They all came running, Lucy from the nursery, Belle, Aunt Fan from the drawing-room, Bessie heavily up the back stairs and old Mrs Fairfield slowly out of her room. Marinda backed away from them towards the bed. Her mother lit a candle so that she could see this fearful deed. She held it high above her head, her face full of alarm and horror.

'You naughty girl! You know you mustn't have scissors,' she said, looking at the uneven shagginess of Marinda's pretty hair and the blood running down her cheek. 'You might have put your eye out. Have you cut yourself?'

'She wants a good whipping,' repeated her grandmother, whose ideas about bringing up children were few and simple.

'Yes,' agreed Belle, but without heat. She was thinking how hideous the child looked and how long it would be before her hair would grow and how she might have blinded herself. 'Of course she can't come to the christening. She isn't fit to be seen.'

Marinda couldn't believe her ears. Not go to the christening! Of course she must go to the christening. She began to stamp and took a deep breath ready to scream.

'Be quiet, Marinda,' called her grandmother sternly. She thought her daughter-in-law was altogether too easy with the children.

But Marinda had begun to scream and she found it so satisfying after all her emotions that she went on screaming. As they forced her into bed she turned quite rigid, but she did not stop screaming.

'Oh, Mother,' called Sue, 'now she has woken Andrew again!'

From the nursery came Andrew's unmistakable wail.

Belle suddenly felt defeated and exhausted. Half an hour ago her children had seemed part of a perfection hard to put into words, but now she felt unable to deal with them. They overwhelmed her. 'Let them cry,' she thought, as she sat suddenly on a chair on the landing and heard cries from both rooms.

On the morning of the christening Joe Locket, the postman, who was the unofficial barber of Farley, came up to Foxholes and trimmed Marinda's hair. In the photograph of the christening party, which was framed in rosewood and hung in the drawing-room, the head of a sad-looking boy peeped out from between Sue and Edward Stonebridge. In the years to come no one recognized this to be Marinda.

Chapter 3 — THE VISIT

'Well,' said Fan, looking up from her embroidery, 'what were they like?'

Belle took off her feather boa and unpinned the big hat from its perch on her puffs of hair, handing it to Marinda to take upstairs. Marinda ran off quickly. She wanted to get back to hear about the new neighbours, but she could not resist trying on the boa and her mother's best hat. At fourteen she was thinner than ever. Her hair, which had only lately been allowed to grow, now hung in two thick plaits to her waist and the fringe, which Fan had cut eight years before, had been allowed to persist. She wished her mother would let her wear puffs and double her hair back with a big bow, but her father liked her plaits, tugging one as if it were a bellrope whenever she passed him, and since the time 'when Marinda cut her hair' (it had become a family horror story) she had bowed to authority in the matter of styles.

'It's just as well Henry's mother is dead,' said Belle. 'I

don't know what she'd say. Just imagine, Fan, Mrs Gray is divorced. She didn't even sound ashamed.'

'Perhaps she had no need to be,' said Fan.

Belle looked at her cousin as if she did not quite understand her.

'It's so odd,' she went on. 'I quite thought she was a widow. Miss Simpson never talked about her niece much, but I quite took it that she was a widow. She has two children, she says. The boy is away at Oxford and the girl is fifteen. It's such a pity. She seemed quite nice and she would have been such a companion for Marinda.'

'Well, she still can be. Surely you don't intend to cut her out of your life because she hasn't a visible husband? It probably wasn't her fault at all. I expect he ran away with a barmaid.'

'No,' objected Belle seriously, 'it was the children's governess.'

'So she told you all about it?'

'That's what was so queer. She was quite open about it. He ran away with the governess to Paris and he never came back. And another odd thing. She writes.'

'You sound as if you think writing is as bad as divorcing,' mocked Fan.

'Well, it is all peculiar. I never met anyone before who did either, and she opened the door herself. Said that she couldn't afford a maid. She didn't try to disguise it a bit. I thought that writers made a lot of money.'

'Depends on what they write.'

'I didn't like to ask because, you see, I'd never heard of her. Reading seems such a waste of time.'

From the expression on Fan's face Belle felt that she was being mocked in a way which she could not understand. 'It's all very well for you to laugh, Fan,' she went on; 'your friends are different. You are probably used to that kind of thing. My friends . . .'

Fan interrupted her impatiently. 'You'd be surprised if you knew the private lives of your friends – even your own family.'

Fan's life had always been an exotic thing apart from anything Belle expected or comprehended. As children they had played together until Fan's father died and her mother took her to live in London. Once Belle and Emma had been to stay with her, a month which was painted in their memories in bright colours, and they had always been good friends, supplying wants in each other's characters in a manner which was refreshing to both.

'Even your own family,' repeated Fan, looking at Belle with the sleek look of a cat, with her green eyes under their long dark fringe of lashes, and Belle had a moment of misgiving. If Fan regretted that at thirty-six she was still unmarried, she never said so. Her engagement to Guy Hale had never been broken off officially, but after a year or two he faded out of her conversation and, thought Belle, now that she was mixed up with all these suffragettes no one would want her. It was such a pity.

Belle had been calling on her new neighbours.

At the gate of Foxholes was a small box of a house with a slate roof. For as long as anyone could remember it had belonged to Miss Simpson, a reserved and respected spinster who had seemed to Belle to have been about seventy for as long as she had lived there. Just when she appeared to be immortal she died, and it was generally known, though how was not certain, that the house had been left to Miss Simpson's niece. Most of the winter it stood empty, and then news circulated that Miss Simpson's niece, a Mrs Gray, and her two children were coming to live there.

The first hint the village had that the Grays were what they called a 'bit cranky' was the whitewashing. The lurid but still good papers on the walls were ordered to be whitewashed. It nearly broke Tom Payne's heart to do it, said his wife. 'And now the place looks like a cowshed.'

Belle was pleased at the thought of a neighbour roughly her own age with a young family. Her own children had few friends and there were no near neighbours apart from those in Miss Simpson's cottage. Belle took it for granted that a niece of Miss Simpson's would be what she called 'suitable' in every way, and was disconcerted and disappointed to find that Laura Gray's divorce should prevent any further friendship. For she had liked Laura. Most people did. She had a small head with her fair, greying hair wound into a knot at the nape of her neck. Belle had been attracted by her unaffected manner and slow smile, and although she realized that she couldn't possibly be friends with Laura, she found something rather piteous in her eyes as she came to the door to see Belle off. Almost automatically she had said, 'You must let me know if there is anything I can do.'

Laura thanked her sincerely as if she really meant to come to Belle if she were in trouble, and Belle realized that in spite of everything she also was sincere in her offer.

She had sighed as she walked down the path, which was half lane, half cart-track, to her home. It was indeed a pity about Laura Gray's husband.

When two weeks later Laura fainted it was Belle to whom her daughter, Carey, came running. She flew out of the cottage and up the track to Foxholes and banged on the back door, because it was the first door she saw. Marinda was showing Andrew how to fish in the waterbutt and they rushed up the stairs to fetch their mother, while Bessie, mystified, but enjoying every moment of the excitement, tried to make the terrified girl sit down and drink a glass of milk and tell her calmly what had happened.

'I gave her some water, but she looks dead,' was all Carey could say when Belle came and asked her gently if there was anything she could do to help.

'Give me the bottle of brandy, Bessie, and my smelling-salts. Marinda, fetch them from my dressing-table. Andrew, call Jim in from the yard.'

Off ran Andrew, the fat nape of his neck swelling with importance.

'Now, child, we'll hurry over and see what's to be done.'

By the time Jim had been despatched for the doctor Laura was induced by brandy, water and smelling-salts to open her eyes. She smiled faintly in recognition. 'How kind you are,' she said.

A quick glance round the kitchen where Laura had collapsed revealed a tidiness which Belle had not associated in her mind with a writer, but on the corner of the kitchen table was a small pile of manuscript with two red pencils like crossed swords lying by the side of all the apparatus of cake-making.

When the doctor had arrived and Belle had put Laura to bed she found that she had offered, with an almost automatic kindness of the country neighbour, to have Carey to supper and to send something over to Laura, and to find someone to help keep the house clean. Young Dr Brickett, who tried to give the impression of knowing everything, because he was acutely conscious of the fact that most of his patients remembered him being born and were likely to compare him unfavourably with his old father, told Laura that she must go to bed and stay there.

'Oh!' gasped Laura in a voice strengthened by dismay, 'I can't! I can't possibly! What is wrong with me?'

'Overwork and possibly worry, I suspect,' said young Dr Brickett, swinging his stethoscope. 'Has anyone ever told you your heart was not in perfect order?'

'Yes,' admitted Laura, 'years ago, after my second child was born. But I took care of myself – and it – it got better. I thought . . .'

'And it will get better again, if you are sensible.'

'Yes, but then it was easier.'

Her mind made a swift flight to the days after Carey was born, when Barney had carried her so carefully up and down the stairs. She looked at this young doctor through sudden tears.

'I don't know how one takes care any more,' she said, turning her face to the window. She was so long past crying over her broken happiness that her weakness surprised her.

Dr Brickett resisted an unaccountable desire to pat his patient. She looked so small and defenceless, but she turned again and lay on her back with an access of that iron strength which had carried her so far.

'All right,' she said. 'I cannot afford to be ill, so I must do as you say. Tell me.'

Dr Brickett put his stethoscope in his pocket and the desire to pat Laura passed. He realized with the perception that even his short medical experience had brought him that here was someone to whom strength of character had been brought by ill-health and unhappiness.

It was only after some weeks of rigid discipline that she recovered. Jeff Oldham had brought her bed downstairs and all those hot summer days she had spent by the low window of the little parlour to the right of the front door. While she rested her body she chased her thoughts and exhausted her mind with the pile of paper always at her elbow.

'I'm going to stop saying "thank you",' said Laura. 'I think you must find my gratitude boring, but you do know how I appreciate it, don't you?' as Belle came over on her daily visit, bringing butter and a custard and the *Marchampton Chronicle*. She had forgotten her original intention of remaining aloof from the Gray household. It was not in her to neglect needy neighbours, and as one so often comes to love those for whom one can do things, rather than those to whom one must be grateful, Belle began, during Laura's illness, to like her, and later almost to love her.

Through Belle, in spite of the erring husband, Laura came to know young Mrs Brickett, the Vicar, old Miss Thornton, and all the props and pins of the limited society of Farley. Carey came every day to Foxholes. She was a year older than Marinda, already at a stage of development when it was hard to realize that she might ever become a woman of even moderate attractions. She had joined Marinda at the Vicarage, where the Vicar's sister, well-meaning, but unqualified, tried to teach them what little mathematics she knew and a modicum of history and geography. In the afternoon the two girls walked back to the cottage, made tea in the kitchen and carried it in to Laura, thinking themselves fine nurses.

'I suppose it is all right for Marinda to spend so much time with those Grays,' said Belle doubtfully to her husband, who stood with his hairy legs poking forth from his night-shirt, looking across his hayfield with an affection in his eyes which no human being inspired. 'I must say I like Mrs Gray – Laura, she asked me to call her Laura – and of course we are friends, only I can't get over the feeling that they are a bit queer. I wish I could meet the boy, but he is going to take a holiday post. They must be very poor if he has to teach all the holidays.'

'Vacation,' corrected Henry.

'Well, vacation then. It's just the same. Do you think they are bad for Marinda?'

'Oh, Lord, no! Let the child alone. It's good for her to have a companion, with Sue away so much. And Carey seems a pleasant enough girl. She wants to learn to milk.'

He laughed. It had never occurred to him to allow his own daughters to learn to milk, and the interest of this sturdy young hoyden in all matters of the farm touched and amused him.

'I shall be glad when Sue comes home.'

'Yes, she has been away nearly three months; it is good of Emma to have her and she does so love a little fun. If we don't let her see some life she will never marry, and you wouldn't like that?'

Henry Fairfield sank into the feather bed and threw back all the covers except the sheet.

'I shouldn't care at all, so long as she was happy,' he said.

'But how can she be happy if she doesn't marry? – and she's so pretty.'

Belle lay comfortably beside her husband and thought of her son, the king-pin of this perfect life. All the land she could see in the moonlight from the windows would be his, the orchards and water meadows, and the tender vines of the hops. There had been a red sunset with turquoise lights over the hills and it was time the gooseberry jam was made.

'All marriages are not happy,' said Henry. His bones always ached so comfortably at night. With a movement that was habitual rather than affectionate he turned and flung his arm round his wife's yielding body. 'Look at Mrs Gray.'

'Yes,' agreed Belle, leaning across to the table at the side of the bed to blow out the candle.

Sue would eventually marry, of course, with those long lashes and curls. Belle would be a grandmother and the old nursery at the top of the house would be used indefinitely. She saw in her mind's eye rows of delightful grandchildren all exactly like Andrew.

But Marinda – Belle was sleepy and could only give a hazy thought to Marinda. She did hope Marinda was not going to be too clever. Miss Spence kept talking about what she called 'Higher Education'. Tomorrow the child must help with the gooseberries and not go dashing off somewhere with Carey before one had time to pin her down to a job.

'Come on,' said Carey. 'I think a fine Saturday is one of the nicest kinds of days, much better than a fine Monday. And it's just like being at the sea.'

She splashed her toes in the little pool and held her skirts indecently high. Marinda, sitting on the bank, dubiously taking off her black boots and woollen stockings, putting her garters inside them for safety, was oppressed by a feeling of sin. Not only ought she to be helping her mother with the gooseberries, but she was expressly forbidden to go near the water. As for paddling, it was something delightful which the village children did and from which, like so many other pleasant things in life, she was mysteriously barred. But Carey knew no such qualms. Her mother did not know of the unexpected dangers of the swift treacherous stream, and the other taboos which restricted Marinda's life had no place in hers. The weir was nearly dry. One could walk across to the salmon jump on the other side, and caught in its broken masonry were fascinating pools which Carey found very tempting on a hot day. She took a book out of her pocket, lifted her skirt, and began to read, moving her feet absently amongst the minnows and mysterious shells.

Marinda never ceased to marvel at the way Carey and her mother spent every spare moment reading. She was consumed with envy because they read at meals, in bed, in the bath. Even in the lavatory Marinda had discovered a row of books, *Essays of Elia, Sketches by Boz, Virginibus Puerisque, The Diary of a Nobody.*

At Foxholes Marinda was forbidden to read before the evening.

'You must find something better to do,' her mother used to say, and she was prepared to accept that reading in the morning was a sin, just as telling lies and not undressing underneath your night-gown.

All this she believed without question until she met Carey. The cottage was piled with books, not like the collected works of Scott and a few Sunday-school prizes in dust-free seclusion in the drawing-room at Foxholes, but good books and bad books, poetry and prose.

'Borrow anything you like, my dear,' said Laura, 'except my own books. I just can't bear to lend those and lose a sale. I don't expect the grocer to feed me for nothing, so why should people expect me to give away my books?'

Marinda took *The Last Days of Pompeii* and *Alice Through the Looking-glass.* She began to carry a small volume about with her as Carey did, but she had less time to read, for although Carey had her mother to look after, nothing stopped her reading. She would open her book and be lost in another more pleasing life while she stirred the custard and waited for the kettle to boil.

The sun beat upon Marinda's back. She took off her hat and began to paddle, looking nervously across the acres of water meadows with her father's cows far away on the other bank. From her pocket she took a handful of gooseberries and a small red book.

'Have a gooseberry?' she called.

Carey did not hear her. She was far away, weeping a little with the pleasure of having her emotions stirred at Beth's deathbed.

Eating the gooseberries, her tongue curling against their tartness, Marinda soon joined her in another world.

Carey and her mother, Marinda discovered, treated poetry as if it was something to read instead of a drudgery of learning by heart. All the poems Marinda had learnt at Miss Spence's and many more besides, of which she had never heard, were quoted by the Grays as if they were old saws. Marinda was impressed and the next time she borrowed a book she took some poetry. It was a thin book by someone called Christina Rossetti, and she took it because she had overheard Laura say to her mother, 'Your Marinda has a Rossetti look.'

It was disappointing that no clue to this was to be found in the book and Marinda turned the pages:

My heart is like a singing bird,
Whose nest is in a water'd shoot.

She read on. Something inside her sang with the rhythm.

She was so happy, it was like Christmas and summer holidays and Aunt Fan to stay and Hop Fair all at once.

Her eyes travelled down the page:

> When I am dead, my dearest,
> Sing no sad songs for me . . .

It was dark suddenly in her mind. Her imagination put herself dead and beautiful into a grave. It was unbearably tragic. Tears welled behind her eyes.

> Be the green grass above me,
> With showers and dewdrops wet,
> And if thou wilt, remember,
> And if thou wilt, forget.

She ate another gooseberry in enchanted misery. The church clock struck twelve and she stretched her legs to dry in the sun. They felt uncomfortably cold, but she did not like to remark on this and drew on her stockings, which stuck a little on her damp shins.

'When does your sister come back?' asked Carey.

'Soon, any day now, when Father can spare Jeff to fetch her,' said Marinda.

'I hope Pen gets here by September.'

Penistone Gray was at Balliol and Marinda was alternately excited and terrified at the thought of meeting him. She had seen his photograph, humorous eyes and a stubborn jaw, but Carey said he was not tall, just two inches taller than she was.

'I like men to be tall,' criticized Marinda, then, realizing that she had hurt Carey's feelings, she added, 'Perhaps he will grow.'

'I shouldn't think so. He is nearly twenty and, anyway, he gets along very well as he is,' said Carey, clambering over the stile with a great display of black stockings and white cambric knickers.

'I must just go in and see if Mother is all right,' she went on as they came to the gate, for most days she had her midday dinner at Foxholes. 'Wait for me.'

'Hurry up. Father hates us to be late.'

'You go on then. I'll catch you up.'

Marinda slowed her steps, looking anxiously over her

shoulder for Carey. At last the gate banged and she came running up the lane, waving fiercely to Marinda to go on. Marinda walked backwards, urging Carey to hurry.

'I am hurrying,' gasped Carey from her bursting lungs as Marinda swung round and opened the gate, drowning its familiar squeak with one of her own.

Neither of the girls ever forgot Sue's homecoming, for it was the first time they had seen one of the new motor-cars in the drive. Like images they watched Sue and Edward Stonebridge and Aunt Emma, swathed unfamiliar beings, disgorged by this monster. Instead of the cries of welcome, Belle and Henry stood silent with amazement to greet their daughter. There was no sound but the spluttering of the motor until Andrew voiced the general alarm with one of his long roars. Instantly Sue emerged from the veil and put her arms round her darling. Tongues were suddenly loosed.

'Well, Sue,' said Henry, kissing his daughter, 'it's good to have you home again, even in that thing.' He gave a cough of disgust in the direction of the motor.

'George thought that you'd like to see it,' murmured Aunt Emma.

'Where is Marinda?' asked Edward Stonebridge, taking off his goggles.

Marinda came round from the back of the motor.

'I suppose you are getting too big to kiss?' said Edward.

'Yes,' answered Marinda, and covered herself with angry blushes when everyone laughed.

Sue had taken off her shroud and revealed beneath a new dress of pale blue nun's-veiling, trimmed with rows of maroon-coloured braid. Belle was struck by the charm of her twenty-year-old daughter, as she twirled round, showing her tiny waist and high youthful bosom. Her curly brown hair would never grow long enough to puff and braid as was the fashion, but its soft waves were kind to her elf-like face, and when she was happy there were moments when people who remembered Sue Fairfield at twenty said that she was beautiful.

Aunt Emma was explaining the motor away. She always felt with her less materially fortunate sister that she must make some excuse for her husband's gradually expanding bank balance.

'George thought it would be good for business,' she said. 'I told you he wanted to open a branch in Corham. He wants Edward to see it, so we came round that way. Such a mercy not to have to consider the horses on the hill.'

'And will George take this new place?'

Her brother-in-law already had another branch at the far end of Marchampton, where he caught the less aristocratic prescriptions from the two young doctors, who, amid much eyebrow-lifting, had put up a plate on one of the new houses in the growing suburb of South Marchampton.

'Of course – it isn't exactly George,' explained Emma. 'It's Edward Stonebridge. He really does have the most astute ideas and George thinks more and more of him. He really relies on him. Sometimes I think he will be quite glad when the time comes to hand it all over to Edward, so that he can do nothing but potter about with his china.'

'Is he really going to pass it all on to Edward?' asked Belle, making a mental note to the effect that Edward Stonebridge was now eligible as a son-in-law.

'Yes,' said Emma.

Both the sisters looked from the window of the best bedroom, where the trappings of the tour were being laid, on to the lawn, at Edward playing with Andrew and throwing remarks over his shoulder to Marinda.

'He is a very nice, good young man,' said Emma, looking with almost maternal fondness at his thin face and pale hair.

The wish that he would marry Sue lay close to the surface, but they did not speak of it. It was to this end that Sue paid such long visits and that Belle did without the services of a daughter in the house. But nothing came of it. Sue's undoubted charms had apparently no effect on young Edward. It was incomprehensible to both women that Sue, with eyes like a sprite and a pert ribbon in her curls, could not charm such a worthy and intelligent man as Edward Stonebridge. But it was so.

'I suppose there's no one else he has his eye on?' ventured Belle at length.

'Oh no,' answered her sister, slightly horrified, as if

Edward had been accused of some form of immorality. 'He doesn't have much spare time, you know, and he spends it all at home, working out figures and prescriptions. Did I tell you he has a very good prescription for indigestion? Quite miraculous it is. People send for it from all over the place. Oh, I assure you there's no one else.'

They began to descend the stairs to the dining-room.

'It's only ham and tongue,' apologized Belle with the comfortable knowledge that the Foxholes home-cured hams and tongues needed no apology. 'If I'd known you were coming I could have killed a couple of fowls. Oh, by the way, we have young Carey Gray in most days to meals. I wrote to you about her, didn't I?'

'Yes,' said Emma. She disapproved of this new friendship, but could not at this moment speak her mind for they were all in the dining-room, where extra places had been laid round the mahogany table, which looked large enough for a game of billiards.

'Oh,' said Marinda suddenly, 'Carey is not here.'

'Run out and fetch her, Andrew,' said Belle.

Andrew, whose young gastric juices were already stimulated by the sight of his favourite tongue, lolling all beparsleyed on a giant dish, was sitting meekly by the side of Sue, who was tying on his feeder. At the prospect of a delay he began to squirm and Belle realized with swift misgiving that if she was not wary at this stage his behaviour would shame them all.

'Go and look for her, Marinda,' said Henry. 'I expect she is feeling a bit shy.'

'She's in the yard,' said Bessie, handing round the plates efficiently, but with a friendly ear to the conversation.

Carey was sitting by the pump with two of the new puppies in her lap and Princess, the old spaniel bitch, snuffling maternally round her legs. The warmth of their bodies comforted Carey to such an extent that she clenched her teeth and half-strangled them with love.

When Marinda brought her in, her hair was untidy and her broad face was sulky with shyness.

'What a great lump she is,' thought Sue, deceived by Marinda's enthusiastic letters about her new friend. Aunt Emma thought the child's manners would have a bad effect on Marinda, as she helped herself to salad.

'Carey,' said Henry, carving wafer-thin slices of ham and tongue with a flexible, worn knife, 'I thought perhaps you might like one of the puppies. Would your mother let you have one?'

Carey's eyes lit up so that they looked a different colour. She took the plate of tongue without even saying 'Thank you', noted Aunt Emma.

'Do you mean it, Mr Fairfield?'

'Of course I do. Why should I say things that I don't mean? We'll go and choose one afterwards.'

'That will be wonderful,' breathed Carey, putting pieces of tongue into her mouth, chewing and swallowing them without even noticing their famed delicacy of flavour.

She was considering a name for her new dog and did not hear the topics of conversation, which ranged from exactly how Belle cured the hams, through the progress of the hops to suitable wear for motoring, but as the Fairfield children were discouraged from speaking at meals unless spoken to, her silence passed unnoticed.

Chapter 4 — THE FRIENDS

'The thing about Shelley,' said Pen Gray, lounging in a shabby deck-chair with his straw boater tilted down over his eyes, 'is that I can't like a man who said "Bird thou never wert". It's an appalling line.'

Marinda was shocked. Of course anything Pen said was sure to be true, because he was in his last year at Oxford and she was only sixteen. But then on the other hand – Shelley . . .

'If Shelley wrote it I should think it must be all right,' she said.

Carey, who was stroking her precious dog, Tray, laughed.

'Marinda always believes the label on the bottle,' she mocked. 'Shelley is a poet. People say he is a great poet. Therefore it can't matter if he said "Bird thou never wert". But personally I don't mind it.'

She pulled Tray's ears together until they covered his eyes. He bore it all with the uncomplaining devotion of the spaniel.

'Well, I think it's a shocking line,' asserted Pen. 'It's worse than Wordsworth at his worst.'

Marinda stared. Wordsworth was also a great poet, or so she thought.

'Don't you like Wordsworth either?' she asked, digging a daisy root from the lawn. She was a little afraid of Pen. He seemed so much older, with his moustache and his stocky figure and his air of authority.

'Of course,' he answered. 'He was a great man. He wrote some wonderful stuff.' Marinda looked relieved. 'But he also wrote some awful rubbish as well.'

'I like the daffodil one,' she said.

'"I wandered lonely as a cloud that floats on high . . ."' began Carcy. 'Oh, bother! I do believe Tray has fleas.'

'You never know,' thought Marinda, 'when the Grays are likely to descend from the heights.'

Carey searched diligently for fleas, at the same time reciting the whole poem in her calm, unaffected voice. '"And then my heart with pleasure fills, and dances with the daffodils",' she chanted. 'And now I must go and milk Juniper. Come on, Marinda, come with me.'

Marinda did not dare to stay on and talk to Pen. She rose reluctantly. Carey was becoming a great deal fonder of the farm animals than any of the Fairfield children. Sue was now twenty-two and the hens and the resultant egg money were hers, but she often was glad for Carey to do the jobs for her and paid her wages in eggs. Soon Carey had some ducklings and a few hens herself. Henry Fairfield was amused and Jeff took her round the cowsheds and pointed out the best of the herd. When the calves were taken off to market she made almost as much fuss as their mothers, and Henry gave her in token the heifer called Juniper. In time Juniper came to be known as Miss Carey's cow and she always milked her charge.

'I shall never be able to sell Juniper,' sighed Henry to Jeff.

'Cor no, that you wunt,' laughed Jeff. 'That young Miss Carey 'ud be a good darter to 'ee.'

Henry agreed and walked on across the yard to the stables. He did not particularly want his own daughters to spend their spare time in the stables and cowsheds, but he thought they might display as much interest in the stock as Carey. Sue, he grumbled to himself, thought of nothing but clothes, and Marinda was forever reading. He did not realize that locked within Marinda was a passion for Foxholes which would bind her to its fields and water-meadows, its very bricks and stones, with an eternal cord woven by her forebears. As for Andrew . . . Henry sighed a little. It was a good thing, he thought, for a boy to have spirit, but Belle did so spoil him. He would have to speak about it. Andrew was not yet ten years old, but already he had the whole house under his thumb. He had only to thrust out his lower lip with a threatened storm, or turn his angelic blue eyes innocently towards you, to get his own way, and the worst of it was that he knew already quite well on whom his various tactics would be effective.

Belle had never encouraged the children to ride. Her own father had been brought home on a hurdle from a hunting accident and died at his own gate, and all her life, as civilization progressed, Belle was to consider horses more dangerous than mad bulls, motor-cars or even Zeppelins.

There was a pony, however, for the children to ride, and later a steady chestnut cob on which Sue hunted as a matter of course, but without enthusiasm. When Marinda fell off the pony at the age of five she went through some years with such a horror of horses that she made a wide detour round old Sultan, who was the mildest of cart-horses, and backed away from the rocking-horse in the nursery. But the blood of his grandfather stirred in Andrew's veins, and from the time he could walk he could also ride, and the sight of his entrancing curls under a hard hat, as Henry trotted him to the meet at the end of a leading-rein, brought soft looks to the women's eyes. No one ever knew exactly how Carey came to be a regular member of the party, so that strangers often thought she was Henry's daughter. She went through stages of clambering on to Sultan's back, riding Sue's chestnut bareback, being given a few lessons by Henry and, finally, when her mother had an unexpected cheque from *Woman's Paper,* there she was perched on Henry's second hunter, which he always meant to sell, in a well-fitting habit, as familiar and regular a figure on Saturday mornings as the Master himself.

'I wish,' said Henry that night, putting the candle by the side of the bed, 'that we could afford to send Andrew away to school. If the hops do well . . .'

Belle released herself thankfully from her corsets, for she was getting plump. She gave an impatient cough, because Henry promised them so many things every year if the hops did well. 'One good year pays for three bad ones' they used to say in Marchshire, but Henry had not had a good year for four years. She looked across the garden to the green hopyards lying like a garland between them and the hills. She did not mind much whether they were rich or poor so long as no one took Andrew away from her.

'Laura was saying,' she remarked, disappearing into her night-gown, 'that he has a really lovely voice and why hadn't we tried him for the Choir School.'

'A lovely voice?' echoed Henry nervously. His children were a constant source of surprise to him, Marinda reading poetry and now Andrew with a voice. 'I never heard him sing, except in church, and he gets out of that if he can.'

Belle ignored this aspersion.

'I always thought he sang rather nicely,' she said, 'but Laura says he really is very good indeed. Something about true pitch. I don't know if it would be worth trying. Laura knows the Precentor at the Cathedral and she says there is a voice trial next week. He'd be educated for nothing, and now the carrier runs every day from Farley he could go in with him.'

'Or I suppose Emma could have him during the week?'

'Oh no.' Belle could not yield Andrew up to Emma. Already Emma had almost annexed Sue and now she wanted to take Marinda to Torquay. 'Besides,' she thought, 'Emma doesn't understand Andrew.'

Emma was one of the few people on whom Andrew exercised his charm in vain. She was unmoved by his golden curls and angelic, deceptive smile. She was also impervious to his storms. And what was more, she would most certainly not want Andrew.

Belle could never understand how it was that Andrew by his screaming had managed to have the upper hand of them all. Marinda, she remembered, had also screamed, but in those days Henry's mother was alive and she supposed, for her sake, the children had been kept in better order.

'Do you think he would like the Choir School?' she asked, watching the candle flicker on the new brass bed. It was the only moment of the day when she had time and opportunity to talk to Henry and all matters of home and business were settled in their bedroom.

'It doesn't really matter if he doesn't,' said Henry. 'No boys like school. I didn't. It wouldn't be natural.'

'No, I suppose not, but I hope he does. It – it will make it so much easier.'

She added a little piece on to her prayers that Andrew would behave well and win a place in the Cathedral choir, staying so long on her knees with the soles of her feet, slightly grubby from her black stockings, sticking out from the night-gown, that Henry said impatiently, 'Hurry up.'

He said no prayers himself although he was Vicar's warden and chairman of the Church Council, but Belle took his sinfulness for granted, as one of the many laws which was right for a man and not for a woman.

'This new tomfool of a bed isn't half as comfortable as the old one,' he said, as Belle murmured a hasty 'Amen' to the Almighty and came to lie beside him.

With this she could not but agree, but the brass bed was a triumph of years of grumbling about the old fourposter on which generations of Fairfields had been born and died. As no one would buy it, it was now in the stables with an outworn governess car, and occasionally a stray hen laid an egg in it.

The subject of the choir trials was broached with much tact to Andrew, for it would be almost as disastrous, thought Belle, for him to dislike the school as for him to fail. But there was no cause for alarm, for he was enchanted at the prospect of going in to Marchampton every day in the carrier's cart, and he was already as tired of Miss Spence as Miss Spence was of Andrew Fairfield.

Laura was a great help.

'I'm going in to see the Frobishers tomorrow,' she said. 'I will find out all about it and teach Andrew something to sing. They won't mind how little he knows, provided he has the voice. I know Mr Frobisher always says it is less to unlearn.'

She came back with a copy of 'Spring, the sweet Spring', and Andrew swung on the gate waiting for her in the dusk. He should have been in bed hours ago, but no one had the courage to insist.

'In the morning,' said Laura, for whose smooth decisions Andrew had respect, 'as soon as school is over, I will give you a lesson.' She did not warn him that he had to be good, but he knew instinctively that it was so.

As Laura listened to the trills of his voice hitting the note with the clarity and precision of a thrush, she regretted for the first and only time that he was not her child.

Before Andrew went for his voice trial Foxholes became very tired of 'Spring, the sweet Spring'. After the first two days only Marinda said 'Sing it again,' but it was the words which fascinated her. The tune merely embellished the words to her and brought her visions of sunlit meadows, light and laughter, overlaid with gambolling lambs and daisy chains.

'Lovely, Andrew, lovely!' she said. 'Sing it again,' and while Sue stuffed her ears and Henry banged the door and even Belle gave a long, tired sigh, she listened in ecstasy to Andrew's voice fluting easily up to high C like the pipings of some shepherd boy in Elysian fields.

'I quite dread to think what will happen if he fails,' said Belle to Laura, as they sat in her garden drinking tea. It was a time of day when Laura stopped everything to enjoy one small hour of relaxation before her pen or her needle or her household claimed her.

'Don't worry, he won't fail, because he is determined not to,' laughed Laura. 'You must admit that when he makes up his mind he generally achieves something.

Besides, his voice is quite exceptional. I can't think how you never noticed it.'

'Miss Spence did say he sang very prettily,' admitted Belle. 'When Mr Lorimer was here he wanted him for the church choir, but, well, he didn't take to the idea. He said he would only go if he could blow the organ, and you know old Sammy has done it for years and – well – somehow it all fell through.'

Thus did Belle gloss over Andrew's grim opposition to the position of choirboy at St Swithun's Church, Farley.

Laura drank her tea slowly and lovingly, as if it were nectar. It was strong and sweet and gave her the strength which, in spite of her improved health, she so often needed.

'And the girls aren't really musical,' went on Belle. 'Sue did have lessons, but somehow she didn't seem to get on and in the end Henry said it was a waste of money, so we never bothered with the others; after the Lorimers went there was no one to give them lessons.'

'What are you going to do with Marinda?'

'Do with her? Why, what can I do with her? I suppose she will marry,' said Belle comfortably. She wished there were more young men round about Farley, for it was unthinkable that the entrancing Sue should be an old maid. She comforted herself with the thought that Marinda would no doubt improve. She was at the awkward age, but with those eyes she would never be really plain, and Belle thought pityingly of Laura's Carey, short and sturdy, with serviceable legs and untidy hair.

'At any rate I must give Carey as good an education as I can manage and see that she is properly trained for something. My brother seems to think there is a future in shorthand-writing. She mustn't be left as I was, but there are so few careers open to women. It's horribly unfair. She really wants to be a farmer or a vet and that hardly seems possible; then she says that next to animals she likes human beings. I don't think she is clever enough to be a doctor even if I could afford it, but I suppose she might make a nurse.'

'A doctor!' echoed Belle. She knew that such phenomena existed, there was even one practising at

Marchampton, but so little faith had Belle in her own sex that she would as soon have consulted the Old Wise Witch of Coppleford.

Laura's mind flew back through her recent years of moderate success and hard work to the days before she had discovered the trick of writing, when Barney's small allowance came irregularly and then ceased. He wasn't dead, she knew, because her lawyers kept trace of his wanderings, though it had become troublesome and uneconomic to try to extract any money from him. Poor Barney – what a fool he was – what a hopeless, dear, delightful fool! She had made her life now without him and the bitterness was gone; indeed, she often pitied people like Belle, because she was sure they had never known the gay idiocy, the tender charm, of her short married bliss with Barney Gray.

'I am thinking of letting Carey have a couple of years at the Blanche Whittle Foundation. Why don't you send Marinda too? You know old Miss Spence means well, but she really doesn't know enough to teach them now. Carey isn't clever, but your Marinda is wasting her time.'

'I never thought Marinda was clever,' mused Belle. 'Miss Spence says she doesn't concentrate. She day-dreams all the time. But she likes history and I believe she does quite well at English.'

Belle realized that she knew much less about her children than did Laura, not only about Carey and Pen, but about Marinda and Andrew. Somehow Laura never took the same interest in Sue, who was so often away.

'I suppose if Carey is to have any sort of training I shall have to go back to London. It will save Pen living in digs. You know he is teaching at a school in Hampstead next term,' said Laura, knitting her hands behind her grey hair and looking out of the windows with sad affection.

'Oh no! Please don't go to London! I should miss you so terribly.'

'Would you?' said Laura calmly. She did not say, 'I shall miss you too.' She had uprooted herself so often and started a new life, just as one began a new chapter in a shiny new exercise book, that she looked forward to the change from the inconveniences of the house and the narrowness of Farley. But this time she disliked the thought of leaving the little almond tree she had planted and the wild daffodils in the orchard.

'Carey detests London and she will hate leaving the farm,' she said. 'She ought to be your daughter and you can give me Marinda.'

Belle thought she could spare Marinda better than Sue or Andrew. Marinda was always the odd one, with her everlasting reading and mooning about.

'I must speak to Henry,' said Belle. 'The Whittle Foundation's not very expensive, is it? You see, it's not as if Marinda were a boy. If Andrew does win the choir scholarship, I suppose it would be possible to do this for Marinda, and if the hops do well, too. Of course he will have to go to school somewhere.'

'They could all three go in with the carrier.'

'Except on market day. Jeff can take them on market day.'

It was an exciting September for the children. The hops did well and Henry brought them all back gingerbread from the Hop Fair and thought with relief that he wouldn't have to part with the second hunter after all. Then – if the hops did well next year . . .

Andrew was given an extra packet of gingerbread, because news came in that day that he had won his chorister's scholarship. He walked about all day wearing his new school satchel and singing hymns, elated at the prospect of endless rides in the carrier's cart.

For over a year the three children, by various means, reached the school gates in time. Sometimes Marinda spent a week with her aunt, sometimes Andrew and Carey rode in importantly and left their horses at the Castle Inn stables in Castle Street. Sometimes Jeff raced them in the dog-cart, or they jogged from the cross-roads to the turnpike, up the hill, down the hill, past the villas and through the West Gate in Borden's cart. But they never missed, even in the snow, and the only prize any of them gained in eighteen months was for attendance.

Chapter 5 — CORONATION AIRS

In order to preserve their energies and their white muslin frocks, Marinda and Carey slept at the Pharmacy in Castle Street for the night of the Coronation Festival. Emma had never, as she put it, 'taken to' Carey, but she found in order to see something of Marinda she had to include the child's friend. They were both about to leave school, Carey with the bright cheeks and cheerful eyes, which were to be in her sturdy body her only attraction as a woman, and Marinda still with the tender gawkiness of a fledgling bird. She was gradually beginning to lose the look of being all mouth and eyes, and at seventeen one realized that her eyes were large and clear and gave a dreamy happiness to her expression, and as the childishly thin cheeks filled, her large mouth curved into proportions which showed generosity and humour.

'Marinda will never be the beauty Sue is,' remarked Emma to Edward Stonebridge. 'But there's something about her – I don't know how to explain it – a sort of lovableness . . .'

'I agree,' said Edward. 'There's depth in Marinda. Sue's all curls and ribbons, but Marinda has always been my favourite.'

Emma looked up sharply from her sewing. She was disappointed that Edward had not fallen in love with Sue as she had planned; now suddenly she became full of plans for Marinda's future. Next year George would retire and they would go to live in one of the new houses on the Corham road. Marinda would be eighteen next year and Edward, at thirty-two, was as worthy and eligible a bachelor as Marchampton could produce. And Stonebridge's Mixture was selling well. Already packets of it were sent to soothe the digestive juices of customers all over England, and George and Edward talked of patenting it and starting a small factory.

All these thoughts, embellished with wedding veils and bridesmaids' bouquets, spun quickly round Emma's mind as she watched Edward Stonebridge turn the *Marchampton Advertiser* back to front.

'Marinda and Carey are staying the night next Thursday for the Coronation Concert,' announced Emma, deploying her forces mentally. 'I hope you will be in to tea.'

Thursday was early-closing day. It was an innovation, a slab of free time which Edward did not always know how to fill. His work was so absorbing to him and he was at the call of the night-bell so often that even in hours of leisure he was seldom free from the tug of duty, until his work became more pleasurable to him than his leisure.

'I was going out to Corham to see how the new branch is getting on,' he said, 'but I shall be back in time; mustn't miss Marinda.'

Emma smiled with as much satisfaction as she might have done had he asked formally for her niece's hand. She considered privately that Edward had been a stick, as she said more than once to George, over Sue, and she took what little compliments he bestowed on Marinda at more than their face value. It was unlucky that on Wednesday George should decide to send him to London to see Fayre and Harrop about a consignment of French perfumes. In spite of Emma's protests George insisted.

'Not go to London just because two gawky schoolgirls are coming! Good Heavens, Emma! Have some sense. Marinda has been in and out of the house since she was a child and likely to be . . .'

'That's just it,' argued Emma. 'As soon as Carey leaves school the Grays are going to live in London and there's some talk of Marinda going too. I don't know what Belle is thinking about. It would be much better to let Marinda come and stay here for a few months and we could take her with us for a nice trip somewhere. The trouble is that, with Sue not married, Belle thinks Marinda should be out of the way. I'm sure I don't know why a lovely girl like Sue isn't married. She's too fussy, that's what. Belle tells me she has refused the curate again. I did think at one time young Penistone Gray would do for her, but he is never home and anyhow he has no money. Then, of course, the doctor went and married out of the county, which was a great disappointment to everybody. As for Edward . . .'

George let his wife's voice run on like a well-known accompaniment to his thoughts. One could not say he did not hear what she said, but it only registered on the top layer of his mind and was quickly forgotten, like the conversation in a dream.

'But of course,' went on his wife, 'if Edward really has to go, he could come back the same night.'

'He might, if he works fast, but Edward doesn't often get the chance of a trip to London and I doubt if he will hurry himself. Not if he has any sense, that is.'

What George called 'sense' was a quality he much admired in Edward. The young man had other qualities such as a quick brain and a certain unflinching honesty, but it was his 'sense' which endeared him to George. If Edward took a risk, it was not a flash-in-the-pan risk, which other men seized, but a risk so well thought out that it almost wasn't a risk at all. The branch at Corham, for instance, nothing when they took it over, but now, with all those new houses, an absolute gold-mine. Yes, if this went on he could retire comfortably in a year or two.

Emma was also thinking of Edward with affection. He had filled out a little since his hollow twenties and now his thin face and direct gaze gave him a distinction which George, fat, bespectacled and untidy, could never achieve.

'Edward might be anybody,' thought Emma with satisfaction. George talked of putting him up for the Council. Why, perhaps he might be Mayor of Marchampton one day. She saw Marinda as Lady Mayoress and Edward's grave smile above the gold mayoral chain. She and George, of course, would have seats at the top table for the banquet. She was so proud of the fantasy of her niece receiving everyone at the Marchampton Town Hall that she was quite surprised when Marinda herself ran in with the pins falling from her newly put up hair under her unbecoming school hat.

'We came through the shop,' said Marinda, as Carey came forward and said 'How do you do?' in her gruff, casual voice. 'Edward said he was going to London tomorrow for Uncle, but he's going to catch the four o'clock train back and he's going to bring us some flowers. Oh, isn't it wonderful? It's the first time I've ever had a frock which was really mine and not an old one of Sue's made over.'

Emma beamed at the thought of Edward's coming home to go to the concert. If he were coming home on the four o'clock, she might ask him to look out for Fan. No, on second thoughts she decided to say nothing. Fan had only said she would arrive some time in the evening, and she might just as easily come on the Midland route. You never knew with her. Besides, there were few men who were safe with Fan, who, on the borders of middle age, could radiate a fascination of which her cousins were alternately frightened and proud, and although Emma was quite sure Edward had too much sense not to see through Fan's wiles, she had earmarked him for Marinda and she was taking no chances.

The Marchampton Festival Concerts were thought by all the inhabitants of Marchshire to rival any concert in the country. And for this Coronation Festival Concert great efforts had been made. Those who had never been over the county's borders vowed that better singing than the Marchampton Choir was just not to be found. Fan thought their provincial attitude ridiculous but affecting, but even she, from the wider world of the Queen's Hall and Covent Garden, had to admit that the choir, if not first-rate, could pass for such to all but the most critical.

By a trick of fortune a well-known composer lived just outside the city and a first performance of his Coronation Airs was being conducted by the great man in person. Marinda was not the only one who was disappointed in his small, shabby figure. Somehow she had pictured a composer and conductor to be large and impressive, whereas she knew that Edward Stonebridge on her right was more distinguished-looking, and her father on her left was more handsome than the conductor, but her mother, at the end of the row, past Sue and Aunt Fan and Uncle George and his wife, did not notice any imperfections, for she had eyes only for Andrew. He was to sing a solo, and he sat, small and round-faced, with the choir, ignoring his relations politely, as he had been instructed. Belle was so proud of Andrew that she forgot music had to be written and choirs assembled and trained and conducted. To her the whole concert was simply an instrument to accompany Andrew's solo.

'Your boy has a remarkable voice, Mrs Fairfield,' Mr Frobisher had said at the school prize-giving. 'The sort of miracle one comes across every ten years or so. Of course, when it breaks he may never sing again for anyone's pleasure, but for the time being . . .'

Mr Frobisher had put his fingers together and looked into space as if he were hearing at that moment the magical clarity of Andrew's voice. If Belle had only known, he was debating as to whether he should ever tell this nice little woman that, apart from his voice, her son was the most tiresome, idle boy in the school. He gave a sigh and held out his hand.

'Good-bye, Mrs Fairfield,' he had said. 'I shall see you at the concert.'

In the interval he came across and spoke to her and Belle felt pleasantly conspicuous as the mother of Andrew.

'Who is the angel-faced child?' said Pen's friend, Mark Studland, who was sitting a little to the side with Laura and Carey and the Frobishers.

'Andrew Fairfield, the horror,' said Carey unfeelingly.

'No, I mean the girl who smiled at you just now.'

'Oh, her. That's only Marinda, the golden-voiced horror's sister. She's a friend of Carey's,' said Pen, taking another look at Marinda. Her plaits had been wound round her head for the occasion and they topped her small heart-shaped face like a too-heavy crown, but the gas-jets shone on the golden lights in her thick hair and her white frills filled out her thin figure and gave one for the first time a hint of beauty to come.

Sue was talking to Fan, her curls bobbing and her little hands fluttering as she talked. She looked round for a moment and saw Pen and his friend and gave a smile which was bright but without warmth.

'And that is Sue Fairfield, Marinda's sister. They live quite near us. If you were staying you could meet them.'

'I am not violently attracted by provincial beauties,' said the young man, yawning behind his programme, but his eyes rested on both the girls, noting Marinda's clear skin and Sue's bright eyes. He thought that, properly dressed, they might look quite well. Unconscious of his interest or his critical eye, Marinda smoothed her flounces and Sue made an excuse to stand up, that Marchampton might better see her new cherry dress with its net bodice and black velvet ribbons.

'I don't think much of this new thing of Poulter's,' said the young man at length, turning to his programme as the orchestra and choir took their places once more, with restrained but unmistakable noise and commotion.

'You know, Mark, if you make such statements you will be thrown out of the hall. Poulter was born within six miles of Marchampton and on that account alone there isn't anyone in this hall who isn't willing to swear he is first-rate. I'm almost willing to swear it myself. The *Watermill Suite* and *Rebecca* were wonderful, you must own.'

'*Rebecca*, yes,' agreed Mark, 'but the *Watermill Suite* is commonplace. I see they are playing it again tonight.'

'Of course. Poor old Poulter will never live that down, but I must confess I like it.'

Mark Studland crossed his legs and made a sound which was half a sigh and half a snort. Though inelegant, it served to show the scorn with which at twenty-five he regarded all things outside London.

It was raining when they left the Town Hall. Swift, wet gusts of wind blew in from the hills and Marinda was glad cabs had been ordered to take them back to Castle Street. As she stood on the steps of the Town Hall and saw the crowds standing in the rain to see the Lord Lieutenant, Jefferson Poulter, and what the women vaguely called 'the dresses', she felt unexpectedly grand, in spite of the woollen fascinator which her aunt had insisted on her wearing, and her old party cape with the rabbit-fur collar. Two more weeks of school and she would be grown up. In fact she was grown up. From now on life was bound to be completely wonderful. For a moment she wasn't aware of anything but raindrops splashing on her face and a great exhilaration. Then she heard a whine from the pavement. 'Have you got a copper, lady? I haven't anywhere to sleep.'

Marinda shuddered. The woman's dirty face and hair were partly obscured by a shawl, a barefooted and ragged child with a shrewd face stood by her side.

'I – I'm sorry, I haven't any money,' said Marinda gently. She looked more closely at the crowd standing in the rain and she saw for the first time that it was shabby and hungry looking. Some of the women carried babies. In the village of Farley there was poverty, but there was generally someone to help. The occasional travelling beggar, if he braved the farm dogs, was never sent away without a mug of cider and a piece of bread and cheese. No one in Farley lacked for food and shelter. It did not occur to her that this woman might be lying.

'Oh, Edward,' she whispered, 'could you give this woman something for me?'

Edward slipped his hand easily into his pocket and pulled out half a crown. To Marinda half a crown was untold wealth, and to the woman also. She hurried off, her voice loud with blessings.

'Oh, thank you. That was very kind. I must pay you back when I get my pocket-money,' said Marinda.

Edward laughed and took her arm through the crowd.

'We must find Carey,' said Edward. 'She is coming with us, isn't she? And the others are waiting for Andrew.'

'Here I am,' called Carey. 'I say, Marinda, Andrew did sing well, didn't he? This is Mark Studland. Pen brought him down. This is Marinda Fairfield, Mark. You thought Andrew sang well too, didn't you?'

'Perfection,' said Mark, and Marinda shot a swift look at him, for he said it as if he meant something quite different. She wanted to introduce Edward Stonebridge, but her tongue became suddenly tied and she could not remember anyone's name. For a horrible moment it seemed as if the world had become anonymous.

'Come on, Carey,' she said, 'the cab is waiting. Good-bye, Pen. We'll see you tomorrow.'

'No, you won't, because Mark and I are going back on the early train.'

Marinda looked back at Mark and noticed through the rain that his hair and eyes were the same dark chestnut colour.

In the cab Edward sat opposite the two girls and looked at Marinda. Carey complained that at least fifty hairpins were sticking into her and she felt like Jael – or was it Sisera? But Marinda was wondering what the beggar woman would do when she had spent the money.

'In a year's time,' thought Edward Stonebridge, looking at her, 'I can ask her to marry me.'

It was ridiculous that the image of a child should have kept him a bachelor until now, but it was so. He had simply waited until the right moment, just as he waited for all his ventures, until he could be sure of success. He would make his intentions plain before anyone else appeared. That young Pen Gray, for instance, but he had no money. No, thought Edward, rejoicing for the first time in the success which he had almost unconsciously been winning for Marinda. He was not rich, but one day he would be. It was wonderful how lucky he was. With a wife like Marinda, whom he could teach and mould and love, there were no heights he could not reach.

Chapter 6 — THE VISITOR

In September 1912 the papers were full of the amazing feats of the new flying machines, but the only topic at Foxholes was the failure of the hops.

'They'll hardly pay for the picking,' said Henry, watching the pickers arrive with their bundles to camp out in the cabins at the far end of Broad Meadow. Across the grass came their rough Black Country voices, and the light of their fires and the tinny uncertainties of Bob Collins' concertina gave a foreign air to the solidity of Foxholes.

'It's like looking at a gypsy encampment,' said Marinda, staring out through the dark.

Some of the pickers had been to Foxholes for the picking for many years and these must be solemnly visited.

'But you mustn't go inside the cabins, mind,' warned Belle.

Hop-picking meant a certain amount of extra work for her, and as she became yearly plumper she found life an increasing effort. She felt the heat, and the corsets, with which she sought to constrict her rolls of fat, chafed her without supporting her. By the end of the day she longed passionately for release from her stays and her shoes.

The days in September began early and ended late, and although there were Bessie and Lucy and The Boy to help her, she found it often simpler to do some of the extra work herself. As she cut off slices of bacon for the hop-drier's supper from one of the sides hanging from the kitchen beam, she thought how easy life was for her sister Emma with her motor-car and her holidays, and now this new house on the Corham Road with electric light and a bathroom.

'Marinda,' she called, 'come and take the hop-drier's supper. Bessie has gone to bed with a headache and Jim seems to have vanished. It's always the same when the pickers come. He's off down to the cabins just when he's wanted.'

Marinda only half heard what her mother said in a voice querulous with fatigue. She was glad of an excuse to leave the house, for as a rule they were not allowed out after dark during the picking. The prohibitions and change of routine at this time gave a subtle feeling of licence to the air and, looking down across the fields, Marinda wondered what went on in the cabins to make them so dangerous after dark.

'I've put in eggs, bacon, bread and milk and a piece of apple pie. He's still got some tea, or he ought to have.'

Marinda took the basket and stood for a moment at the kitchen door looking up across the yard to the starlit sky and the far distance where she knew the Marchshire Hills lay crouching, as if to protect them, in the darkness. It was still and fine with only night's chill breath in the air. To-morrow, after the flaming sunset, there would doubtless be what her father called a 'hop-picking morning,' with the hills hidden in September mist which would later dissolve into a warm day.

She heard Carey's voice in the lane. 'Is that you, Marinda?'

'I'm just taking over old Joseph's supper. Come across with me to the kiln.'

She saw Carey's light frock emerge from the darkness and heard Pen's voice. 'All right. Wait for us.'

They were all there in the dark yard lit only by the squares of soft lamplight from the kitchen windows. Suddenly she realized that there were two men with Carey.

'You remember Mark Studland? I believe you saw him at the Festival Concert.'

'How do you do?' said Marinda. She met few young men and she did remember Mark Studland, but she said indifferently with the innate but awkward coyness of eighteen, 'Did we meet? There were so many people there.'

'You look like Little Red Riding Hood with that covered basket of yours,' said Pen. 'Where on earth are you off to at this time of night?'

'It's only the hop-drier's supper.'

'Oh, do let us come with you,' said Carey. 'I love old Joseph. He's the most wonderful old man. He knows all about hops and comes every year. How long has he been coming, Marinda?'

'Oh, I don't know. As long as I can remember.'

They walked across the yard.

'What does he do the rest of the year?' asked Mark Studland.

'I've never thought what he did,' answered Marinda, wonderingly. She realized she took so many things on the farm for granted, which excited slightly condescending interest from the various people who came to stay with the Grays. What could happen to old Joseph during all the months when the hop vines were growing? He came in the spring to help with the tying and to know if the Master wanted him again this year, and he was always given a plate of ham and a mug of cider at the back door. In September he came again with his bundle. He was part of the cycle of the year at Foxholes, like the first swallow and hay-making and the Christmas bell ringers, but she did not even know his surname. The drowsy smell of the drying hops met them at the door of the kiln. Joseph was stoking the fire and he finished the job deliberately before he took the basket without thanks.

'These are friends of mine,' said Marinda.

'Ah yes,' said Joseph, nodding. 'I know Miss Gray.

See'd her yesterday at milking time.' He looked at the young men as if they were slightly troublesome children.

'Good year for hops?' asked Pen.

'Noooaw,' said Joseph in disgust. Everyone in Marchshire knew it was a bad year and at Foxholes it was one of the worst pickings he remembered, but you couldn't explain that to these city folk. He took the bacon from the basket and prepared to toast it on the tip of his knife. A can was already boiling for his tea. All night he would be up at intervals to test with his skill and experience the heat of the kiln, unable to foresee the days when he would be replaced by thermometers and thermostats. Against the flamelit chamber it all looked warm and comfortable.

'Like a rather cosy little hell,' said Mark Studland, after they had said 'Good night', and walked out again into the rickyard.

'Something for you to write a poem about,' mocked Pen.

'An idea,' murmured Mark. 'I say, those hops have made me thirsty. Is there any cider left in that barrel?'

Marinda looked at his thin face with its scornfully humorous mouth and unexpected colouring. Was this man a poet? She must ask Carey. So many of the people who came to stay with the Grays had such curious occupations and Marinda had always imagined that poets wore large black hats and looked at the stars and were not red-haired young men clamouring for cider.

'There will be tea, anyway,' said Carey. 'Come over to us, Marinda. Mamma is bound to be having some tea.'

'I must ask Mother. Wait for me.'

Marinda's pink muslin skirt whirled round her ankles as she ran off to Belle with her basket, and her mother said if she weren't back by ten her father would be angry and pointed to the clock which said nearly half past nine.

'And if you see Andrew,' went on Belle, lighting the lamp in the drawing-room and looking half-heartedly for some sewing, 'tell him to come back at once. It's lucky your father is still talking to Mr Price or he would have noticed. Tell him to hurry and go straight to bed up the back stairs.'

There was a tacit agreement in the family that Andrew's

misdemeanours should be hidden when possible from his father. Henry Fairfield was a mild man, but he disliked being defied, and if he discovered that Andrew, in spite of his ban, spent most of his spare time with the hop-pickers, his slow wrath would be kindled and Andrew would be beaten. Belle would cry and Andrew would take his beating as a matter of course, but would be in no way deterred from repeating the disobedience.

'Henry doesn't understand Andrew,' thought Belle. She did not understand him herself. She did not realize that in his search for admiration he was happier with the Lees and the Jacksons and the Collinses, who were flattered by his preference for them.

Marinda thought she knew where he was to be found. He was probably only listening to Fred Collins' concertina or off rabbiting with the Jackson boys. Her mother was afraid he would catch something, and her father was afraid he would 'learn bad ways', but the lasting effect of their flattery and hero-worship did not occur to them.

'I only hope he doesn't start to sing,' thought Marinda. 'He won't realize how the sound carries.'

'Hurry, Marinda,' called Carey. 'We're going to walk down to the bridge while the kettle boils.'

Marinda shivered a little. A small night breeze was rising, but she did not go back into the house for a wrap, in case her mother forbade her to walk down the lane in the dark.

'Marinda?' repeated Mark in a musing voice. 'I've never heard that name before.'

'Then you can't have been to church in these parts,' answered Marinda. 'There's a Marinda Fairfield at Farley and one who married into the Farley family at Farley Cross and there's a tiny baby's monument there too, really rather sweet. She died in 1792 and it just says, "My babe, sweet innocent Marinda".'

'Might be you,' said Mark.

She felt suddenly uncomfortable. No one had ever paid her a compliment, either implied or direct, and she had a secret feeling of indecency which made her blush.

'It's short for Mary Belinda,' she went on, thinking her name was a safe topic.

The old bridge, with its deep embrasures at the sides, where pedestrians might take refuge when the coaches went by, had been there in Cromwell's time when the river was said to have been red with the blood of Prince Rupert's followers.

'I just don't believe it,' laughed Carey, explaining the local tradition to Mark. 'The banks are red anyway with Marchshire clay.'

Marinda never became used to the way Carey and Pen refused to believe unsubstantiated local traditions.

'Of course, it couldn't have been true. Think how much blood there would have been. Diluted, mind you.'

'But there must have been. I mean if they have said so all these years.'

'When I say a thing thrice, it is true,' murmured Mark, and Marinda couldn't think what they were talking about. She looked across the field to the outlines of the 'Jubilee Bridge' on the New Road, which took away the usefulness of the old bridge.

'One of the Fairfields was wounded here,' she said. 'He lay down by the mill all day and then at night he dragged himself across the valley to the Manor, where the Fairfields lived in those days, you know, and there was a trail of blood all the way, so they followed it, the Roundheads, I mean, and they shot him. He stood up so that he should die like a man, and he did die just as they fired, but it missed him because he had fallen to the ground. You can see the bullet hole in the wall at Farley Manor.'

She told all this as if it had recently happened and this time Mark did not scoff. He felt suddenly surrounded by ghosts.

'My mother's people fought here too,' went on Marinda, 'but they were on the other side.'

Thus simply did Marinda unconsciously define the distinction between her paternal and maternal ancestry.

'Just imagine a family living here since the Civil War,' said Carey, looking back on her own uncertain childhood.

'Oh, but they were here before then,' said Marinda, as if 1646 were only yesterday. To her it was nothing to cause pride or even surprise. There were many families in Marchshire, from old Lord March to Tom Cleek the blacksmith, whose forebears were in the Parish Records in the days when the monks fasted on the product of the Grimston fish-ponds. Occasionally 'foreigners' such as the Grays came from Marchshire's barbarous neighbouring counties and were likely to endure mistrust and hostility for many years.

'Of course,' explained Pen, on whom a year's schoolmastering had already set its imprint, 'it's quite understandable. The March Hills cut them off from Wales and the roads beyond Marchampton went through bog and forest. Things will alter now with railways and motor-cars.'

'And aeroplanes. I saw one the other day. Looked most unsafe,' said Mark.

They began to walk 'round the island' back towards Foxholes.

'I think progress is a pity. I like stability, security, roots,' Mark went on.

'What rubbish!' said Carey. 'Why, you never settle to anything.'

'I wish I could say my ancestor died on this bridge. Well, for all I know of my forebears he may have done, but it's more likely he kept swine and died in a hovel eaten by vermin.'

There was something about the way Mark declaimed this to the stars which gave his words a ring of insincerity. Carey instantly pounced on what it was.

'If you mean pigs, for heaven's sake, say so,' she protested hotly. 'There's no need to say "swine" unless it has to rhyme with something.'

'My poems don't rhyme,' answered Mark loftily.

Marinda wondered if they didn't rhyme why they should be poems, only of course there was blank verse. She wondered if he wrote something in the style of Shakespeare, and wished that she knew more about him. Then suddenly she had a flash of memory. It was 'The Silver Tree'. This was the man about whom they had all been talking last year. How stupid she had been not to remember. Although she had read the long poem, there was a great deal of it which she had not understood or liked and, being afraid to say so, she could not join in the conversation.

'I must say,' said Carey, with a backward glance for her

dog, 'that I think it's time you wrote something else, Mark; one poem is nothing, even if it does make you a bit famous at the time.'

Her voice was lofty with magnificent ignorance.

'But, Carey,' objected Pen, 'he isn't like Mamma. He can't turn them out to boil the pot.'

'Of course I can't,' said Mark.

Carey fixed a lead on to Tray as they came back to the farmyard. It was the terror of her life that his chicken-chasing propensities might be discovered.

'Mark doesn't have to,' she said in her gruff voice, looking at him with her penetrating eyes. The lights of her mother's room lay ahead of her. She knew that only when the tea was made would her mother lay down her pen with an air of exhausted finality. Her longing to protect her mother and her admiration for all she did made her impatient with most of the people, who came to stay and idly watched her work and ate the food which her driven pen earned, while despising the words which brought comfort, and even lately a certain luxury, to the cottage.

One of the luxuries was Beatrice Bristowe, who for twelve pounds a year gave, in those unregenerate days, not only long hours of work, but an interest and devotion which no money could buy, either then or now. Beatrice was looking forward to the move to London in the spring and a rise of two pounds a year with pride and excitement. Already in Farley it was talked of, and Mrs Bristowe thought thankfully of Beaty's round plain face and clumsy manners.

'She won't get into no trouble,' she said optimistically to her husband. 'They say Mrs Fairfield won't let Miss Marinda go.'

Nothing was hidden in Farley and Belle's opposition to Marinda's leaving home was well known. Beaty, opening the door, looked pityingly at Marinda in her new pink muslin dress, because she was not going to London.

For the winter Laura had been lent a small house in St John's Wood, which belonged to a friend of hers who was going to Italy and said she could not be bothered with letting the house to strangers. Laura felt this was an unexpected gift which she must repay to Fate, so as the tea cleared the tired corners of her mind, she said impulsively to Mark: 'You say you've nowhere peaceful where you can work. Take this place for the winter. I'll lend it to you, if you promise to keep it clean, and then you'll have no excuse for not working.'

Mark thanked her and made no protest against a generosity which he knew she could hardly afford. The world he lived in was casual and freehanded.

'When can I come?' was all he said.

'In the middle of October. The Fairfields will be kind to you, won't they, Marinda?'

Marinda was sitting a little way from the lamp like a quiet ghost. The thought of having Mark as a neighbour warmed her with sharp pleasure, but some perverse instinct made her say: 'I shall be away until November with Aunt Emma. We are going to Fladbury Spa for Uncle's gout.'

'But Sue will be there,' said Carey. 'You know, Mark, Sue and Marinda are like those little weather men. They are never out together. Their Aunt Emma always has possession of one of them.'

'Then,' said Mark, 'I must make do with Sue.'

He looked mockingly at Marinda, and she was tortured for the first time with the fear of Sue as a rival. The two girls, owing to the disparity in ages and the fact that they were so often separated, had little of the friendly intimacy of sisters. But it had never occurred to Marinda that Sue's short curls and kitten's eyes could one day menace her happiness. Mark looked again at Marinda. 'And I shall look forward to the end of your stay.'

By the following morning Marinda was quite certain that she was in love with Mark. Love, other than a romantic emotion, had never been explained to her and even if she had understood more biology and the ways of the world, it is doubtful if her immature body and inexperienced spirit would have withstood the violence of the feeling for Mark which now overwhelmed her. In spite of her upbringing on a farm, her ignorance was ridiculous and profound. She had once asked Bessie some pertinent questions on the facts of life and Bessie had said briefly, 'Much the same as cows and dogs.' This explanation had struck Marinda as being so revolting that it did not occur to her to consider it seriously. But all the knowledge and wisdom in the world could not save her from the inevitable poignancy of first love. She hugged her secret and gave herself up to days of alternating excitement, happiness and disappointment.

The click of the cottage gate brought her, like a shot fired from a gun, into the lane; a message to take to Laura from her mother was charged with hope and uncertainty; each stray observation of Mark's was treasured and reconsidered, until the visit to Fladbury at the end of the week became an impending tragedy. It was impossible for her to see her life stretching forward in endless variety of adventure and experience until Mark was but an episode. She walked by the side of the river and contemplated exile with her aunt and, as a pleasurable alternative, suicide.

'This is a favourite walk of yours, I think.'

She looked across the river with startled pleasure. On the other side, separated from her by the deep, red banks and swift water, was Mark Studland.

'I've seen you here a good many times,' he went on, bending a fishing-rod.

'You must have remarkable eyesight,' answered Marinda, and then wished she had said something else. Their conversation came clearly across the water with the unreality of stage dialogue.

'As a matter of fact,' said Mark, 'I saw you through my telescope.'

'Telescope?'

'Yes, I have a telescope.' He swung his fishing-rod gracefully over the water. 'I am interested in astronomy.' Then he laughed. His laugh was mocking but agreeable and Marinda had no idea which of his statements was true.

'I say, can't I get across? I'll wade.'

'No, please don't try, it's very dangerous. The current – people drown,' shouted Marinda. 'There's a footbridge further on.'

'Watch me,' he called. 'I'll come across those boulders at the bend.'

Like a tightrope walker he balanced on the stones, holding his rod carefully out of reach of the willows. Marinda's mind became empty of everything except anxiety. Strangers knew nothing of the treachery of the Brene, which claimed the bodies of the over-adventurous in its seductive waters every year. As he jumped from the last boulder to the bank his foot slipped and he dropped his fishing-rod. Marinda put out a hand and saved it while he caught the willow branches above his head.

'Well, here I am, only a little wet,' he said, wringing out the knee of his Norfolk suit, 'and thank you for saving Pen's rod. I only took it to give me an excuse. I hate fishing.'

'So do I,' said Marinda, struck with the miracle that they both hated fishing.

'I like sitting by the water and thinking, but I do so dislike taking the fish off the hook. A very good thing, as I seldom get a bite.'

'But there's a bit I liked in "The Silver Tree" about fishing, about the "cool trout, artful in the weeds".'

'Oh, so you've read it?'

'Yes, I've just read it again. I mean, I'd read it ages ago when the Grays were all talking about it, and then, when I got to know you I thought I'd – well, I read bits of it again.'

'And did you like it?'

'Yes, I liked it better the second time, but then it was mixed up with you, personally I mean, and that made it difficult to judge.'

'And do you like me?'

'Yes,' said Marinda solemnly, 'I do.'

'Well,' said Mark, picking up his hat, which lay between them at their feet, 'isn't that a good thing, because –'

He paused, dropped his hat again, and put his hands on her shoulders. Her eyes were nearly on a level with his, because in the last few years she had grown until she had overtaken Sue, and their limpid sincerity was fatally attractive to him.

He slipped his arms across her shoulders.

'Because I think you are beautiful,' he breathed into her hair.

He kissed her gently on her yielding mouth, tenderly and then with passion as his hands tightened on her unresisting body. He knew nothing of the fire that his kisses aroused in her, but he thought she was very sweet and that it was a pity she was going away and he said so.

'But when I come back, you will still be here, won't you?' said Marinda. She was as vulnerable as a trapped animal.

'I expect so, I never know very far ahead. I hate being tied by my own plans, but perhaps if I am to see you again –'

'I will write and tell you. Could I do that?'

'Of course you could. But don't expect an answer. Letter-writing bores me.'

He kissed her again, and at the farm gate he left her and went off to Laura's cottage, his sensitive emotions stimulated, so that words, after a long silence on the part of his muse, began to trickle together into his mind. He wanted to be alone with them and he walked off across the orchard in a state of exhilaration, while Marinda, dazed, ignorant and young, walked slowly through the side door into the house. She, too, wanted to be alone to revive in her memory every word and look of Mark's. She fancied she was deeply and irrevocably in love, and there was nothing in her pitiful lack of experience to disabuse her of the notion.

From the front windows she noted that the Souths' motor-car was in the drive and she supposed that her aunt had come over to collect some of her luggage, for the journey to Fladbury was to be taken in the new monster, in preparation for which Marinda had been fitted out with veils and dust cloaks and a new, small trunk. From the dark little gun-room on the right, which her father used as an office, came the deep murmuring of male voices. Edward Stonebridge must have driven over, thought Marinda. Her Aunt Emma must be somewhere in the house or garden with her mother, but the drawing-room was untouched since its turn-out of the previous day. On the table in the window the bold faces of the dahlias dropped a petal as she banged the door on the empty room.

'Where is Mother?' she asked Bessie, who came awkwardly up the passage from the kitchen with a heavy tray, to lay in the dining-room the cold supper which was the custom at Foxholes.

Bessie jerked her head in the direction of the kitchen garden. 'Cutting some lettuces,' she said. 'There warn't enough with Mr Stonebridge staying to supper, I shouldn't wonder. She was asking for you. I said you'd gone off somewhere, but I saw you come up the lane.'

She gave a loud laugh and Marinda felt for a moment that everything about Bessie, from her red hands to her suggestive grin, was somehow revolting. She walked out through the front door and beyond the mulberry tree towards the kitchen garden with her nerves taut and a vague feeling that the world would be a better place if she, and of course Mark, lived alone in it. Bessie looked after her, resting the tray on her hip and her good-natured grin faded.

'Such a madam as she's growing,' she thought. 'She'll be even more trouble than Miss Sue.'

Belle straightened her back and shook the earth off a couple of lettuces. 'Oh, Marinda,' she called, 'come here, dear, I have some wonderful news for you.'

Marinda came slowly up the cinder path and stopped by a large marrow which was being saved for the Harvest Festival. She looked up at her mother with mild interest. Belle had often had what she called 'wonderful news' which only turned out to be a new washerwoman or the result of the Missionary Fête.

'It's Edward Stonebridge, my love,' she said with shining eyes, stepping over the lettuces towards Marinda. 'Just think, he wants to marry you.'

Marinda stood still, but for the trembling of a little nerve in her neck, just where Mark had kissed her she thought.

'Well, darling, what do you say? Isn't it lovely for you?'

Belle stopped, looking at her child with sudden misgiving.

'You would like to marry him, wouldn't you, my darling?' she went on, holding the lettuces in her hand like a bouquet. She was so overjoyed at the thought of either of her daughters marrying such a suitable and worthy young man, that it did not seem possible for Marinda to view the proposal with anything but enthusiasm.

'Wouldn't you, darling?' she repeated.

'Oh, Mother, no! No, of course not! I couldn't possibly!' said Marinda. 'Not in a million years,' and turning, she ran blindly away. Her mother dropped the lettuces and hurried after her as fast as her corset-constricted plumpness would allow. But she was gone.

'Oh dear,' sighed Belle, deflated as a broken balloon. 'Who would have thought it?'

She went slowly back for the lettuces, deciding that Henry was right and perhaps she had spoilt her children. Marinda must be talked into it.

Chapter 7 — FLADBURY SPA

The snow, which half an hour ago had been cold rain, melted in rivulets on Marinda's new blue coat, as she shut her unmanageable umbrella. It was Aunt Emma's best silk one, with a long crook tipped with mother-of-pearl, and she thought it better to risk the white wings in her velvet hat than to let the snow break the umbrella. She was nearly at Eversleigh Gardens, and already the towers of the Eversleigh Hotel broke the beauty of the Georgian street.

The porter opened the door and smiled. It was not often that anyone so young as Marinda was seen amongst its arthritic patients.

'How is Mrs South today, miss?' he asked.

'Better, thank you,' said Marinda. 'The doctor says the bone is knitting nicely.' 'Two plain, two purl', thought an imp in her mind. 'And it won't be long before she can be moved, I hope.'

She shook the snowflakes off with a certain grace. Thin and supple as a birch sapling, she now moved, not with the rawness of a schoolgirl, but with something bordering on elegance. An old man, sitting by the fire in the hall, watched her with a warm wave of pleasure which now took the place of desire in his withered body.

'So you're leaving us soon, Miss Fairfield?' he said, turning awkwardly round, like a screw which is wrongly set.

'I hope so, Mr Binns. It was so awful spending Christmas away from home, but I expect to be back for the New Year.'

All the ritual of seeing the New Year in at Foxholes, Jeff's ceremonial walk through the house because the Fairfield men were all light-haired, the waits, the laughter, the good wishes, swam in a melting picture before her eyes.

'Well, it was nice for us that you could be here for Christmas, but that accident of your aunt's was unlucky for her, most unlucky. Of course it might have been worse.'

Marinda, climbing the stairs (for she was secretly a little afraid of the newly installed lift), thought it could hardly have been worse. She was not as fond of her aunt as was her sister Sue, and when the poor woman slipped one frosty morning in late November and broke her ankle it was only a strong sense of duty and long admonitions from her mother which kept her from running home for Christmas.

Uncle George had come to join their sad little party, but Edward Stonebridge had astonished everyone by discovering cousins in London and spending Christmas with them. For this Marinda was deeply thankful and his understanding of her refusal of his love made her gradually sorry for him. Her aunt, however, comforted herself with the thought that girls of that age were very awkward and Belle had probably blurted it all out and frightened the child. Because she thought she would 'come round in time', she ceased to nag Marinda and contented herself with singing Edward's praises, but in those days Marinda thought of no one but Mark. She was so sure that he loved her that she thought she had only to return to Farley and then nothing could prevent endless happiness. The two months' absence, now stretching into nearly a quarter of a year, had been a penance, but she had been comforted by the knowledge that Mark's acquaintance with her family had deepened. In the same way that Belle had added Laura to her family, so now in Laura's vacant place there was Mark. Belle refused to believe that a young man living alone could do other than starve. He was not at all her idea of a poet, being neither penniless nor long-haired, but he was thin and neither Belle nor her sister Emma could bear to see anyone unduly thin without wishing to nourish him.

It was thus on a diet of home-cured ham and her own butter that the idea of a Christmas masque was born. Andrew was to sing and Sue could declaim quite prettily. Other talent was discovered in the neighbourhood, and for weeks all the letters from Farley were about the masque. Marinda thought she would die with disappointment when she realized it would all have to take place without her, although the thought of having an active part in such an affair made her knees quiver.

That Mark never wrote her a letter she did not consider strange. She knew he hated writing letters and there were messages from Sue which she hugged to her heart. 'Mr Studland hopes you are well and says he misses you.' 'Mr Studland hopes you will be back in time for the masque', and then 'Mark hopes you are well.' At Christmas he sent her a card, an odd one, she thought, just a woodcut of a thrush on a bush. All the other greetings she had were vaguely flavoured with Dickens, but she treasured this because it showed his handwriting for the first time, small and neat, almost like printing. 'Best wishes, Mark Studland.'

'Did you change my book?' asked her aunt as Marinda hung up her damp coat.

'No, they said it would probably be in this afternoon, so I will run down for it after lunch. I like a walk.'

Any excuse served Marinda to escape from her prison.

'Oh no, child, not in this weather.'

'It may have cleared up by then.'

They both looked out at the swirling feathers of snow, white only for an instant in flight, to become, under hurrying feet, the brown slush of the town.

Seeing Foxholes soothed by its snow blanket in her mind's eye, Marinda thought 'I hate this place', but aloud she said brightly: 'I think I will start my packing. It's only four more days.'

Emma's face folded into offended lines. Three months away from home in the lap of luxury, you might say, and the child had never stopped longing for Foxholes. But before she could speak Marinda added, 'If I pack now, it will give me more time to help you.'

Three months with her aunt had coated her youthful frankness with a veil of polite insincerity. She had unconsciously become one of those who must avoid hurting her aunt's feelings. She did not know, and if she had known she would not then have understood, the cause of Emma's sudden fretful depressions. Her childlessness and the gradual withdrawal of her husband's love, made her long to possess such young things as Marinda, Sue and Edward Stonebridge. Of the three she thought Edward was the most satisfactory.

'I have bought my going home presents. Would you like to see them?' said Marinda. 'I spent some of the money Uncle gave me. He wouldn't mind, would he?'

'No, of course not, but he meant it for you.'

Emma smiled. Money had not worried her for so many years that she was amused by Marinda's habit of keeping it in mental compartments as if The Money Uncle George Gave Me was of different currency from The Pocket Money Father Sent.

'I bought Andrew a game. It's called "Counties of England". I thought it would help him with his geography. He's very bad at geography.'

Andrew was also very bad at history, Latin and spelling, shining mysteriously at mathematics.

'And for Mother I bought some handkerchiefs and these stockings are for Bessie and Lucy, but the most beautiful thing of all is this scarf for Sue. It will be useful now that she is staying with Aunt Fan – but I shall have to post it to her.'

Marinda let the scarf rest lightly on her own fair hair and the soft net gave her a bridal look. Then she whipped it off and folded it lovingly into its box. 'I haven't thought of anything for Father,' she said.

Aunt Emma's bright eyes hardened. She liked to feel that Sue and Marinda were hers and she disapproved of Sue's visit to Fan in London and hinted gloomily at disastrous consequences. Sue was now twenty-four, gay with a certain pertness, due less to her manner than to her upturned nose and dark curly hair. Her eyes were round and green, like a kitten's, with a feline mixture of innocence and mystery. The clothes of 1912 gave her an air of maturity and already people wondered why Sue Fairfield had not married. Sometimes in sudden fright she herself wondered if she were not turning into the counterpart of the spinster sisters of the Vicar or old Miss Cox who lived at Cuffley Manor with thirty-five cats.

It was not that Sue's charms did not attract men, for the few who crossed her path were always intrigued by her bright colouring and the slender contours of her figure, revealed here and hidden there in the constricting whim of fashion. She came to believe that a husband such as she desired (for her ambitions did not range beyond her wedding) would be easy enough to secure if only she could meet this paragon, not foreseeing that the emptiness which lay behind the pretty lines of her face might detract, as the years passed, from her charms. Her letters about the impending visit to London were full of the joys of anticipation, 'Aunt Fan was taking her to Lady Silcourt's ball, to "The Great Adventure" and to hear Caruso. Of course, it wasn't the season, Aunt Fan said, but . . .'

Marinda never understood how Sue could bear to be so long and often away from Foxholes. It was the only place in the world, Marinda thought, where one could be perfectly safe and happy. It was as if a moat surrounded it to keep out the world, and once over it she was sure of the welcome and love which seemed lacking outside. As she packed away her presents and began slowly and blissfully to spread her clothes in neat piles on the bed she imagined the creak of the gate and the surging forth of the family, dogs barking, and the front door open wide. The picture remained clear in a corner of her mind as she packed, helped her aunt, saw to the matter of cabs, trains, and started on the short but tedious journey, with its long wait at Headley Junction, before picking up the slow train to Marchampton.

They approached the city from the north, which gave her a different picture of the March Hills, lying across the country at an unfamiliar angle. It was after two o'clock when they arrived, and George South suggested that he should drive out to Farley with Marinda in order that he could be back by dark. George still used his motor-car as if it were a horse which needed a certain amount of exercise, and almost felt that twenty miles at a stretch, if indeed it proceeded so far without breaking down, was all that could be asked of it.

Marinda put on her dust-coat joyfully. She did not forget to thank her aunt for her lovely stay at Fladbury but it was the thought of home which brought the excited sparkle to her eyes.

'You've been a good child,' said her aunt. 'I don't know how I should have managed without you, indeed I don't.'

Edward Stonebridge did not come out of the dispensary. Uncle George said he was busy and it was market day, but Marinda knew that it was she who was keeping him away. She was thankful to be saved embarrassment, but in her relief there was a trace of disappointment. Edward had always been there, and it was not until he was missing that one realized the amount of space he occupied in her homecoming thoughts. As she tied a veil over her hat and nestled under the fur rug by the side of her uncle, it seemed as if she had slipped right out of her childhood and that even her homecoming might not be the same.

Yet they were all safely there. Here at sheltered Foxholes the little snow which had fallen had quickly melted in the pallid sunshine, but it was cold and Andrew's cap was tied on with a blue scarf to protect his ears, as he swung on the gate waiting for them. Marinda could hear its friendly creak above the distress of the motor's engine.

She could not tell how she knew that this homecoming was different, for they stood there as usual in the porch: Mother, hastily shrouded in the old cloak which hung in the hall for this purpose, and Father with his meerschaum and the *Marchampton Advertiser*. The dogs were there and Louis the cat was spitting from the wall which separated the garden from the rickyard. It was all inevitably the same and yet Marinda felt a disappointing chill of foreboding that the good, happy things were slipping away. No one ran down the path to meet her. The dogs barked unchecked as Marinda kissed her parents.

'Ah, child! I am glad – oh so glad, you've come home.'

George gave his sister-in-law's soft, fat cheek a platonic peck. There was always a pause before he decided whether he should or should not kiss her, thus making his embrace a matter of importance rather than a custom. This time Belle put up her cheek unconsciously. It was unlined and silky under George's moustache.

'You'll never believe what has happened,' said Belle, moving into the drawing-room, warmed by a log fire and freshly cleaned and opened for the occasion, so that everything smelt faintly of *pot-pourri* and old books and furniture polish.

'Don't be alarmed, old fellow. Belle is all worked up. You know how she gets . . .'

Henry looked at his wife with deprecating affection.

'Whatever has happened, Mother?' said Marinda, untying her veil.

Belle began to tell her story. Distressed as she was, she was enjoying the drama of the situation. 'Well,' she said, 'I suppose it's not very terrible. It's only so sudden, so entirely unexpected. When she went off to Fan's, who'd have thought of such a thing?'

'Really, Belle,' said George, 'do get on with the story. Whatever do you mean? I expect when we get to the point, it will be nothing at all.' His sister-in-law's method of telling a story always infuriated him.

Andrew stood in the doorway rubbing his ears, which had been tickled by his scarf. Regardless of his dirty boots he walked over the plush slip-mat leaving wet tracks on the polished boards.

'If you want to know,' he said calmly, 'it's only that Sue is married.'

'Is that all?' grumbled George. 'Surely that's a good thing. You can't have two daughters on your hands for ever, Henry, with hops at the price they are.'

It then occurred to him that the name of his nephew-in-law might be of interest.

'Who is the chap?' he asked.

'That's what is so extraordinary,' said Belle. 'All the time he was here I never thought of such a thing. It seems as soon as Sue got to Fan's they ran off and –'

'Are they married?' asked George with sudden ferocity.

'Oh yes, of course. She was married yesterday – to Mark Studland.'

'Never heard of him,' said George with such emphasis that one might have thought his ignorance of Mark made him cease to exist.

'Oh yes, George, you remember. He was staying with the Grays and then he took their house when they went to London, and we thought he was going to stay until the spring. He wrote a sort of play which they all acted. Sue was really sweet in it and Andrew sang . . .'

Her soft voice went on and on and Marinda had a curious feeling of unreality. 'This isn't happening to me at all,' she thought as she saw her oval face in the big gilt mirror over the fireplace. The lustre ornaments on the mantelshelf, the photograph on the wall of her mother's wedding with the bridesmaids in improbable hats suddenly had no connection with space or time. This moment simply was not. She did not dare to sit down while her elders stood in an agitated group by the fire, but she leant back on the arm of the sofa, for her legs seemed to be melting like hot candles.

'Don't sit on the arm of the sofa, child,' admonished her mother with maternal habit.

Marinda straightened her back and smoothed the antimacassar. They were all talking at once and of course it wasn't true at all. It simply wasn't true. It couldn't be. Unnoticed, she walked out through the front door across the lawn and into the lane. The trees were black with winter, as if they had died for ever. A robin sang thinly on the gate of the Grays' cottage. Not knowing what she did, she walked up the path, dismal with neglect. The box-like house stood before her like a mocking face. She gave a little cry, as if she had suddenly seen a ghost, and turned and ran back to Foxholes.

Book Two

Chapter 8 — THE SOLDIER

The train to Marchampton was late and it was already beginning to get dark. Sue looked at the drunken soldier, singing and lurching a few feet away, with distaste and annoyance. She used to be frightened of drunken men, but now she was merely anxious that he should not wake three-months-old Duffy, who was sleeping peacefully as yet on her arm. Just within sight she could see Mark's back, different from the others even in his uniform. There was a casualness, almost a grace, about the lines of his body as he stood gazing down the track, far enough away, he hoped, for no one to connect him with his wife and son on the seat and near enough that he need not fear charges of neglect from Sue's tongue. For the uncertainties of marriage with Mark had sharpened everything about Sue, her tongue, her wits and her expression. Even her tip-tilted nose seemed more pointed as her eyes darted round the familiar dreariness of Headley Junction.

She had not been home since her marriage over two years ago, and though her unconventional behaviour had long been officially forgiven by letter, this was her first visit.

When the war broke out she and Mark had been in Paris. Their married life seemed to have been passed in trunks and suitcases, for as soon as Sue had put out her family photographs and settled the spirit stove for making tea and found someone to talk to, Mark would come flaming in and say: 'I can't write a word in this place. Let's go to Fiesole', or 'Rapallo', or 'A little place outside Dinard.' At first Sue loved the gaiety and change and then Mark became less gay, so that it was only the change which attracted her. At length even the constant change palled. It was about this time that she had lost the beginnings of her first baby, almost before she had time to unpack in that dreary room in Bruges.

Mark was sorry for her then and she was too heart-broken to nag or sharpen her tongue, so that for a time they came nearer to each other, but when she wanted to leave Bruges to escape from its quaintness, burnt in pretty, heartrending pictures in her memory, for once Mark would not. He had friends there with whom he drank and laughed and talked what he called 'his language' while Sue wept unexpectedly when spoken to and lost her looks.

'Why don't you go home for a bit?' he had said, but she would not go to Foxholes without him. It was Aunt Emma who finally saved her. In July 1914 she and Uncle George, greatly daring, came to Paris. There had been talks of war and Uncle George was full of misgiving, but Aunt Emma, once her plans were made, was determined to see Paris and she overruled her easy-going husband. Sue's spirits rose and she packed her trunks and told Mark she was going to Paris to see Aunt Emma for a week.

It was like a tonic to Sue to whirl round the city with her obviously provincial relatives behind her and show off her knowledge of Paris and the Parisians. She became voluble to waiters, cab-drivers and station officials in order to demonstrate how easy it was to speak French and her uncle and aunt were amazed and proud. She wore the bright colours she loved with such an air that her hobble skirts became miracles of elegance. When Mark came, after ten days, chased to Paris by rumours of war, he fell in love with her very slightly as if she were not his wife at all, but one of the women who had inevitably punctuated his life with affairs of varying depth and about which she knew nothing.

He had always declared himself to be a pacifist, but as soon as they were back in London, staying in lodgings which Pen Gray found for them in Kensington, he was chased into uniform by a mixture of emotions. In these there was a certain amount of patriotic idealism, but he also wanted to escape into some other life, and in his gloomier moments he wished that he might be killed. He would be better dead, he would say, and Sue would cry and cling to him while he gently freed himself from her as if she were some tiresome briar. Sue was unhappy without knowing quite why, until she found she was again expecting a child.

They were in Yorkshire where Mark was undergoing

training, and Sue, with her heavy body, followed him to Wales where she could see the March Hills from the far other side, and thence to the Scottish borders. Her baby was due in three months' time and it was arranged that she should go back to Foxholes for its birth, though she herself, embarrassed though she was by her ungainly figure, was terrified of leaving Mark. There were continual rumours of a move to France and the casualty lists contained many familiar names. With what, Sue considered, to be great luck, Mark broke his leg on a training exercise and was thus safe from the enemy for a time, but her baby was born unexpectedly at Dunbar two months too early. She was very ill and it took all the skill and kindness of a strange Scottish doctor to keep them both alive. As soon as she was well enough Mark had ten days' leave and they made the long journey to Foxholes to recuperate. The baby was small but healthy and Sue recovered more quickly than anyone expected. She realized that if she was to keep Mark she could not afford to be ill, and in those days was born in her a fortitude which removed for ever the soft lines of her mouth and made her impatient with the sufferings of others.

When the Marchampton train came in it was full of soldiers, and in spite of first-class tickets in his pocket Mark battered helplessly against the crowd in the corridor. If it had not been for his wife and baby he would have found it difficult to board the train at all, but a way was miraculously found for Sue and later a seat into which she sank gratefully. Mark stood in the corridor just out of sight and smoked. Everywhere was pervaded by the sharp smell of wet uniforms and hot bodies and tobacco. Duffy wrinkled his nose and coughed and Sue patted him gently, horrified lest he should cry.

Dusk deepened gradually into darkness and hid the familiar landmarks as Duffy and Sue, gathering comfort from each other, spent the journey in little bursts of conscious tiredness or snatches of merciful sleep until the train drew in at Marchampton. It was so long that it pulled up awkwardly with their coach just out of reach of the platform. In the gloom Sue thought she could see Marinda as she waited for the engine to jolt on a few yards and allow them to alight.

'Sue darling! How are you? And is this Duffy? Why, he's like you, just like you, except –'

Mark held out his hand. 'How are you, Marinda?'

'Hallo, Mark,' she said briefly, looking him full in the face with an uncompromising gaze. Then she turned back to the baby. 'Duffy has Mark's eyes,' she said. 'You must be frozen and starved. Edward has Uncle's car and is driving us out to Foxholes. It is a new Riley and it really goes. I told him to wait at the barrier in case we missed you. There's an awful crowd. A hospital train just came in on Number Four and I expect Aunt Emma is there somewhere. Cups of tea for our gallant heroes. You lose a leg and they give you a cup of tea. Lord, how I hate the war! Shall I take the baby? Or do you think he will yell?'

'If you would,' said Sue thankfully. 'My arm is breaking off and Mark can't of course – not in uniform.'

Marinda glanced at Mark. He looked younger in uniform, as if indeed his wife and baby were incongruous appendages.

'I'll see to the bags,' he said.

They left him standing by a flat-footed porter as if he were commanding a battalion, but in the end it was Edward who helped to find the luggage and grappled with straps and ropes to fix it on to the car.

At Foxholes the war seemed very far away, partly because the papers, with news of the bombardment of Zeebrugge and Zeppelin raids and the long lists of casualties, did not arrive at breakfast, so that one spent the day trying to find time to read them; and partly because everyone at the farm was absorbed in the importance of its routine. But although the guns were remote, the war had much affected the Fairfields. It had in fact saved Foxholes, for in the spring of 1914 Henry Fairfield had been kept awake at night by the gathering volume of his overdraft. Now he was making money. How much he did not know, because his ideas on finance had always been vague, but at last the bank manager was more friendly. The accounts which Marinda had started to keep looked good enough to him.

The war had changed Marinda's whole existence, sending

her ambitions off in another direction and stiffening her with a sense of purpose. The unhappy months after Sue's marriage now seemed the experience of some other young and infinitely more stupid person. At the beginning of the war her father was taken ill with a gastric ulcer and from his bed he gave orders to Marinda and Andrew and Jeff, who thus found themselves running the farm; indeed more than running it, for Andrew took his turn with the hoeing and muck-spreading and Marinda learnt to milk. Her mother took the dairymaid's place and made the butter. The farm became again a compact community, everyone with a job, necessary and important. When Henry was well enough to work again he did not praise them, for that was not his way, but he walked round his acres with more pride than he had done for many years. The wheat was in and if it was anything like a crop it should fetch a good price. The hunters, except for old Monarch, had been commandeered, and although the empty stables were a sad sight, there was no temptation to hunt twice a week. Instead he rode round gently on old Monarch and grumbled about the foxes.

It was Edward Stonebridge who suggested to Marinda that she should help with the accounts and even showed her a method of doing so. Marinda was not good at figures, but she was neat and accurate and in time came to see in her ledgers the whole history of her beloved Foxholes. It was in the dark, so-called gun-room, amongst her father's pipes and the curling copies of the *Farmers' Weekly* and her father's single twelve-bore, that Edward once more asked her to marry him.

He had closed the ledger.

'Well, that's getting to look more shipshape,' he said. 'Nice to see your father about again.'

'He has aged a lot.'

'Oh, he will pick up. Why, he's not much past sixty.'

Marinda had looked through the inadequate window across to the stables, which made the room so gloomy, to where her father stood stroking Monarch's nose before Jim took him to his box. She had never felt near to her father until she grew up and was old enough to realize and share their common passion for the farm.

'Marinda,' said Edward, 'you won't change your mind? I would give all I have to marry you.'

'No, I am sorry, Edward. I do like you so much. It would be lovely to say "Yes" and make you and everyone happy, but it would be wrong. I don't love you.'

She did not mean to show little heart but she did not love him and she said so, yet as she spoke he gave a long sigh and she caught a glimpse of his pain, because of all that she herself had suffered two years ago.

'Edward, would it – would it be easier for us not to meet? I always seem to be needing your help over something, but if it makes it difficult for you –'

'Ah no, don't talk of it. I won't ask again, but if you change your mind, don't forget that I shall always be glad to hear it.'

'Oh rubbish, Edward! There's that nice Miss Cheriton and I hear Uncle is taking in a lady dispenser. You can marry her. Think how suitable it would be.'

She had laughed, gently teasing, but Edward did not smile.

'I don't think I shall change,' he had said.

And now as Marinda saw Edward struggling with the luggage in the darkness with his thin, clever hands, she felt impatient with him that he could not light the spark which one glance at Mark could dangerously kindle.

There was so much more to be said than had been told in letters and the two young women began a whispering chatter in the back seat across the sleeping Duffy.

'The war has given Uncle George and Aunt Emma a new lease of life. Uncle can't retire because all the assistants have gone. Edward keeps saying he will go too, but so far we have persuaded him that he is doing as good a job at home.'

Sue looked complacently at Mark's uniformed back. Although she had stormed, wept and cajoled to keep him by her side, she was now proud that she had not succeeded.

'And Carey is coming back,' Marinda continued. 'Isn't that wonderful? She is going to help us on the farm. She hasn't been well and the doctor thinks it will do her good, so Mrs Gray is bringing her back at the end of the month.

Their house has been let all this time, first one person, then another, mostly army people. There's a big camp at Overbury. I expect you will notice a lot of changes. Andrew is quite grown up and he's a great help. I believe he will make a farmer after all, only we've all spoilt him so terribly. It's a wonder he's even human, Edward says. His voice? Oh well, of course he only croaks now. It may develop later on, Mr Frobisher says, and if so, he will try for a scholarship at Kings, if we can spare him from the farm and if the war is over. In another two years he will have to go, but it could never last until he has to go, could it?'

'I don't know,' said Sue soberly. 'They said it would be over by last Christmas.'

'Edward is terribly gloomy about it and he is the only intelligent person I meet. I mean the only person who doesn't think Foxholes comes first. I shall be glad when the Grays are back. Did you know Pen is in the Navy? Oh Sue, it is fun to have you home again! Does it feel queer?'

In spite of all the welcome it was queer, thought Sue, and that night as she lay in bed and saw Mark's Sam Browne belt hanging on the chair where Marinda's clothes always used to be she had a strange feeling that her husband was an interloper.

Marinda had moved out of the room she used to share with Sue, partly because she thought Sue would like to be back in her old bed and partly because there was more room in it for Andrew's old cot. Mark stood looking at her bookshelves where the product of Christmas and birthdays gave hints of Marinda's gradual development, from *Little Women* to *The Hound of Heaven*. *Little Women* was shabby, because it had remained a favourite.

'Rossetti,' murmured Mark, fingering the titles, 'I remember she used to love Rossetti.'

He picked out a thin volume which bore his own name and read a stanza here and there, thinking with a shock of surprise: 'That's not bad. Not bad at all – did I write that?'

He had not produced anything worth while since 'The Silver Tree'. Perhaps it was the war, perhaps it was his marriage. Whatever the cause he resented it, not considering for a moment that such fault might lie within himself.

'Mark, do come to bed,' whispered Sue, for Duffy was stirring and she dared not speak aloud, although she knew that whispering always annoyed Mark. 'What on earth are you reading?'

'*Little Women*,' said Mark.

Foxholes was still lit by candles and he snuffed them one by one.

'Do you know I haven't written a word for months?' he said angrily through the bedclothes. He would not whisper. Let the child wake.

But Duffy did not wake. He screwed up his face and turned and sighed. Before the last candle was extinguished Mark had looked at his child and his face had suddenly softened. It was at such rare moments that Sue's world became cosy. She blew out the candle for him and sought his hand across the space between the beds. It was not there, and although she was at Foxholes again, where she had so often longed to be, although she could hear the dogs barking across the field and the church clock striking eleven and the far sound of water rushing against the weir, sounds so familiar that she felt they had been there since the beginning of time, yet because her husband's hand did not touch hers in the darkness and she could not feel the warmth of his body against hers, she felt lonely and fearful.

Mark walked round the farm with his father-in-law and saw something which to Henry Fairfield was not there. He saw not the good crops and the bad crops, the mended gate, the broken fence, but some melting quality of earth and sky which turned into poetry in his mind and became locked there. The wind blew uselessly against the March Hills and the willows swayed until their bare branches touched the water. The two men sheltered against a hedge to light their pipes and watched Marinda in the far corner of the field talking to the shepherd.

'She's a wonderful girl,' said Henry proudly. 'Don't know what we'd do without her. Of course, she doesn't know much, but she learns and learns fast. Belle says it's no life for a girl, but I often think it's a good thing for us she didn't marry young Stonebridge.'

Mark had never known that Edward had wanted to marry Marinda and he looked across the field at her thin figure hidden in a riding mackintosh, her legs lost in Andrew's fishing-boots. Only her coronet of hair proclaimed that she was not a slender youth.

When her father called her she was about to slip over the stile and down the river-path home, for she found Mark sufficiently disturbing to wish to avoid him, but her father called and she walked obediently towards him down the furrows of the field, with her dog at her heels.

'I was just showing Mark the Starveacre now it's ploughed up,' said Henry complacently, as if the sight of its bracken and rabbit holes turned into neat furrows was a proper amusement for a new son-in-law, but Mark's eyes were looking higher, across the hedges and the willows and the stone roofs of the village to the long line of the hills. Marinda's eyes, too, looked up at the view, ever-changing, ever familiar.

'"The Vision of Piers Plowman",' said Mark. 'I don't wonder Langland could write there.'

> 'In Somer Season
> When soft was the Sonne
> Ac on a May morwenying . . .'

quoted Marinda dreamily.

'So you know it?'

'I learnt it at school. All Marchshire children learn it, but it sticks because I love it.'

The top of the hills was lost in the clouds.

> 'When March Hills wear a cap,
> Men in the valley, beware of that,'

quoted Henry. 'There's poetry for you and damned good sense, too.'

He was surprised to find that he did not dislike his new son-in-law as much as he wanted to. Poet indeed.

He lifted the broken gate and pushed it through the mud, breaking it a little more as he did so. Together they all came into the lane leading back to the farm, and as Henry crossed the road he said: 'Better take Mark back to the house, it's beginning to rain. I'm just going to see Jeff about the cattle feed.' He turned back across the field.

'You don't write much now?' observed Marinda. The rain began to spit gently into the puddles as they sprang from island to island along the ruts. 'I saw a poem in the *Signal*, just a short one, a month or two ago, but that's all.'

'Did you like it?'

'Oh yes, I did, but it hadn't – I don't know how to describe it – that sort of magic there was in "The Silver Tree".'

'But there were parts of "The Silver Tree" which you criticized.'

'Yes, I know. That wasn't polite of me, but I am only just beginning to distinguish good from bad. The Grays taught me that. At one time I thought writing poetry was so clever that it must be good.'

'Like Sue,' said Mark.

'I suppose you get all the admiration you want from her?'

'More than enough. That's why I can't write. "What do you think of this?" I say, "That's wonderful, dear," is all I get. "That's wonderful, dear,"' he repeated, his voice harsher. '"How much will you get for it?" If I wrote verses for Christmas cards that's what she'd say. The sight of my name in print and the cheque is all she wants. I had a talent, a gift, a trick of words. Lord knows I had, and it's going like some childish oddity – like Andrew's voice.'

'Perhaps it's the war,' comforted Marinda. One put everything down to the war, from a lowered milk yield to the drying up of Mark's muse. 'Don't you hate it?'

'I hate the waste of people and time. Of course I do. It's loathsome, but there are parts of it I like – even enjoy. It horrifies me.'

'Like me with the farm. I hate the mud and cold mornings and pig-killing, but I love the lambs and the even curves the plough makes and all the different greens and browns and that queer grey. I wish I could paint.'

How easy it was to talk to Mark, she thought. She had almost forgotten that he had ever kissed her, that she had fancied herself in love with him. The hateful sensation of being jealous of her own sister had faded and here was Mark, a delightful friend who knew what she meant even when what she said was only half explained.

'This is my embarkation leave,' said Mark. 'I haven't told Sue. I can't face the tears, but I'm telling you, Marinda. It's a secret.'

They went on walking slowly through the rain, and suddenly into Marinda's quietly busy world came the reality of mud and guns and death.

'I suppose it had to come,' was all she said.

Sue met them at the gate with Duffy in Andrew's old perambulator, fetched from its shabby exile in the coach-house. She enjoyed showing off her baby's charms to all her friends and relatives and pushed him happily from house to house, sure of welcome and interest.

'Mrs Bristowe has been in the Grays' place lighting fires,' she announced. Already she had fallen back into the Foxholes habit of relating the tit-bits of news from their small world and forgetting the importance of anything that happened beyond its boundaries. The pettiness of it irritated Mark, partly because he seldom knew the people who had become the news of the moment, and the explanations were often so involved that he was no wiser at the end. Sometimes Marinda would catch his eye and grin, as if she knew what had annoyed him and brought his lips together in scornful superiority, and then he would lift a corner of his mouth in recognition.

At Foxholes dinner was still in the middle of the day, white damask on the long dining-table, dishes piled high with vegetables at one end, served with anxious lavishness by Belle, joint carved ceremoniously with the precision of a surgeon by Henry at the other end. The meat was invariably roast, hot or cold, for Henry disliked what he called 'fallals' and his tastes regulated the menus, so that the food, though delicious and cooked to perfection, had acquired in time a certain dullness. As yet there was no hint of shortage. The butter was piled high and the dogs were given as good food as Jeff's children down at Coppins Cottage.

The time when Bessie would at length marry the man

with whom she had been walking out on and off for nearly twenty years, and her place in the kitchen be filled inadequately by girls of varying degrees of skill and charm, could not be foreseen, and although Belle did most of the cooking and dairy work, the washing-up and the arduous work of the inconvenient house was done by Bessie and the cowman's wife, a thin, grey creature, who seemed perpetually on her hands and knees scrubbing out dark passages. Both these women were part of the life of the family, and it now struck Sue, as she sat by her father's side, that Bessie was too familiar.

The new motor bus to Marchampton, run by Mr Tibbins, the carrier, as a greatly daring venture, was under discussion.

'I wonder what time it runs,' said Mark, seeing in it a means of escape from Foxholes.

'It goes from the Red Lion about a quarter after ten and just before three,' volunteered Bessie, putting a vast apple pudding in front of Belle and carrying away the dishes.

'It's best to be there in good time,' she admonished, lingering in the doorway, the tray caught by the ledge of her stomach. 'For Mr Studland has no more idea of time than a fly,' she continued in the kitchen to Mrs Cribbage, as they took their plates out of the oven and began their belated meal.

Mark was always amazed at the Fairfields' unconscious preoccupation with food. Possessed of good appetites, they made a business of their meals. He now begged Belle to give him a smaller portion of apple pudding, not because he was not hungry, for he was interested in taste and flavour and often drove Sue to distraction by demanding something of which she had never heard, but because the sight of everyone round the table giving their whole attention to vast portions of apple pudding, passing the cream and sugar and obviously enjoying each mouthful, sickened him. Belle took no notice of his protests. Her apple puddings were feather light with butter and eggs and Mark looked, as usual, half-starved. Mark was surprised to find that he had soon finished it.

'If you are going to Marchampton,' said Sue, 'you'll be seeing Uncle George. Would you ask him if he has an

"Elixir" feeding-bottle?'

'Why should I be seeing Uncle George?'

'Well, we always do see him when we go to Marchampton,' persisted Sue.

The rest of the family began to give him commissions.

'Ask at the station about the cowcake.'

'Tell Emma we shall be pleased to see her on Sunday,' said Belle.

'Oh, Mark,' murmured Marinda, 'I wonder if my book has come in at Smith's.'

'Please, please,' said Mark irritably. 'I shan't have time for any of these things. I am going to see a chap at the barracks.'

Sue's eyes were on her baby and she said without looking at him, 'I hope you have a nice time.'

'Surely one can go and have a drink in Marchampton without being made to feel neglectful and licentious.'

There was a moment's silence.

'Edward will get my book,' said Marinda, folding her napkin and stuffing it into its heavy silver ring. 'I will telephone him to bring it on Sunday.'

The telephone was still so much of an innovation that no one thought of using it except in dire emergency. Bessie was frankly terrified of it and Belle never could remember to press the middle part of the receiver, so that she heard nothing, and came away helplessly, saying that 'So-and-so won't speak up', while Henry shouted 'Are you there?' as loudly as if his voice alone could dispense with telephone wires.

As a result of chiding and a certain amount of falsification as to whether the grandfather clock was or was not fast, Mark shot out of the house and arrived at the bridge with twenty minutes to spare. Although he could see the chimneys of Foxholes through the trees he felt suddenly unfettered and cheerful. 'If I'd thought of it earlier I might even have run up to London.'

He jingled a few coins in his pocket at the happy thought of spending money, for he loved spending, buying everyone drinks, overtipping the taxi-driver, giving a beggar a sovereign, but when he had come to the end there was nothing, so Sue often said, 'that you could see'. His income, which in peace-time was sufficient to dull any incentive to earn more, was in fact not enough to keep Sue as she liked to live, with her bills paid promptly and a new frock when she needed it, and although the war had excused him from providing for the expenses of a settled home, and he was now a captain, he seemed eternally in want of money. Again he wondered, as he had wondered at intervals since that cold December day four years before, what had possessed him that he had allowed Sue's kitten charms to lead him into the irrevocability of marriage.

Chapter 9 — THE BROTHER-IN-LAW

'Primrose three gallons, Patsy three and a half gallons,' wrote Marinda in a new account book provided by Edward, where she recorded the daily milk yield. Then she laid down her pen, stretched her legs in their shabby riding-breeches and tilted her chair back from the dining-room table to face Sue, who was knitting by the fire. The clock on the mantelpiece struck eleven bright little pings, and a log dropped off the grate.

'Well, Mark has missed the last bus,' said Marinda. 'You go to bed, Sue. I expect he will find somewhere to sleep in Marchampton. Aunt Emma would put him up, or Edward might run him home in Uncle's car.'

'Oh, I do hope he doesn't go there. He has been late so often this week. I know Mother and Father disapprove of him for going off like this. If Aunt Emma starts I shall flare up, I know I shall. They don't understand a man like Mark. He has always been used to going round – you know – and drinking with people. I don't mean he gets drunk. He just likes to go out – and it's so awkward that Father won't give him a key or let him lock up or something. It will annoy him to find us both sitting here.'

'Well, that can't be helped. Father always has the house open all day so that everything could be happily stolen by any passer-by, and at night when no one stirs out in these parts it has to be bolted and barred and chained by his own hand as if it is Marchampton Gaol. My dear Sue, you don't understand what a privilege it is that he has let me do it, and that's only because he knows I've got to go out at twelve and dose poor old Primrose. You go to bed. I think Mark is lucky that he has such an easy-going wife.'

Sue picked up her knitting and stuck her pins in the ball, as if she were stabbing somebody.

'It's the only thing I am good at, and even that he doesn't appreciate. You know, with a man like Mark you have to let him have his own way, and I can manage that generally – only . . .' She stood up and the lamplight was kind to the thin lines of her jaw and the bitter twist of her mouth. 'It's only,' she went on, turning her back so that Marinda should not see the tears that came so easily to her eyes nowadays, 'it just –'

'I know,' said Marinda gently. 'It's so often and I expect you looked forward to the leave.'

'I am always so scared of him being sent to France. If he'd only take me out sometimes.'

'Never mind. I don't suppose you'd have enjoyed being stranded in Marchampton. Go to bed, my dear. He'll turn up.'

'He could have telephoned,' said Sue.

Having defended Mark hotly against her mother's accusing hints, she was too tired to hide the fact that his behaviour on this leave had hurt her deeply.

She took her candle from the table in the hall and lit it. The flame flickered up the stairs so that the ugliness of the wallpaper and the umbrella-stand was hidden in the dim light and only the pleasing curve of the staircase was revealed. She was out of the habit of carrying a candle and she tilted it, dropping spots of wax on the carpet.

'Mind the wax,' whispered Marinda, in joking imitation of her mother's nightly admonition since they were old enough to carry their own candles. She saw the light catch Sue's mouth as it smiled in tolerant amusement. Marinda adjusted the wick of the hall lamp and went back to the dining-room.

At midnight she took the lantern and went out to the cow-shed. She wished Carey were here to help her, for she did not love animals with Carey's passion, and sick animals repelled her. But they were all part of Foxholes and she did what she was called upon to do with much the spirit of a mother who wipes up her child's vomit. She washed her hands in the icy water from the yard-pump, for the kitchen entrance was barred, then she picked her way through the garden to the front door.

She hoped the policeman had done his round for it was open and a wedge of light lay like a piece of cheese on the path. Mark's hat and belt were on the chest. She pulled off her boots in the hall and tiptoed across the floor to the dining-room door.

'So you are in, Mark,' she whispered. 'I want to lock up.'

He was sitting in her father's chair with his eyes closed, but he opened them at once, although he did not rise.

'Yes, sorry I'm late. I missed the bus so I started to walk, and then old Knighton passed me with his trap and he gave me a lift as far as the bridge. Sorry you had to wait up for me. Where's Sue?'

'Sue has gone to bed and I wasn't waiting for you. I had to stay up because Primrose is ill.'

'Primrose? Who on earth –?'

'One of the cows,' explained Marinda. 'Are you going to bed or shall I put on another log?'

'Better go to bed, I suppose. Was Sue very cross?'

'No, only disappointed.'

'That's worse.'

'Mark, have you told her about going to France?'

'No, she'll know soon enough, and if I get killed it will be a good thing. She'll have enough to live on and the minute I die you see if they don't all say I'm a genius. She'll like being the widow of a genius.'

'Oh, Mark, don't die, don't talk like that! You've got so much to live for – Sue and Duffy –'

'But I haven't got you,' said Mark solemnly.

Marinda looked at him sharply. There was something about him which seemed different and yet more honest. Her experience of drunkenness was limited to the cheerful incoherence of the farm hands on Saturday nights and at harvest suppers. She had never seen her father or uncles or any of her friends after they had exceeded their limits, or if she had they had concealed it, so that she now did not realize at once, as Sue would have done, that Mark was drunk.

He put out his hand to touch her arm.

'Give me a drink, there's a good girl,' he said.

'The whisky's in Father's cupboard and he has the key. Come on, Mark, go to bed.'

'You're so pretty, you know, Marinda, not so pretty as Sue – there's something fascinating about Sue, damn her, but there is more behind you. I love that beautiful wide look in your eyes. God, I wish I'd never married!'

Marinda thought he was talking wildly and strangely, but Mark's behaviour had always been incalculable and she might never have known he was drunk had he not told her.

'I'm drunk, Marinda darling, not drunk enough to frighten you, but just drunk enough to tell you the truth and you know what the truth is, don't you? It's you I love and always will. I was crazy to marry Sue. Marinda, why did you go away and make me marry Sue?'

'No one made you marry Sue,' said Marinda sternly, backing in sudden terror to the door. Horror swept coldly over her that he should be saying these things.

'Yes, I was made to marry Sue,' argued Mark. 'I couldn't get her any other way and I had to have her, you see.'

'Mark, stop! You don't know what you are saying.'

'Oh yes, I do. I'm speaking the honest-to-God truth for the first time in years and it's a blessed relief. She fascinated me; fascinated me absolutely, I tell you. How was I to know that there was just blankness behind those kitten eyes? And then I found to solve the mystery that wasn't a mystery at all, I had to marry . . .'

He laughed disagreeably and Marinda stared at him, hating him

'Can you imagine me marrying anyone? But at least we made no fuss about it. Sue wanted to drag me back here and be suffocated in bridesmaids and orange blossom.'

'Poor Sue,' said Marinda, having a swift vision of a wedding at Farley church where Fairfields had been married for centuries.

'Poor Sue, indeed,' said Mark. 'What about me? She has everything she wants, a husband, a child, a certain amount of amusement, but as far as I am concerned I am finished. I can't write, I can't even feel – and what does Sue care? But perhaps these things are an excuse. Perhaps I haven't got it in me to do more. Already people are saying "The Silver Tree" was a flash in the pan. Ah well, in a few months none of it will matter at all. I shall be dead.'

He gave sepulchral emphasis to these last words as if they were the start of a dirge.

'Mark, you must go up,' urged Marinda, feeling that she must get him safely back to Sue before he told her any more.

'All right,' he said suddenly. 'I'm cold sober now, fit for the connubial chamber. Don't worry. The walk did me good and talking to you. Kiss me good night, Marinda.'

He came close to her and she found she could not hate him, though his breath was sickly sweet with whisky and his lock of reddish hair fell out of its new army sleekness into its old disorder.

From above came small sounds and then the rumble of her father's voice. It separated them and broke their dangerous mood as no other force could have done. Marinda opened the door.

'It's all right, Father, Mark is in. I will lock the door and we're just coming,' called Marinda softly as she saw her father holding his candle and peering down the stairs, ludicrous in his night-shirt, like some enormous bug. His voice came down to them in an urgent half-whisper of authority.

'Time too, just about. Put the lamp out, Marinda.'

Marinda obediently turned down the wick and blew gently at the lamp. The room was filled with the familiar smell of paraffin vapour, a smell which in all its nausea would bring back Foxholes to Marinda's mind all her life, with a swiftness which even the drugging perfume of hops and clear scent of water blowing off the reeds could not surpass.

There was a moment of darkness while Mark fumbled for his matches.

'That's my candle. Sue took yours.'

Marinda gave a last tug at the door and put up the chain, turned the old key and pulled the bolts at the top and bottom. Her father watched from the top of the stairs as if he were surveying important preparations for a siege.

'Hurry up, child,' he said.

They climbed the stairs and Mark began a whispered explanation about missing the bus. Henry Fairfield gave him a discerning look and ignored him.

'How was Primrose?' he asked Marinda.

'All right, I think. Jeff is going in about five to have a look at her.'

Mark slid into Sue's bedroom and as Marinda walked down two steps and past Andrew's door on the left she heard her father testing the bolts.

Since Mark's and Sue's arrival Marinda had slept in her grandmother's old room, now reserved as the second-best spare bedroom and seldom used. 'Prepare to Meet Thy God' in red and gold greeted the newcomer, for something of the old lady's grim personality seemed to linger about the four-poster brought from Fairfield Manor, and the stern engravings on the walls of the more bloodthirsty events in the Old Testament. There was always a faint smell of mustiness and lavender which even the open window could not dispel. It was at the back of the house and missed the view of the hills, but from here the old lady had had a commanding position for watching everyone who came up the lane to Foxholes.

Marinda climbed thankfully into the high bed and lost herself in the feather mattress. In the next room she could hear voices like bees caught in a bottle, and then a thin protesting cry from Duffy. Someone pushed up the window and an owl shrieked in the copse. Then there was silence until the small sounds of dawn gathered together and became the noises of the day.

Sleep came with difficulty to Marinda. Her emotions fought with each other and banished the relaxation which as a rule sent her into a deep sleep a few moments after she had snuffed her candle. She ought, she knew, to be horrified to find that Mark loved her more than his wife. This excitement and exultation within her were bad emotions and must be resisted. Mark, when he was sober, would regret his outburst, might even not remember it, but as long as she lived she would know that he loved her. She was young and she believed in permanence, the roof of Foxholes over her head and the stray words of a man who she knew was untrustworthy. She found she could not be jealous of Sue, only sorry for her. She forgot that she was younger than her sister, that she knew nothing of the strange world outside Foxholes where Mark had taken Sue to live. She was taller than Sue and she knew that she was also stronger, immeasurably stronger; and Mark loved her.

'Poor little Sue,' she murmured aloud as she lost herself in sleep. 'Poor little Sue.'

Miss Finch, the postmistress, always delivered the telegrams herself, leaving her niece in charge of the shop. In this way she became part of every unexpected happening in the village, and when Marinda thought of the day Mark left for France she thought also of Miss Finch with her thick shoes and long serge skirt, hovering in the background, an incongruous harbinger of death.

'It's a telegram for Mr Studland,' said Miss Finch. 'I'm afraid you won't like the news.'

Andrew ran off to Mark's room with the telegram. Mark's breakfast was being kept hot by a disgruntled Bessie, and the seductive smell of gammon rashers floated up to him as he moved his tongue round his dry mouth.

'Got any aspirin, Sue?' he asked, wincing a little at Andrew's wholehearted knock. By the time Andrew came downstairs, the news that Mark had been recalled and must catch the midday train was forestalled by Miss Finch, now sitting in the kitchen and being given a cup of tea by Bessie.

'And I tell you what,' said Miss Finch, 'there's trouble for the Oldhams.'

She patted her pocket as if she herself pulled the strings of fate.

'Not Jeff's boy?' said Bessie, her kind eyes soft with pity.

'Yes, perhaps I could catch Jeff if he's round about and

save myself a journey. Of course it's confidential, but you'll know soon enough. "The Army Council desire to offer you their profound sympathy." They put it well, don't they?'

Belle paused as she came out of the dairy, where she had been searching on the shelf where the vases were kept for a small pot for the first daffodils growing under the lime trees.

'Poor Mrs Oldham,' went on the postmistress. 'Young Steve was always a bit of trouble to her and now he's the first to be killed from Farley. I suppose you'd call him a hero.'

'He is a hero, Miss Finch,' said Belle.

Stephen Oldham was one of many heroes, for in the early spring of 1916 began the Battle of Verdun and the Marchshire Light Infantry distinguished themselves in a manner which brought pride and sorrow to almost every home in the county. If you want to refresh your memory of that war to end wars, their names are engraved on the memorial in the little park behind the Cathedral, opened after much controversy in 1920 by Lord March, whose brother's name was on the stone. But in 1915 all this was mercifully veiled by the future. And as Belle's heart contracted with pity for Mrs Oldham, she looked thankfully at her own lusty son shouting in the yard. In two more years he would be old enough to die too, but the war could not last another two years. It was unthinkable, yet he was already longing for the time, and Belle was thankful that his baby good looks had persisted, so that he looked no older than he was and could not run off and falsify his age as young John Selsey had done. The flute-like voice of his childhood had passed the cracked stage and had now acquired the depth of manhood and the Marchshire burr. He was the first of the Fairfields to speak with the county accent since Regency days, for he was the first whose opportunities for education and travel had been denied through lack of money, and although his father often corrected him and his mother sighed at the length of his vowels and roughness of his consonants, there was a pithiness about his sudden country expressions that suited his curly hair and strong, well-built body. Sue had called him 'Farmer Giles', with a slight air of disparagement, and her mother had said, 'Well, he is a farmer, and the son and grandson of a farmer.'

It was useless to criticize Andrew to his mother.

Belle put on her hat and made automatic preparations to go to Jeff's wife. It was a distasteful errand but she had been brought up to consider Henry's work-people as part of her family. She did not find this solicitude incongruous with the fact that she would hardly have housed a dog in a room like the kitchen at the Oldhams' cottage. Warm easy sympathy welled up in her soft heart as she went to ask her husband if she could take Mrs Oldham some brandy.

The death of Steve Oldham, the prelude to many, seemed to make the parting with Mark even more dramatic. Henry found himself able to overlook his son-in-law's irritating habits, such as the way he looked beyond you when he was supposed to be listening to you and his abysmal lack of interest in all things of the soil except as romantic survivals. To Henry, Mark was simply not a real person as Jeff and Andrew and old Sandway were.

Sue fluttered round her husband, like Amelia on the eve of Waterloo, incapable in her misery of doing more than get in the way. And as Marinda tramped and rode round the farm in the soft rain she was thankful that the cause of the turmoil in her heart should now be going out of her life, perhaps for ever. She could not believe that she could still be in love with her sister's husband, or he with her, and the possibilities and complications which chased themselves round her imagination alternately fascinated and revolted her.

The shades of all dead soldiers seemed to surround Mark and he enjoyed his brief moment as he polished his belt and buttons and wished that his batman were there to do the work. Now that he was leaving Foxholes, he became fond of it and recaptured the feeling of beauty which the compact outlines of the hop-kilns and barns, the feudal survivals of its life and the blue eternity of the hills had given him when he first came to stay with the Grays. The unknown horrors which confronted him seemed far away, separated from him by the wall of farewells.

He could not find Marinda anywhere and the morning was slipping by. Belle had returned in a quiet mood from the Oldhams' and was cutting ham and tongue sandwiches, in spite of his protests that he never ate in the train.

'You will be sinking, my dear boy,' protested Belle, calmly slicing the ham.

'Please don't bother,' pleaded Mark. 'I say, Mamma, have you seen Marinda? I – I want to say goodbye to her.'

'She will be in before you go. She was riding over to Farley St George about some fencing, I think she said. She won't be long.'

Mark walked out into the lane and stood there for a while looking at his watch. Sue saw him from the dining-room window, where she was gazing with maternal satisfaction at Duffy asleep in his perambulator on the lawn. There had been a long argument with Belle as to whether he should be allowed out on a damp morning and Sue had won. Duffy lay pinkly asleep, sheltered from the wind by the angle of the house. Now that Mark was so nearly gone, Duffy seemed to Sue more loving, more important than he had ever been. With a last look at him she turned and went into the hall for her hat and mackintosh to follow Mark in a way which she could not resist, even though she knew it would not please him. But when she reached the gate there was no sign of him. The lane forked and she hesitated a moment wondering which way he could have gone, then she walked with slow uncertainty towards the village. When she realized at the bend in the track that he must have taken the other way she hurried back, taking a short cut across the field into the rickyard. She looked at the time on the stable clock. In another hour he would be gone and she felt lost and helpless that he should not choose to spend this hour with her, but soon the feeling of hurt changed to anxiety that he might miss his train. Belle brought the sandwiches and laid them on the hall table. Bessie brought his bags down and Andrew harnessed the pony and tied him to the gate. There was still plenty of time if only he would come. Henry came in from the barn and compared his watch with the grandfather clock.

'Run out to the gate, Andrew,' said Belle, who always

thought that if someone were posted in an advanced position the latecomer would arrive sooner. Andrew had passed the age when he enjoyed swinging on the gate and keeping a look-out.

'Don't fuss, Mother,' he said, 'if he is here by twenty past I can manage it.'

'I will go to the gate,' said Sue, but Duffy awoke and began to cry and, bending over him, she did not see her husband jump the stile by Foxholes Cottage and hurry up the path.

He dismissed their anxiety with a laugh.

'Loads of time,' he said.

He began to say goodbye quickly, as if he would be gone, shaking hands or kissing them in a row. When he came to Sue he kissed her with the rest. She ran after him and he kissed her again, patted her shoulder, told her not to worry. Sue's easy tears made it impossible for her to speak, but she looked at him with all her heart in her eyes, while the river between them grew wider.

'You've missed Marinda,' said Belle. 'I wonder where she can be.'

'I saw her – by the bridge. I've said goodbye,' said Mark, detaching Sue's clinging hands. 'Where is my valise?'

'In the trap – hurry, hurry!'

'We will take care of Sue and Duffy for you. Don't worry, dear boy.'

'Good luck,' said Henry briefly.

'Good luck!' they all echoed, as Andrew untied the pony and Mark jumped into the trap.

It began to rain and they all crowded back into the porch as he turned and waved, an indistinguishable bunch of people in mackintoshes, like a slice of the crowd at a football match. The love they had for him slid off him as he was borne away to fresh scenes, scenes perhaps both dangerous and horrible, but new and, therefore to Mark, enticing.

Henry put his arm round his elder daughter as they went into the hall.

'Oh dear!' cried Belle, looking at a package on the table. 'He never took his sandwiches.'

Chapter 10 — THE CASUALTY LIST

In 1917 came one of those periods of movement and change which come once in a while to every family, particularly in war. Bessie put it all down to such signs and portents as broken mirrors, dropped knives and the snowdrops which Marinda brought into the house.

As the war dragged on, hardly a week went by that the casualty lists did not contain the name of an acquaintance or friend, and in March 1917, Marinda, reading the paper as she waited for the bus to Marchampton, saw 'Penistone James Gray – missing . . .'

Carey and her mother had been living at Foxholes Cottage for the past eighteen months, but at the moment they were in London so that Laura could see another specialist, for lately Dr Brickett had grown gloomy about her heart. Marinda knew she was in no fit state for prolonged anxiety. 'Missing', she read again, hailing the bus absently and pulling her unaccustomed skirt over her knees as she sat down.

Carey had become a better friend to her than any other. She took the place of Sue, who had been living in Devon with the wife of a friend of Mark's. They shared a small house and it was here that Mark came to spend his brief emotionally upsetting leaves. Once Sue discovered he stayed in Paris and never came back to England at all. Now he was in Egypt and there was apparently no chance of his returning.

Mark, who had been so sure he would die, was safe in Shepheard's Hotel, and Pen, hopeful phlegmatic Pen, was missing. Even Edward, who had joined the RAMC as a pharmacist in 1916 and was now a sergeant with no hope of further promotion, was in the thick of brutal fighting round St Quentin.

With the men away and her responsibilities growing daily heavier at the farm, Marinda's social life disappeared. There were girls who were taken to the new tea dances at the March Arms by the officers from the camp at Overbury, but Marinda was not one of them. As a rule she had no time, and when her mother urged her to take a holiday she found that she felt strange in her best clothes and conscious of her sunburnt skin (which in 1917 was not considered elegant) and her roughened hands. In the end she found she preferred an afternoon with Carey climbing the March Hills and looking into another world on the other side – the blue haze that was Wales. Sometimes, if Pen were on leave, he came with them, or Andrew bicycled ahead and met them on the far side of the hills. They became very fond of one another, as if they were all one family, and sometimes when Marinda was older she was able to forget the slaughter and the anxieties which they all hid so desperately from each other, and remember only the smell of the gorse and the chequer-board of Marchshire at their feet and the sound of their laughter.

And now Pen was missing and Andrew was praying that the war would not end too soon for him to have some share in it. The years of hardship and responsibility had done for Andrew what boarding-school and parental strictness might have effected. His work was arduous but appreciated, the men liked him and concealed his youthful shortcomings from his father and Marinda, who both became proud of him. His mother's besotted admiration he came in time to feel weighty and tedious, and in his later adolescence he turned to his father, who was surprised to find that his spoilt son was a delightful companion.

Marinda jumped off the bus as soon as it turned into the London road for her first port of call, her Aunt Emma's house. The Laurels, carved with awful permanence in stone by the gate, had lost its first air of newness, but not its intrinsic ugliness. It sprouted turrets and balconies, porches and parapets, which Marinda vaguely disliked without knowing why. In the garden beetroots and carrots flourished in precise and patriotic patterns in the beds which used to be livid with geraniums. Since Jinny had left, Aunt Emma's conversation had been full of servant trouble, and the door was opened by a pert girl in a crooked cap.

'Dear child,' said Aunt Emma, rolling bandages in the new morning-room, a room so cosy that she often found herself still there in the evening, with the meagre dust in the large rooms in the front of the house still unstirred. 'You've just caught me. I have to go to a meeting at three o'clock, and then tea with Lady Spence.' Her war work had given Emma a social status which, though precarious, she treasured. 'This afternoon we expect two trains of wounded.'

She spoke as if some commodity were being delivered and rolled bandages swiftly as she talked.

'You're looking thin,' she went on – 'not exactly thin, but peaked.'

'I'm very well,' said Marinda uncomfortably. She knew that her aunt was disapproving of the shabbiness of her best felt hat and the cut of her brown tweed coat.

'If you go on like this you will lose your looks,' said her aunt severely.

'I didn't know I ever had any,' laughed Marinda. 'Sue is the beauty in our family.'

At the back of her mind there was Mark's faint echo: 'Marinda darling, did you know that you were beautiful?'

'Don't be silly, child, of course you were a nice-looking girl.'

'I note the past tense.'

'Well, dear, all this hard work has made you look older. It's a pity you have to do it. You never meet anyone, stuck away in that backwater.'

As a successful farmer's daughter, who had never done more than a little butter-making, her aunt disapproved of her niece's work on the farm. She thought that to scrub floors at Lady Spence's Convalescent Home for Officers was less degrading, because Lady Spence's daughter did it, and besides, the girls met the officers, such charming fellows some of them.

'I had a letter from Edward this morning,' said Emma proudly. She had come to regard Edward as her own son, and although she resented the fact that by joining the RAMC as a pharmacist he could never flaunt elegantly round Marchampton with at least one pip on his shoulder, she loved him enough to forgive him. It was Marinda whom she could not forgive for not marrying him.

'He wanted to know how you were getting on. Your uncle took the letter with him, or I would show it to you.'

'How is Uncle? I must try and see him as I go by. I've really come in to see Knowle about repairing the cabins for the hop-pickers. They look like pigsties and Father keeps putting everything off, and you know, unless they are better, we simply shan't get pickers with the wages people are paying in the factories in the Black Country.'

'Yes, do call and see your uncle. He works too hard, of course. Edward should never have gone off like that and left him.'

Emma was not happy that her husband, after his brief years of retirement, should be back at the shop in Castle Street, working harder than ever, but she was aware that retirement had not brought him the happiness he had expected. When Edward joined up, he had looked out his old alpaca coat and soon people forgot that he had ever been away from the huge coloured bottles which threw gay, incongruous shadows on the dark mahogany cabinets and showcases.

'I must be going,' said Marinda, dropping her unaccustomed burden, her best gloves. 'By the way, Pen Gray is missing. It's in today's paper.'

'Yes, I saw it, and young Elham from Settlefield. You remember the Elhams, very nice people, old customers. Young Elham is a prisoner. I met his mother yesterday. I heard from Sue last week. Mark hasn't been back on leave for some time. I suppose he won't get back from Egypt very often. You ought to go down and stay with Sue. It would do you good.'

'Aunt Emma, dear,' Marinda said patiently. 'How can I? Father has never picked up since he had that gastric trouble. He relies on me for so many things and Mother gets so fussed now that Bessie has gone.'

'They would have to manage without you if you married.'

They were at the front door now looking down the steps at the green swords of the daffodils in the grass, kept in check by the chilly winds

'I shall never marry,' said Marinda.

'Oh come, child, don't be silly.'

'It's true,' said Marinda earnestly, and for the first time Emma South wondered why her niece had not married, wondered indeed if beneath that calm, energetic exterior lay some hidden unhappiness.

'There ought to be one old maid in every family.' Marinda laughed as she left the gate, but she shivered a little. There was something icy in the words 'old maid', and although she was sure she would never meet anyone who would stir her heart as Mark had done, there were moments when she felt cheated and lonely. She went on down the road towards the town, a thin, tall girl who walked well, but her coat was three years old, and her hat did not suit her. She was just twenty-three, but tiredness fought the youth in her face and gave it maturity. The sight of the twin towers of the West Gate on an awkward curve into the city, unseen for many weeks, filled her with the usual automatic pleasure which she would not have thought of analysing. She had seen no foreign country and very little of England. An aeroplane was to her just a black speck in the sky and she had never been to London, but she considered that there could not be many things in the world more beautiful than the West Gate of Marchampton. Even in her parochial ignorance she may have been right.

Her business with William Knowle and Son, Builder and Contractor, took time because, even though the war had quickened his pace a little, he was a slow man and did not care to be hurried. Before any business could be done, questions must be asked of the Fairfields' health and Marinda must enquire after the health of Miss Knowle, a nurse in France, and young Alice, still at school. Fred Knowle, for whom William had so proudly added 'and Son' to his sign in 1913, had been killed in the retreat from Mons. The paint was peeling from the sign. Fred had been dead for nearly three years, and the war still went on.

After all these preliminaries William Knowle said that he would come out the following week and see the cabins, and Marinda picked her way out of the yard over the pipes and plumbing fixtures, indelicately visible.

'If this war ever ends, Mr Knowle, I hope my father

will get you to put in a bathroom at Foxholes.'

'Oh, I dare say we could do that very nicely, Miss Fairfield. Some of these jobs would suit you a treat.' He looked lovingly at a stack of lavatory pans.

It was Sue and Mark who had put into Marinda's mind that the plumbing arrangements of her home were unnecessarily inconvenient. She looked shyly, but with envy, at the lavatory pans. There were many words in the English language which Marinda found she could never say aloud without self-consciousness, and lavatory was one of them.

The streets were crowded, wounded soldiers in blue, kilted Scots from the camp at Overbury and Marchampton, soldiers and sailors on leave. There was a life in the old city, new and transitory, which in spite of its grim origin seemed to quicken its pace. Marinda walked quickly down Castle Street and stopped at the Square to look at the fashions, but Amberley and Down's window was black with mourning. With a chill she thought of Pen and Fred Knowle and young Elham and all those dead and yet to die. The mud splashed her cashmere stockings and strong shoes. Her face, undisguised by make-up, showed the soft clearness of her skin and the fatigue which a day in the town always brought her. After a call at the seed merchant's and cornchandler's and a short browse in the bookshop, she turned to the old chemist's to give her uncle the customary greeting of all Fairfields who spent a day in Marchampton.

But his familiar figure stooping over his bottles, his untidy moustache fluttering with his breath, his kind, vague eyes, his sympathetic smile, were not there. Miss Harlow, the startling innovation who had now become a commonplace necessity, was bursting with the pleasure of imparting news of a sensational character.

'Mr South went home about three it must have been. Mrs South telephoned; it's Mr Stonebridge. He has been very badly wounded, very badly indeed.'

Chapter 11 — AGE SHALL NOT WEARY THEM

There was a protected angle at Foxholes made by the addition of the monstrous bow window to the drawing-room in 1880 and the pale pink bricks of the south wall. On a warm October day in 1918 Edward Stonebridge lay there, looking alternately at the account of the capture of Le Catelet in *The Times* and the milky sky. Ten days before he had been discharged from hospital and had accepted Belle Fairfield's invitation to spend a few weeks at Foxholes, where she was sure she could fill out the hollows of his cheeks, her thoughts running pleasantly over menus of beef-tea and illicit butter, for Edward was thinner than ever. The hollows of his mind and the tired horror in his eyes passed her by.

He did not lie watching the wide view over the river, but facing the garden wall, for in this way he shielded the casual visitor from the shock of his appearance. Edward Stonebridge's distinguished good looks had been scarred away from the left side of his face by the whim of blast, which had injured his leg. He took a melancholy interest in the shock or surprised pity he thought he saw in people's eyes when he turned his head and displayed the silky distortion of his scars.

'Egg and milk,' said Marinda's voice through the open window. 'Now, don't groan. The kitchen is full of chicken-and-bread sauce and a monumental ginger pudding. Mother is convinced she can make a new man of you alone and unaided.'

She gave him the milk and balanced herself on the window-ledge, sticking out her slender, straight legs into the weedy flower-bed with its dying chrysanthemums.

'I don't know how it is, but I'm not as hungry as your mother thinks,' said Edward, warming his hands on the tumbler.

He smiled and felt the now familiar tug of his skin as his mouth twisted to one side.

'Never mind. It gives her an object in life, now Andrew is in the Flying Corps. I think if she could have done Andrew's breathing for him she would have done it. Do you want anything from the shop? I'm going past it to see why Mrs Cribbage didn't come this morning.'

'Would it hold you up if I came with you? I haven't done my little stretch today and I think I could get as far as the village.'

Marinda had intended to race down the lane and across the village green to the Cribbages' cottage on her bicycle, but she had the good sense to conceal the pity she felt for Edward, which made her smile brightly and say: 'Oh do, and you can pay your "respecks", as Jeff says, to our new postmistress. Miss Finch has really got past it at last and retired.'

Edward swallowed his egg and milk, levered himself up and forgot his face as he concentrated on hiding the stiffness of his left leg. He unhooked the stick from the back of his chair.

'I've just read a bit about Mark in *The Times*,' he said as he shut the gate behind them with his stick. 'That lecture tour of his in the States seems to be going very well. It's a funny way of being a soldier, but I suppose it helps.'

He could not keep a scornful note out of his voice.

For the past eight months Mark had been in America displaying a surprising talent for oratory. On the back of a wine card in Shepheard's Hotel in Cairo he had in the winter of 1917 suddenly produced eight lines of verse with the hard edges of truth and the certain beauty of simplicity which he had, so the critics said, demonstrated in 'The Silver Tree'. The wine card on which the poem was written was sold in aid of the Red Cross, and Mark found that in writing 'The Hero' his military career had taken a new turn. He stood on platforms all over America and recited extracts from 'The Silver Tree', finishing up with 'The Hero', in his pleasant compelling voice, and spoke almost, as his critics unkindly said, 'with second sight' of the horrors of war on the Western Front. From the generous Americans money poured in for whichever cause he was instructed to plead.

'Sue says it's absolutely wonderful. The hospitality and

the excitement must be thrilling, and even Duffy enjoys himself. And the war must seem a long way off,' said Marinda.

'Do you envy her?'

Marinda looked sharply at Edward. As he always walked carefully with the good side of his face next to her he stared straight ahead so that by turning he should not dispel the illusion that he was not disfigured. She could not see the expression in his eyes. For a moment she was horrified lest he might know that Mark's image lay always perilously near the top layer of her thoughts, oppressing her with a mingled feeling of guilt and resentment.

'Oh, I don't mean as a husband,' he continued. 'Anyone can see that as a husband Mark is a bad proposition. It's just that I thought you might envy all Sue's travels and adventures while you are stuck here at Foxholes.'

Marinda laughed. The only thing she had ever grudged her sister was her husband. That her life was more interesting meant less to her. Indeed she seldom thought of it. It was the thought of Mark's nearness to Sue, his physical nearness, which sometimes caught Marinda unawares and fatigued her with longing and disgust at herself.

'I would as soon be at Foxholes,' she said, stopping for a moment, for she had without thinking been walking too fast for Edward. 'Sue never loved it as I do. She was always away with Aunt Emma or Aunt Fan, and if she wasn't away she was itching to get away. I'm afraid I spend most of my days wondering how we shall cling to the place.'

'I thought it was doing well. I know your father has been ill, but you and Carey seem to be doing a wonderful job together. Only you both work too hard.'

He looked anxiously at Marinda's thin figure. She was nearly as tall as he, but there was a tautness about her, and her graceful bones seemed to have no spare flesh on them. She had had a hard time since Andrew had gone, but now that October had come and the hops were sold and the harvest in, Jeff could be seen with his age-old picture of the plough against the sky and she could relax for a while.

'Carey is simply marvellous with the animals, but it isn't

Foxholes she loves. It's my home and my father's land and I hate to think of anyone else having it.'

Marinda whipped fiercely at the hedge with the dog's lead.

'But surely,' said Edward, 'no one else will have it. There's Andrew to come and he will pull the place together. It always seems to me it makes enough money but the money isn't well spent.'

She was reminded of something of Blackmore's which she did not repeat to Edward. It was something which Mark would have liked, she thought.

> I am an English girl and I care very little for the things that I don't see, such as justice, liberty, rights of people and all that. But I do care about my relations and our friends and the people that live here and the boats and all the trees and the land that belongs to my father . . .

'Poor old Father. The Fairfields have been hopeless spenders for generations.'

'They have no idea,' said Edward, thinking of his own ventures, 'of profit and loss.'

'None at all.'

'In fact they think it's rather vulgar.'

'I believe you're right,' laughed Marinda. 'And the really frightful thing is,' she went on, 'it's so frightful it's unbelievable, in fact I don't know if I shall tell you.'

'Oh come on, now that you've roused my curiosity.'

'It's Andrew.'

Edward looked sober. There were so many things gay, spoilt Andrew, with his Fairfield irresponsibility, might do in a war to shock Marinda, and he thought swiftly of prostitutes and blackmail, debts and deceit, so that when Marinda said, her voice deepening with horror, 'He wants to go on the stage,' Edward stopped still and laughed. He had a pleasant but not very ready laugh, and Marinda realized she had not heard it for a long time.

'But my dear Marinda, there's nothing tragic about that. It's like wanting to be an engine driver.'

'No, I tell you he is quite earnest. You see his voice is really rather nice now, and last summer a friend of the Grays got him all puffed up about it. And now it seems that Roger Rainham is at his station and they get up concert parties. He has taught Andrew to dance and he says – or at least Andrew says that he says – that he could really make something of Andrew for musical comedy. Have you ever heard of such a thing? Father would have a fit; and besides we need him desperately at Foxholes when – if – he comes back.'

'Ah yes, there's always the chance that he might not – come back.'

'That's why I haven't worried them at home about it and maybe it will blow over. Only he's so fixed on it and you know it might be the right thing for him. He has always wanted the limelight. It was all that singing, probably. His voice was the most perfect thing when he was little. Don't you remember?'

Edward nodded. Snatches of the perfection of Andrew's trills remained embedded in his memory.

'Look, I must go in here, you go across to the shop and see Miss Billows.'

'I'd rather sit here and wait for you,' said Edward, perching himself on the foot of the stile, remembering his scars and nervous of strangers' questioning eyes.

Marinda gave him a little half-smile to show that she knew and understood why he wouldn't go on to the Post Office, and suddenly he was filled with courage. He stood up again and walked as quickly as his dragging leg would let him towards the green.

Marinda came slowly out of the Cribbages' cottage.

'Edward, I do hate this war. Why doesn't it end? Those poor Cribbages. Now young Sam has been killed and he was such a nice cheerful boy, just about Andrew's age. Edward, I'm frightened. Do you know that almost every young man in the village is dead or a prisoner –'

'Or like me – a mess,' said Edward bitterly.

Marinda felt embarrassed. She herself was not acutely conscious of his disfigurement, the long white scars across his left cheek which stiffened his smile and blinded his eye. Never having thought of his physical charms she was not revolted by his scars. The stiffness of his leg and the apathy of his mind after long spells in hospital appalled her more.

'At any rate,' Edward went on, 'at least it has stopped me from asking you to marry me. I can't do that again.'

'I shouldn't stop. I should miss it,' said Marinda, laughing.

'No, I couldn't ask you again.'

His voice was quite firm with a note of obstinacy. Suddenly Marinda realized that her heart was full of a curious sensation, pity, deep friendship, something quite different from the feeling she had for Mark, something which might be – she did not know – but it might, she thought, be a kind of love. She turned to Edward with her eyes full of bewilderment.

'I could not marry just now,' she said. 'But then you haven't asked me, have you?'

'Oh, Marinda darling! I can't. It wouldn't be right or fair. Your parents would never let you.'

Edward was horrified to find weak tears welling in his eyes. He put his hand on Marinda's arm and she felt his whole body shaking.

'Well then,' persisted Marinda gently. 'One day, when you are stronger and everything is all right at Foxholes, perhaps I will do the proposing.'

The two lamps in the drawing-room at Foxholes made islands of light in the gloom. By the side of one Marinda was trying to make herself a dress, going through the usual periods of optimism, disappointment, despair and a sort of resignation summed up in her words, 'Oh well, it will have to do.' Later, when the dress was nearly worn out, she might come to regard her handiwork with affectionate pride. At the moment, her mouth dangerously full of pins, she was trying to understand the pattern.

By the other lamp sat Edward, with his finger in a book and a cup of milk at his elbow, and her father grimly reading the casualty lists. The door of the drawing-room, owing to Henry's father's experiments in architecture, opened awkwardly on to whoever was sitting on the left-hand side of the fireplace, and this necessitated a constant shifting and regrouping which gave the room a restless air. This time it was Carey's round, cheerful face.

'Don't get up, anybody,' for the men gave signs of polite

uneasy stirrings, and then at her words sank back into their chairs. 'I just came to say that Monarch is a bit lame. I thought he was, but I think it's only a strain. I'll send for the vet if you think I should.'

Henry looked at Carey with approval. He had a great opinion of her power over animals.

'I dare say you're right,' he said comfortably. 'We'll see in the morning.'

'Look at my Paris model,' said Marinda.

'I can't stop, I'm afraid. Uncle Syme is with Mother and he complains that I am never at home. By the way, he seems to think we are coming to the end of the war.'

'Oh, Carey,' whispered Marinda, 'if only it could be.'

For over four years, in a country no farther away than Scotland, men had been struggling and dying in horrors which one could hardly conceive, though in Farley no one had heard the sound of a gun or heard so much as an air-raid warning. And yet, through four years, this horror took their men and did not return them. John Lark, the Swithin boys, the young man from the mill, Pen Gray ill in a prison camp. There was not a house in the county which had not its sorrow and anxiety. If only it all could end while Andrew was still safe and before Pen died of tuberculosis in Mühldorf.

But it did not. By November the eleventh when England, so it seemed, went mad with delirium that it should be over, at Foxholes there was no rejoicing, for by then Pen was buried in enemy country and Andrew had crashed to his death while still in training.

In his pocket-book was a cutting from the *Yorkshire Echo* which said that 'Andrew Fairfield, whose singing and dancing had given so much pleasure at troop concerts, had a great future.'

Book Three

Chapter 12 — DANCE AT MY WEDDING

'I can't get used to these pink stockings,' said Marinda, looking dismayed at her legs conspicuously slender in flesh-coloured silk stockings.

'Rubbish!' snorted Carey. 'Everyone has been wearing them for years, and you can't possibly be married in black stockings.'

The two girls were in a fitting-room at Amberley and Downs, waiting to try on Marinda's wedding dress. It was March, and through the small window one could see, across the medley of Tudor and Elizabethan roofs at the back of West Street, the rooks busy in the elm trees of the Cathedral Close. In a pool of chilly sunshine, with the dust flying like specks of gold, Marinda stepped out of her black coat and skirt and stood hugging herself modestly, her arms hiding her small breasts and her best lace-trimmed camisole.

Miss Calendar, who had made her mother's and her grandmother's wedding dresses, now appeared with two lesser menials, one who carried the new pale blue delaine wedding gown and a notebook, and another who crawled miserably about with pins in her mouth adjusting seams.

'So few are being married in white nowadays,' said Miss Calendar. 'And this will be so useful afterwards,' murmured Miss Groves, slipping on the dress. A tack gave way with a sharp sound of destruction. 'Never mind,' said the least menial of all, rushing forward with a pin.

'I remember your mother's wedding dress. Beautiful it was. No expense spared. Of course this is very nice, very nice, but – your mother's was in white satin. Everything was boned in those days. One had to be able to cut and fit. Nowadays I say there's nothing to it. A sack, but it's young-looking. You ought to cut your hair, Miss Fairfield.'

Marinda looked at herself in her wedding dress. It was the first time she had worn anything but black since

Andrew was killed, and she felt there was something gay and abandoned and completely incongruous about the blue, short, shapeless thing which she now wore. But such is the whim of fashion that she was also conscious that it suited her; and as she turned her head she had a momentary pleasure in her reflection in the mirror, and wondered if she would ever be brave enough to cut her hair.

It was to be a quiet wedding, for with Andrew's death the heart of Foxholes seemed to have stopped beating. There were no laments from Belle about Fairfield brides in white veils as there had been when Sue was married.

'If it weren't for Aunt Emma,' said Marinda, as she and Carey held their hats in the stiff breeze half an hour later, 'I could put the wedding off for another six months.'

'Surely you don't want to?'

'I don't mind much either way,' admitted Marinda. 'To tell you the truth, the thought of going to live in London makes me take a deep breath. I just can't picture it, and when I said I'd marry Edward I must confess I never thought of going any further from home than Marchampton. I know it sounds horribly provincial.'

'It isn't merely provincial,' said Carey, peering up the road for the tram, 'it's parochial. It's a very good thing that Edward has launched forth with this new factory. Marchampton would never have kept him, anyway. He was bound to go further, and just now when he needs confidence the change will do him good.'

'I don't believe I could have gone if Father hadn't decided to sell Foxholes. I just don't feel it matters what happens to me when the place has gone. It's a great comfort to know that you will still be here to help Mother and Father with the move. It's such an uprooting sort of time, marrying and moving – I like things to stay as they are.'

'Whatever would you have done with Sue's life?'

Marinda considered momentarily being the wife of Mark, and rejected it with a stab of conscience.

'When is Sue coming home? They have been in America for ages, haven't they?'

'They won't be coming home just yet, Sue says. They

never seem to have any money, at least not for that. I wish they would. Duffy is getting quite big, and Mother and Father long to see him again. America seems to have swallowed Sue. She seems so far away that writing letters is quite an effort. Let's walk out to Aunt Emma's. This tram seems as if it will never come.'

As she spoke its clanking progress was heard coming round the Square, hulking, incredible, ugly, but taken for granted since the turn of the century.

'Let's go on the top.'

Undeterred by a south-west wind, which began to sprinkle rain gently over them, they 'went on top', as they had always done since the time when they were at school together. Although Marinda's thin gawkiness had made way for a certain degree of good looks, due to the delicate fineness of her features and the clearness of her eyes, she still had no make-up or permanent wave to make the soft rain an enemy. Sitting on the hard, slatted seats, their skirts protected with a mackintosh cover, they swayed with a delicious sense of danger down Tile Hill ('What if the brakes give way?') and dragged wearily up the slope on the other side. Both girls clutched the wet iron rail with one hand and their black velour hats with the other, knowing that their faces and headgear were rainproof.

From their perch they could overlook the whole of Mrs South's half-acre of garden, but the inside of the house was hidden from prying eyes by stiff and spotless Nottingham lace.

The end of the war had left Aunt Emma at a loss. Her 'boys', who had visited her and written to her, suddenly became strangers with all the shyness and inhibitions of civilians, and there were fewer letters and no visits. Marinda's wedding filled her life with sudden bustle again, and she talked ceaselessly of monograms and frilled night-gowns. She felt as if she were father and mother of the bride and of the bridegroom too, and this pleasant multiple function was almost as good as the war to her arteries.

'Of course, it's just like Marinda to refuse Edward when he was one of the most handsome – well, anyhow, distinguished – men in the town, and to marry him when the poor boy is so sadly changed . . .' she complained to Carey as the girls reported on the progress of the wedding dress.

Marinda felt a knife turn in her heart. She only minded Edward's looks when other people noticed them, and because they upset his confidence and would, if she did not fight, change his nature.

She demurred gently.

'There's a new man in London who is very clever at mending faces,' she said. 'Plastic surgery, they call it. I dare say later on something can be done. Thank God he is getting strong again and he hardly limps at all.'

'Yes,' agreed her aunt, 'he is beginning to eat as he used to.'

Like her sister she considered that a stomach adequately filled was a safeguard against plastic surgery, neurosis or the pangs of love.

'He told me not to give you too big a trousseau, as he wishes to buy you everything you want in London.'

'Lucky creature,' said Carey, helping herself to quince jelly.

The two girls seldom spoke of their brothers, both horribly vanished in the war, but their common loss drew them together with the kind of friendship that could survive until they were old women. The news of Pen's death in a prison camp did not filter through until after the war had ended, and although they knew he had been ill for some time, Carey had feared that the shock would also be the end of her mother, now so thin and little, relaxing slightly from her labours as her royalties increased, but always resilient and self-contained. As the years passed a fierceness showed in Laura Gray's eyes, whose colour seemed deepened by her white hair. She had never grown into the life of Farley, escaping when she could to London, and if it had not been for Carey's friendship with the Fairfields she would not have stayed longer than was financially necessary, but now, with middle-age past, she was surprised to realize how attached she was to her home, and found herself making plans for a decent bathroom and a garden room.

It was Laura who helped Belle most through the days

after Andrew's death. Belle's life, cushioned physically and mentally, had not conditioned her for a loss such as this and she lay plump and weeping in a desolate household when Marinda ran across for Laura, just as ten years ago Carey had come hurrying across the lane for Belle. On the uncomfortable horsehair sofa of the morning-room the two distracted women, so unlike in everything but their terrible troubles, spoke of their sons and found courage together.

Emma South had never grown out of a faint disapproval of Carey, indeed of the whole Gray family. She held them responsible for Sue's marriage and for Marinda's preoccupation with books, both of which she considered regrettable. Now that Foxholes was to be sold and Marinda was at last marrying Edward, she hoped she would escape from them.

For Foxholes, after four hundred years in the Fairfield family, was to be sold. If it were not so Marinda knew she would not be marrying Edward, and in his deepest heart Edward knew this too. It gave an earnest sadness to the wedding preparations, and it was endlessly talked of.

'Of course, it's the only thing, Marinda dear,' said Aunt Emma, handing the seed cake. 'Now that Andrew has gone, there is really no purpose in struggling on with it, and you know your father, even when he was stronger, never really made it pay.'

'It was doing better lately,' said Marinda faintly. Carey stroked Aunt Emma's middle-aged spaniel, snuffling round her shins.

'Of course I know that people expected your uncle to buy it for your father –'

'Oh no,' murmured Marinda.

'Yes, they did, but one has to realize that Henry is no relation to your uncle, no blood relation that is, and the way those Fairfields have always wasted their money vexes him, you know. And in any case, although one can't tell everybody this' – Emma always prefaced her copious confidences with these words – 'although one can't tell everybody this, he is putting all the money he can spare into this new factory for Edward at Acton.'

She looked pointedly at Carey, and Carey gazed at an enlargement of George's father as if she were not listening at all to this family discussion.

Marinda changed the subject skilfully. There were now so many topics to be avoided: Andrew's death, Edward's disfigurement, the sale of Foxholes, that her conversation was becoming quite different from the things that went chasing round in her mind.

The new factory was a great thing, she said. It was so very good of Uncle George to help with the extra capital which Edward needed, and had they sent the embroidered pillow-cases?

'They're upstairs, in the spare room. If we've finished we might as well go and take a look. The pink blouse came. It's real *crêpe de Chine,* very nicely trimmed with faggot stitching – all hand done.'

Aunt Emma's generous but managing soul was soothed by providing most of Marinda's trousseau, and Marinda found that continual gratitude was an effort. She followed her aunt upstairs over the drugget which kept the new stair-carpet from wear and view.

'She might just as well have the old one and cover it with a drugget if no one is ever to see it,' she thought, registering vows that when she was married she would not, like her ignorant and benighted elders, do this or that.

The thought of this freedom and of all her new clothes was to Marinda a great deal of all that marriage with Edward would mean. She knew she did not love him as she had loved Mark, but she was young then, she told herself with the lofty wisdom of twenty-four years, and such things happen when one is young. Her ideas on life had been taken largely out of books and she had little knowledge of what marriage would really mean, either spiritually or physically. But she was happy to be marrying Edward. She trusted him with a completeness which almost overwhelmed him, and the knowledge that she had made life worth living for him again made him very dear to her.

She picked up the blouse. 'Yes, Aunt Emma, it's very nice. Aren't I lucky, Carey?'

'Anyone can have *crêpe de Chine* blouses,' remarked Carey tersely. 'You're lucky to have Edward.'

Aunt Emma, although agreeing with Carey, looked at her sharply, and Carey met her eyes disconcertingly and almost stared back. Marinda felt a vague shaft of hostility cross the room.

'What a nuisance it is,' she thought, putting the blouse down, 'that nothing will make Aunt Emma like Carey.'

Edward drove them back to Foxholes in the Souths' car, Carey sitting in the back balancing two wedding presents on her knees. It was nearly dark as they slipped away from the outskirts of the town which stretched yearly farther and farther towards Venning, now almost a suburb of Marchampton. Farley itself was beginning to change and two new houses had been built by the bridge in Starveacre. In the headlights their red bricks looked alien and unloved. Marinda never passed without feeling that everything about them was wrong, even their very existence, but in one of them her parents were to live, with all the comforts of water and electricity, as soon as they left Foxholes. The sale of the other half of the field to a retired ironmonger from Marchampton had helped with these innovations.

The house had not originally been intended for themselves, but after Andrew was killed the fact that it existed had proved a blessing in providing an interest for Belle and a convenient home in their own village.

'If we leave Foxholes,' Marinda had said when the project was first suggested, 'I shall never want to come home. I couldn't pass the gate. It would hurt me to know that anyone else looked at my view.'

Three months later, on the eve of her marriage and departure to London, she felt no less violently, and as Edward stopped to drop Carey and then headed the car for the lane to the farm she turned her eyes thankfully away. There was now none of the old welcome as one approached Foxholes; no Andrew as advance guard; no crowded porch. Bessie had married at last and Belle had to be careful of the cold since a bad bout of bronchitis the previous winter. The gate was open and the car's wheels on the weedy gravel gave notice of their approach. While they sorted out the parcels Belle and Henry made slow progress to the door with the dogs barking and the lamp in the hall behind them flickering in the draught.

Marinda had a sudden stab of pain when she saw how much older they both looked. Her father was only sixty-four, but his leg stiffened from an old riding injury and his face pale from chronic gastric troubles gave him an appearance of age. Her mother was seven years younger, but her hair was white and she too looked as if her spring had broken. She was laughing. 'It is a long time,' thought Marinda, 'since she looked so bright.'

With some of her old impetuosity her mother began to talk, while they were wiping their shoes on the mat and putting the parcels on the old card table in the hall.

'Isn't it wonderful,' she said, waving a telegram in her hand, 'to think of seeing them all again before I die?' for Belle now often talked with wistful drama of dying.

'Who's coming?' asked Marinda, wishing her mother would not take so long in coming to the point, for in spite of her impetuosity it took time to extract an accurate version of what she wanted to say.

'I'm telling you, dear. We've had a telegram. They're all coming to the wedding.'

'More relations,' thought Marinda, taking off her hat and starting up the stairs. Then she heard her father's voice translating his wife's tangle of words.

'Sue and Mark and Duffy are coming to England for the wedding,' he said.

Marinda stumbled on the stair and turned.

'Here's the telegram, or rather cable, I suppose you'd call it, from the boat. They'll actually be here by the end of the week. I must make a Dundee cake and do a tongue. They always come in . . .'

She held up the telegram to Marinda, who came slowly back down the stairs. By the inadequate light of the hall lamp she read:

All three arriving to dance at Marinda's wedding Mark.

Chapter 13 — MARINDA AND EDWARD

The elusive confetti invaded every corner of the bedroom, and Edward, at Marinda's bidding, had tried to gather it up, so that their marital inexperience should not be known to the chambermaid.

'I think that's all, darling,' he said, 'hateful stuff and the floor is uncommonly dirty, what's more.'

Marinda's mouth curved downwards with disgust.

'Never mind. When we have found a house I promise to turn out on all the right days,' she said. 'Darling, when shall we start house-hunting?'

'Sick of our honeymoon already?' he asked, and she shook her head. Of course she wasn't, but it was all so different. Edward was gentle and kind, but she hadn't been entirely prepared, only nebulously, romantically, not factually, and she was tired. The day before had been her wedding-day, the day before had been long and exhausting. The day before she had seen Mark again.

In order to save extra work at Foxholes, Sue and Mark and Duffy had stayed at the Souths' and were only moving into Foxholes when Marinda had left, so that after the first family meeting Marinda had not seen them until she was signing the register. So many people kissed her that she was only conscious of Mark being one of them, and then Edward had taken charge of her and she had walked back down the aisle of the tiny church of Farley St George with the whole village packed into its pews to see her.

It was a quiet wedding, but the champagne helped everyone not to see Andrew's ghost, and it was a gay one. The best man, the county surveyor, flirted with Aunt Fan, who didn't look a day more than forty, and Sue, with her newly-acquired American slang and her well-groomed curls and her quiet small boy with a startling accent, enjoyed almost as much attention as the bride.

As for Mark, he had an air of success which was mostly conceit of himself, born of the knowledge that he had progressed under the acid criticism and unfettered adulation of the Americans. He was now deep in a new volume of collected poems and in a corner of the room he talked excitedly of this with Laura Gray, while the other guests felt either neglected or relieved.

It was not until the end of the little reception that he spoke to Marinda. The best man was consulting his watch with a warning to Edward, and Carey had moved across the room to remind Sue that Marinda must now go and change into the grey travelling suit and cherry-coloured hat. Suddenly Marinda found Mark by her side looking at her over the edge of his champagne-glass.

'I drink to your everlasting happiness,' he said. 'If I am unhappy there is no reason why you should be.'

'Are you unhappy, Mark? I'm sorry,' said Marinda gently.

The noise made by thirty guests in the drawing-room at Foxholes made it possible for them to say anything they wished to each other. To make himself heard he came quite close to her, his arm touched hers, his breath was warm against her ear.

'I shall never be happy as you understand it,' he said. 'If I had married you – even then I might not have been happy.'

Marinda remembered that there were always a great many 'I's' about Mark's conversation, Carey maintained.

'But there would have been moments of utter perfection,' he went on, 'complete and utter perfection.' His bright eyes narrowed until he looked like a fox, thought Marinda. Then Carey and Sue and Edward converged upon them, and as they went through the doorway into the hall she saw Mark finish his glass and help himself to another from the table by the window.

'My dear husband seems to be enjoying Father's champagne,' said Sue, with a short laugh. 'It makes him very talkative.'

'Yes,' said Marinda, and Edward put his hand on her arm as they went up the stairs. At the top they divided as if it were all part of a square dance with prearranged moves. Edward turned into Andrew's old room and the three chattering girls went on down the passage to Marinda's room to clothe the bride in further, but slightly more restrained, splendour.

'Mark's talk is like the bubbles in champagne,' observed Carey. 'I know he's your husband, Sue, but he never means a thing he says, does he?'

Sue laughed uncomfortably. She was painfully thin and when she spoke her voice sounded brittle, but as it occurred to no one that she was skilfully rouged, everyone remarked on her apparent well-being.

'He gets carried away,' she said. 'I expect it's being a poet.'

'Rubbish!' sniffed Carey, helping Marinda off with her blue dress so as not to disarrange her hair, and failing. 'More likely the champagne.'

Sue's mouth hardened a little. There was something about Carey's gruffness which she had never liked.

Marinda felt suddenly hopelessly tired. Mark's words rang in her brain; London seemed as far away as Australia, the view across the hills inexpressibly dear and marriage a frightening reality. Her mother appeared, breathless and a little tearful, and caught her up in her soft embrace.

'Are you sure you've had enough to eat, dear?' she said. 'It's a long way and you seemed to me to be eating nothing. Aunt Fan is bringing you a sandwich.'

'Oh, Mother, I couldn't, I simply couldn't,' said Marinda. But while Sue and Carey found her handkerchief and her handbag and put her new silver hairbrush in her suitcase, her mother fed her with pieces of sandwich as if she were a bird. Marinda's last impression of her dearly loved home was of scurry and laughter and the taste of ham.

Her wedding journey was the first time Marinda had ever travelled in a first-class carriage, and as her slender body relaxed comfortably on the wide cushions she closed her eyes and thought how wicked it was of her to be starting her honeymoon by thinking not of Edward, whose calm eyes and sensitive mouth faced her, but of her sister's husband and his fox-coloured hair and eyes and his mocking disturbing words. She could remember all that he had ever said to her from the time that she met him at the

Coronation Concert until her wedding-day. All that he had ever said to her had misled her senses and confused her actions. Even now she did not know if any of it had been true. She knew that it must not be true, but at the back of her mind she knew that she wished it might have been. The train's wheels rang a familiar rhythm, 'It might have been, it might have been . . .' She opened her eyes and saw that Edward was looking at her with tender concern. He leant forward and took her knees between his hands.

'It's a pity I haven't a car of my own, we shall miss your uncle's. Darling Marinda, you look so tired.'

'It's been such a day,' she answered, stroking his hair and the taut scars on the side of his face, 'such a day –'

'They put a restaurant car on at Oxford. Shall I order you some tea?'

'Yes, please, in a minute. Don't go for a minute.'

She felt enveloped in Edward's kindness, safe, content, as if a great danger had passed her. 'I can believe Edward,' she thought. 'Nothing he will ever say to me will be anything but the truth.'

He crossed the carriage and sat beside her. Outside in the corridor the broad back of a stranger enjoying a cigarette blocked the flying view.

'I will always be good to you,' he said. 'So far as in me lies, I swear it, my darling, my darling.'

'I know,' answered Marinda softly. 'I'm not afraid.'

Painstakingly Edward burnt the confetti in an ash-tray. It smouldered and gave off a faint acrid smell.

'I dare say a house won't be so easy to find. I've sent our name to several agents already, but now let's be gay for a week. Tell me all the things you want to do most.'

As he spoke he jingled his pockets as if the contents were the answer to everything. Although he was by no means a rich man he was prepared to try to do everything Marinda wanted. When it turned out that this was simply to buy a present for her mother, go over the Tower, see *Chu Chin Chow* and visit Kew Gardens, he rapturously accompanied her, delighted with her delight, happy with her happiness.

He had been advised to dance in order to improve the muscles of his damaged leg and now he knew the foxtrot, the one-step and the tango. All these he taught Marinda, and they danced through their honeymoon like blown thistledown.

Marinda had never been to London before, but Edward knew it well. He had a few business friends and a cheerful family of distant cousins who lived at Putney, and on Sunday they went to a service at St Paul's and in the afternoon set off to see them.

After her week of gaiety Marinda was glad to spend an afternoon in a home again. The door of the Yeadons' grey stone house opened to disclose warmth and light and, to Marinda, regiments of people. But when she had been kissed by Mrs Yeadon, and had shaken hands with Mr Yeadon, the family in the background somehow simmered down to Elspeth, whose husband had been killed early in the war, Jack, who had lost an arm at Jutland, and Margaret, a serious child born as a surprising afterthought eleven years before. They were all pale and sandy-haired, resembling for some reason their Scottish mother rather than their father. It gave them a curious family solidity, when one saw them at first, though as Marinda came to know them better she realized that Elspeth's hair, red paling to gold, shining against her white skin, amounted to beauty, whereas Jack was just a lanky Scot with sandy hair and undistinguished features, and Margaret was a freckled child with a short crop of tawny curls. Their mother was a worn replica of them all, self-contained, seemingly detached, but with a quiet wit accentuated by the accent of her native Peebles.

Mr Yeadon was a successful tea-broker, over-stout, with the obvious cheerfulness of the fat man.

'I hope you won't feel lonely, my dear. London is a funny place to come to as a stranger. I well remember my own first impressions. Dirt and rush, rush and dirt.'

'You will have to wash your curtains every three weeks,' said Mrs Yeadon, looking round complacently at the muslin frills hiding a degenerate sycamore in the garden.

In the warmth of the fire, surrounded by the friendly faces, Marinda said she was sure she would soon get used to everything.

But the Yeadons, for all their kindness, were too anxious

to smooth the Stonebridges' path, and Edward, who had managed his own affairs since his mother died, began to wriggle under their offers of hospitality and their suggestions for a house.

'You could do worse than live in Putney,' said Mr Yeadon, 'and of course if you want any help you need only say, my boy. Are you going to buy?'

'I didn't want to, but I suppose renting a house is not easy in these days.'

'One can. Sometimes one is lucky. I will see what I can do for you, for of course if you buy you stand to lose when the market drops. In Putney for instance –'

Edward interrupted him.

'We shall have to live more west than that. I had thought of Ealing. You see, the factory is at Acton.'

'Ah yes, quite so, but Ealing . . .'

He gave a large, fat sigh which seemed to shake him with visible sorrow. 'Ealing,' he repeated, as if it were some outpost miles from the touch of white men.

'They had better come and stay with us until they find somewhere, eh, Mother?'

Mr Yeadon gave his wife a commanding smile and she looked quickly at Elspeth, and Marinda saw their eyes meet and telegraph something to each other.

'Why yes, of course,' said Mrs Yeadon.

Edward protested. For one thing he was so happy in his possession of Marinda that he did not wish to give up the anonymous seclusion of a hotel. Marinda protested too.

'We shall be such a bother,' she said.

'Nothing is a bother to us,' said Mr Yeadon, and Marinda discovered a week later when she was installed that this was indeed so, for Jack had moved into a bed in the study; Elspeth was in Jack's room and her small son's cot had been pushed into Margaret's room, in order that a distant cousin and his new wife might occupy their best bedroom.

Marinda thought that it might be pleasant to live near the Yeadons, but she was now to find that there were many moments when Edward's work, his new-born factory, the mysterious white powder which fed and clothed them, the workers who made it, came first in Edward's mind. It was not that they were more important to him than Marinda, but he felt for her he must be a success, not realizing that she would often have preferred his company and companionship to his increasing absorption in his work. For the house had to be in Ealing, and it was here that at last they found it. It was not at all what they originally wanted, but by the time they found it, it seemed so. It was number seventeen, Allington Road, West Ealing, and it was exactly like number nineteen, to which it was attached, and slightly different from number fifteen, whose front door was not a dozen yards from theirs. Marinda had never lived at such close quarters with anyone in her life, and she thought at first that it was a friendly arrangement and would prevent her from being lonely. The first time she saw her neighbour, an elderly woman, well-dressed and purposeful, she let her mouth slide into a friendly half-smile. The neighbour quelled her with a glance and the strange house swallowed her. Marinda's smile slipped off her face, and the fresh confidence, which marriage and new clothes had given her, received a jolt.

'You'll soon find that your neighbours are the last people you'll get to know,' explained Elspeth, when Marinda told her of the incident. 'I suppose Londoners have to build up a reserve in case you are a burglar or something undesirable.'

'But why should people suppose I'm undesirable? I didn't think she was a burglar. I just felt neighbourly. In Farley we –'

'Oh, Farley,' laughed Elspeth. 'I expect you knew who people were, back to their great-grandfathers. We do in Glenmorrow when we go up there to stay, even just as visitors we know them and they know us. But here it's quite different, and when you do get to know people, you won't know much about them really. There's a man who lives near us and Mother always used to call him the undertaker. We have nicknames for all our neighbours, 'Mrs Pink Curtains', 'Mrs Frills', 'Lady Bighat', and so on. Well, one day Mother found out that he *was* an undertaker.'

Elspeth's laughte disconcerted Marinda. At Farley Mr Floate, the carpente and joiner, put up shelves and made coffins and now and then appeared in funereal garb and was in no way remarkable. Certainly Marinda had never thought there was anything the least bit humorous about Mr Floate. She remembered the solid bookshelves he had made in her bedroom at Foxholes.

'And there was an awfully charming person who lived in the big house on the corner. You know, you pass it coming from the bus. Father used to talk to him in the train. He turned out to be a forger. It was in all the papers and he's in prison now.'

Marinda opened her eyes. She had a swift mental picture of her respectable neighbour slowly poisoning her husband with arsenic.

These new vague suspicions made her even more lonely. She had no friends beyond the Yeadons, who now lived a morning's journey away. She missed the cheerful chatter of their household, and with an efficient maid provided with the aid of a registry office, for the first time in her life she found more than enough leisure for reading. She joined a library, and at the end of three weeks she had read twenty-one books, and a sharp pain stabbed between her eyes.

Chapter 14 — FARLEY REVISITED

'"Little by little the spring begins",' quoted Carey.

'In Marchshire it is better than all other springs,' said Marinda, as the two-forty from Paddington began at last to slacken its pace and stop at insignificant stations lost in frothing blossom.

'Japan,' murmured Carey, 'and Montreux and, oh, Marinda, Italy. Italy has the most exuberant spring.'

'Ah, you've travelled.'

'I've never been to Japan.'

'But you have travelled. Surely, though, it isn't better than this.'

Marinda sighed with delight when the blue of the March Hills came into sight as a background to the bridal landscape. 'It isn't white exactly – it's just as if chinese white has got into everything. The greens, the yellows are all lighter. It is fun to be back.'

'You have never really settled down, have you?'

'Of course I have. I'm practically a Cockney already, only London makes me restless. I don't know how it is, but you know unless you are perpetually going to something or other, which Edward is too tired to do, I find London so dull.'

'Don't be ridiculous. Why, everything goes on there that any mind could possibly require.'

'Well, perhaps "dull" isn't the word I want, but it's so impersonal. Now if I go for a walk at home I come back with all sorts of news, even if I only walk across the fields. The fish are or aren't jumping, the primroses are out, or a tree has blown down, and if, of course, you meet anybody, well, you can be sure someone has died or beaten his wife or done something else worth noting.' She laughed. 'But in London –'

'You can't say nothing happens there!'

'Well, I don't hear about it.'

'I wonder what Dr Johnson would have said –'

'I know, that bit about being tired of life, if you are tired of London. Well, perhaps I am tired of life.' Marinda laughed at anything so ridiculous as being tired of life. As the hills gradually grew from the shadows of distance she felt invigorated and happy. She walked restlessly in the corridor, and as the train began to stop at the smaller stations she let the roughened vowels of the Marchshire accent refresh her mind and bring back her childhood like a short, lost dream.

The wind was too cold for her father to venture out, but her mother was at the station to meet her. Enveloping her in her warm embrace her mother wanted to know all the news before they were half out of the carriage, so that the last porter had gone before they realized they were alone on the platform.

'I'll go and find one,' offered Carey.

Belle looked helplessly for her platform ticket in her glove, in the deep recesses of her bag, and then in her glove again.

'Never mind, we'll get another one,' said Marinda.

'No, I know I had it, it must be here, and of course they know me at the gate.'

In her happiness at seeing the familiar landmarks of the station, the faint, damp smell, old Ives at the barrier, the hideous ornamentation, approved by Queen Victoria when she visited Marchampton in 1859, now hanging like blackened filigree above them, Marinda let her mother ransack her bag without a word of impatience, laughing with her at the triumphant discovery of the platform ticket, an innovation much resented by everybody. Old Ives whistled up an ancient porter.

'There's a car outside, Major Shipley's. He was coming into Marchampton, market day, you know, and he very kindly said he'd bring us out to Farley.'

Marinda had never met the man who had bought Foxholes and she looked his stocky figure over, disapproving that he sat firmly at the wheel and gave no hand in helping them settle themselves in the dirty Ford car. It was not until she was sitting by his side balancing a bag of seed on her knees that she realized and remembered that he had lost a leg at Ypres.

Belle called excitedly to her from the back seat. Aunt Emma was in Torquay and Bessie's husband wasn't much good and she was coming back to help with the spring cleaning.

Robert Shipley drove on without speaking. The car had been specially arranged to suit his disability, but he appeared to need to concentrate. In fact he was a man who threw himself generously into whatever he was doing, and just now it was driving to Farley. When they reached the bridge and passed the old turning to Foxholes, Marinda's heart was wrenched. He pulled up outside what were already christened simply 'New-houses' by the village.

'I hope you and Miss Gray will come up to the farm sometime and see what I have done there.'

'Major Shipley has worked wonders with it,' said Belle.

'Don't you wish you had never sold it?' persisted Marinda, looking coldly at the small boxlike outlines of the new house.

'No,' said Belle, 'there was no point in wearing ourselves out with – no one to come after.'

Andrew's ghost chilled the atmosphere for a second and was gone, while Robert Shipley sorted out the suitcases and Marinda felt her father's lean arm across her shoulders. The fragility of his skin and a certain soft vagueness in his manner frightened her. Her mother had now become the strong partner. She bustled through the house with cheerful energy, explaining to Marinda why the old sideboard would not fit in and how the geyser worked. Marinda looked through the window across the fields to the line of poplars which hid her old home.

The next day she pushed open the gate of Foxholes.

'Carey,' she said in horror, 'the squeak has gone!'

It was true. A timely drop of oil had silenced the warning voice of the gate.

'I can't forgive him that,' muttered Marinda, and then she stopped and said nothing, looking with something like envy in her eyes at the effect energy and money had had on the untidy old garden – daffodils everywhere, wallflowers, forget-me-nots and the promise of tulips in the beds under the windows. The exuberance of the Albertine rose cut back and restrained to the porch, the honeysuckle and the wistaria with separate existences on the south wall and not hopelessly intermingled.

'Don't you like it?' said Carey.

'Of course I do,' said Marinda resentfully, realizing that this was the first time in her life that she had knocked on the door of Foxholes. She lifted the heavy knocker and as she did so she noticed the new electric bell. It gave a far-away discreet buzz as she pressed it.

At the moment the door was opened Robert Shipley appeared at the yard gate.

'There you are. I thought I heard you. Come and see the cowsheds first.'

He led the way down a new concrete path. Everything about him was brisk, even his limp. There was a general air of tidiness and order which made the buildings seem vaguely foreign.

'I've put electric light in here. I'm going in for dairy work good and proper later on. I've thought of buying an electric milking machine . . .'

Carey burst enthusiastically into the conversation and captured it while Marinda walked round feeling sentimental over the lost cobwebs and the broken-down traps and perambulators which had littered the barns in her childhood.

The contour of the walnut tree outlined against the dark mass of the hop kilns was the only familiar sight in that corner of the yard. A ginger cat, spitting fiercely, fled by her ankles, a strange man and a boy went unobtrusively through the barred gate into the field.

'And the pigsties,' continued Robert Shipley. 'I don't know much about pigs, but I'm going to raise Berkshires. They're pulling down the old sties now. I'm going to put in brick ones. No need for them to live like pigs.'

He smiled as he realized he had made a joke of sorts, but Marinda looked obstinately at the space where the noxious old sties had been and saw one more change.

'And now for the house.'

They walked in single file along the concrete path. Their shoes were not even muddy, thought Marinda resentfully. She did not want to go into the house. To her it was like visiting an open coffin.

Robert turned the knob of the front door. It still wobbled. He looked back at the two girls with hesitancy.

'I suppose it's a bit hard to come back to your old home?'

Carey said briskly that it had got to be done some time and they were in the hall.

The red paper had gone and it was lightened by white paint and walls. A new door on the west side gave a vista of the garden at the back of the house, the neglected paddock of the Fairfields' day, now restrained into a lawn.

'I've shut up the old kitchens and made them into storerooms. This used to be the dairy, you remember? It makes a nice kitchen, don't you think?'

An elderly woman and a young girl looked up self-consciously from the table where they were making marmalade. The crisp smell of the oranges filled the air. Marinda peered through the door where gargantuan Fairfield meals had been cooked. It was bare, lifeless and empty, the old stove rusting in a corner.

*

'It was a perfectly horrible morning,' said Marinda to her mother. 'I felt just as if I was being cut up alive. My bedroom is a bathroom, if you ever did.'

'But you were always on about our having a bathroom put in.'

'Yes, I know, but not in my bedroom. The only thing he hasn't touched is the nursery. It's just as it was, bars at the window and the gate at the door.'

'He said he hoped to use it one day,' said Carey. 'Rather nice of him, I thought.'

'Why, Carey,' exclaimed Belle, 'he's just the man for you!'

Marinda could see her mother filling the nursery with the imaginary offspring of Carey and Robert. Carey's red face turned an unbecoming brick colour.

'I must say I liked his pigsties,' she laughed. 'He wants us all to go to tea with him any day next week except market day, but I told him I had to be back by the end of the week.'

Chapter 15 — PROFIT AND LOSS

'Why don't you ask someone to stay?' suggested Edward one evening in the autumn, as Marinda walked to the window and back to the fireplace, picked up some sewing and put it down again.

'I have asked Carey,' she said, 'but she can't come until the end of November.'

'Well, Sue and Mark then, there's plenty of room.'

Edward laid down the pencil with which he had been writing, working out some figures on the edge of his evening paper, and felt suddenly as if he were confronted with a child with nothing to do.

'I don't suppose they would come and, anyway, I don't want to ask them.'

'Why ever not? They'd come fast enough.'

He thought privately that they might be difficult to eject. He could not understand how they could live their life in a ceaseless round of wanderings, overstaying their welcome with some friends, leaving unexpectedly with others. He preferred Marinda to himself, but if she was lonely he was prepared to put up with them. He pursued the subject.

'They've been in Ireland six weeks and they're due for a move. I shall write and ask them. Where do they intend to go next? Back to America?'

'I believe so, eventually. Sue said something about Paris,' answered Marinda.

'Well, ask them for a bit. Sue looks to me as if she could do with a settled existence and a few early nights.'

'She goes to bed early enough. It's what Mark complains of. But she says she's always tired. I'd really rather not ask them, Edward.'

'Oh well,' Edward shrugged his shoulders, 'I suppose your mother and father will come for Christmas?'

'Yes,' said Marinda, going over to the window again, 'I expect so.'

Edward looked at her slight figure, its outlines blurred against the light, and was stricken by a certain pathos in her listless attitude. At Foxholes one had so seldom caught her idle. She was always snatching a moment from the farm to cram in a hasty gulp of reading, or an urgent job of mending, and her conversation had been quick and vivid, punctuated with gusts of laughter with Carey. Seldom had anything been discussed which happened farther away than Marchampton, but in its very narrowness it had a virility which was now lacking.

'What are all those figures?' asked Marinda. 'Now don't say I shouldn't understand, because I did the farm book-keeping, didn't I?'

'You did. Oh, I dare say you'd understand this well enough, only it isn't very cheerful. The costs at Acton are higher than we estimated.'

The costs of the house were also higher than Marinda had thought possible. The maid's wages and the laundry, the price of eggs, poultry and vegetables, continually surprised Marinda, products produced, as one mistakenly supposed, for nothing at Farley, but she merely told Edward and was given a larger allowance. After the haphazard finances of her father, Edward seemed not only wealthy but securely wealthy. She was now to learn that this might not be so. In his gratitude to her for marrying him he had wanted to hide it from her, but now she began to wriggle into his worries like a ferret.

'Get a proper piece of paper and then I can see what you mean,' she said, sitting on the arm of his chair.

He reached up to his desk by his elbow for a sheet of paper. It was embossed with their address. 'Not that,' she protested. 'Extravagant. If we have to be careful, it's not a good way to begin.'

All her life she was to have unexpected economies, odd scraps of paper, knotted string.

He smiled and changed the paper. And as he wrote down the figures and explained them, what he had expected to earn, what he might earn, and what he had in fact earned, it became less disastrous. Marinda understood better than he had supposed. Managing the chaotic finances of the farm had, after all, taught her something.

'It's not so dreadful. The mortgage on the house is a nuisance, and of course we can't have a car just yet, but we can cut down a bit.'

'I hate to ask you to cut down anything, anything at all,' argued Edward vehemently. 'You've just begun to enjoy theatres and concerts, so they must stay.'

'Now and again,' murmured Marinda, keeping the regret out of her voice. 'Maud is the first casualty. Out she goes.'

She drew a line through Maud as if she had murdered her successfully and disposed of the body.

'But you must have someone.'

'I've never liked her, and the way she puts her indigestion down to anything I happen to cook is maddening.'

'Does she?'

'She gives a very genteel little heave and then says: "Pardon! That would be the shepherd's pie." And if I ask her to use anything up she says afterwards, "I suppose that mince really was all right?" as if I were trying to poison her.'

Edward laughed, and over their economies Marinda's spirits rose, and he reflected as he halved her dress allowance that she had not looked half so cheerful when he gave it to her. But she had at last something to achieve, and just as she threw herself into farming, without actually liking it, for the sake of Foxholes, now she transferred her interest to economies for the sake of Stonebridges Ltd.

'If you say I must have a maid, let's get one from Farley or round about. As soon as I had engaged Maud, Carey wrote to know if I'd like Nellie Spender. She's younger than Maud and less experienced. She'd never want Maud's wages. Eighteen pounds a year. I've always thought it was outrageous. And then when I've got her into the way of things I can come and give you a hand.'

'Oh no, that wouldn't do at all.'

'All right,' answered Marinda with misleading meekness, 'then bring me something home to do. You say you need another book-keeper's clerk. Bring the work home and you and I can do it between us, and, another thing, that man who comes to dig . . .'

He brought her small jobs to pacify her and she did them eagerly, and with a certain pride in her efficiency, so that he was surprised to find that she was indeed helping him. He withdrew the advertisement for a second clerk, and on Saturday afternoons he dug in the sooty cat-ridden patch which was their garden.

In the New Year Nellie Spender arrived to fill the place of the expensive and departed Maud. Before she had unstrapped her basket she and Marinda were gossiping furiously about Foxholes. Did Miss Marinda know that young Elms had thrown over that girl from Upper Farley and was marrying someone from Marchampton?

'You will have to call me "madam" now, Nellie,' said Marinda, but she felt as she talked to Nellie that her life in London was as untrue as the plot of a novel.

'Yes, miss,' said Nellie, inspecting the saucepans with a roving gaze. Her eyes had a look of hardness and humour which seemed unsuitable to her immature body. For Nellie Spender, for all her two years' experience and middle-aged hat, was but fifteen years old. Though she was young she learnt slowly, and there were moments when Marinda sighed and thought of the efficient Maud, but Nellie had other qualities, qualities which the word loyalty does not wholly cover. Trustworthy she was, and honest, but that was not all. Though she never became a perfect servant and was liable to announce the wrong people in the wrong places and speak her mind when her feelings were strong, her life began and ended in the kitchen of number seventeen, Allington Road. When she spoke of Farley it was not in a voice soft with homesickness, like Marinda's, but with the affectionate scorn of the emigrant.

She adopted a large black cat which made Edward, a cat-hater, shiver as his skin pricked with loathing.

'It's lucky,' she said. And when the factory's teething troubles began to end, Nellie, who knew when Edward was worried as quickly as his wife, took the entire credit on the cat's behalf.

The door of Stonebridges Ltd bore a notice inviting one to walk in. Marinda turned the knob nervously and gave her name to a wise and wizened boy who sat in the outer office sucking sweets. When he heard it he pushed the bull's-eye under his tongue and became all eyes and deference. Marinda found herself ushered through the door marked 'Mr Stonebridge' into a small box of a room filled by a desk, a filing-cabinet, a hat-stand and the tall figure of her husband, who rose and, ignoring the presence of the boy, kissed her.

Marinda was always surprised by Edward in the office. He seemed to have no connection with the creature who lazed in the chair opposite her in the evenings and slept with her at night, the helpless male who needed feeding and nursing by turns. She returned the unexpected kiss.

'Give this to Miss Pillar,' said Edward, 'and ask Mr Sprake to bring me over a sample packing.'

'Yessir.'

'And,' said Edward, suddenly becoming awe-inspiring, 'for heaven's sake stop sucking sweets.'

'Poor child,' said Marinda when he had gone, violently crunching bull's-eyes, 'didn't you suck sweets at fourteen?'

'Discipline, and anyway, I can't bear the smell of peppermints.'

'I shall have to buy him some toffee,' said Marinda; then, in a whisper, 'How is Miss Pillar?'

'Better, I think. My God, you women! If only you wouldn't cry!'

'I don't cry. When did you last see me cry?'

Edward thought. 'When you married me,' he said triumphantly. 'When you left Foxholes.'

'Ah, Foxholes!' Marinda looked out of the window on to the back of Grant's Products, lit by an unwilling sun.

'And your crying or not crying has nothing to do with Miss Pillar. That's another thing women do.'

'What?'

Marinda's mind made the swift journey from Marchshire to Stonebridges Ltd.

'Turn everything back to themselves. Look! What do you think of that?'

He produced from a drawer a small phial with a red cap. 'Neat, eh?'

'Very. Let's look.'

'It's just come in.'

While he leant over her she sat down in his chair and turned the phial in her hand.

'Oughtn't it to be flatter?'

'Oh, I don't know.'

He looked deflated. 'No, it has to be round.'

Marinda realized that she had spoken out of turn. Edward took suggestions of improvement as criticism, and to criticism he was sensitive.

He put the phial in his pocket. 'Come over and see the new machine,' he said.

He did not know that Marinda was not interested in the new machine, although she had come ostensibly to see it, but she was interested in the three men and two women working at the bench.

'This is Stevens,' said Edward. Stevens gave a slow turn to his machine and wiped his hands, nodding briefly at Marinda.

'Oh,' said Marinda, 'you are the one with the twins?'

Stevens' thin mouth twisted into a Cockney grin. He looked proud for a moment, and then sheepish.

'Mr Stonebridge told me about them,' she went on; 'two boys, aren't they?'

Stevens nodded. The two women went on packing small

bottles into boxes with a swift rhythm, their heads turned a few degrees that they might miss nothing.

Marinda walked over to them and watched them for a moment. Then she smiled. 'Does it make you nervous for me to watch you?'

Mrs Dane, the elder, said roughly, 'Oh, we get used to all sorts.'

The younger one gave an embarrassed giggle.

Marinda felt suddenly that she must know these women, that they must not dislike her.

'I suppose it's difficult to be as quick as you are?' she said.

The younger girl stopped. 'It's just knack.'

Mrs Dane looked sideways at Marinda.

'I'll show you.'

Edward had walked across to speak to Sprake, and when he returned with him he found his wife had packed a dozen small bottles in a carton. She knew that Mrs Dane was a widow and that the thin girl's name was Louie.

'This is Mr Sprake.'

Marinda smiled at the women and was now ready for Mr Sprake. He was Edward's right hand and she had heard much about him. But no one could become acquainted with Tom Sprake except after long study and research. He held out his hand defensively, as if it were a gun, and the tone of his 'How do you do?' gave her to understand that her place was in the home. Marinda left the enslavement of Mr Sprake to a later date.

'By the way, Sprake,' said Edward as he walked back to the office, 'oughtn't that new phial to be flatter?'

Sprake's face folded into obstinate lines.

'I only hope he doesn't say it's my suggestion,' thought Marinda. But Edward, as he was often to do, took another's view which he had first rejected and brought it forth as his own. Indeed, he had now forgotten, as he persuaded the reluctant Sprake, that Marinda had given him the idea.

'Well,' said Edward, 'you look completely at home.'

They were back in his office now, cut off by a glass door and partition, behind which shapes hurried like driven phantoms in another world.

Marinda leaned back in Edward's chair, slightly disconcerted by its swivel, and drank a strong cup of tea that was no longer hot.

'It's queer about you, Marinda. You melt into your surroundings. You used to be part of Foxholes, and now you're part of Stonebridges. They liked you. Oh, I could see it. Do you know what I heard Stevens say? "Pleasant, ain't she?"'

The bitter tea was warmed by Edward's praise.

'I'm a chameleon,' she said.

'So you are. Why, I could even imagine you fitting into Sue's life if you had it. I can even imagine you married to Mark.'

Mark and Sue had been living for the past month with friends at Primrose Hill, and the day before, Edward had spent an uncomfortable evening listening to Mark and Ernest Webbe discussing the libretto which Mark was writing for Webbe's new opera *The Harvesters*. On the way home he had volubly disapproved of his brother-in-law, of his treatment of Sue, of his conversation, which Edward only half rightly put down to exhibitionism; to the lateness of supper and to the fact that when it did appear Mark made a great show of preparing it himself, and after much talk produced an inadequate and tough omelette.

'He was simply showing off,' Edward had said, producing a latch-key from a chain to open his own front door with a few neat motions.

To his surprise Marinda had turned from the hall table, where she was examining a bill, to defend Mark.

'Mark isn't like other people, at least people like us. Farming, patent medicines, how can he have anything in common with us?'

'I bet he takes my dope when he has a pain. As a matter of fact I saw a bottle in the bathroom, and I should think by the way they live and the food they eat he'd be a good customer.'

'I could listen to them talking all day,' said Marinda dreamily. 'It's like another language, like being in some strange country.'

Edward bolted the door. His mind was on the morning.

By his hat and gloves he put some papers that he might not forget them, and Marinda's words fell on an inattentive ear:

'You're coming in to the office tomorrow, dear, aren't you?'

'Oh, tomorrow? Was it tomorrow we fixed? I'd forgotten. Yes, what time?'

And here she was in the office, melting into the background as if she was provided with protective colouring. 'I can even imagine you dealing with that fellow,' Edward was saying. 'It's a great gift – adaptability. Imagine being married to Mark.'

To his surprise Marinda's expression changed completely. 'Don't say anything so horrible, Edward,' she said.

'But I didn't, I meant . . .' Edward stammered with distraction. What curious things women were! Here was Marinda suddenly nearly in tears with all the unaccountableness of Miss Pillar. 'What on earth is the matter?' he said, giving a hasty glance at the door. 'You can't cry here.'

Marinda thought of her recent boast and made what was obviously a great effort. Of course she could not cry at Stonebridges Ltd, and yet the desire for tears tied her tongue and pressed against her heart. She picked up her bag and gloves. The desk lay between them. From a moment of close companionship she had slipped across a cold, lonely chasm.

'I'm sorry,' she said, looking for her umbrella. 'I expect it's because I'm going to have a baby.'

'What, darling! What are you saying?'

He looked at her across the desk, transfixed with the suddenness of the announcement and the inappropriateness of the moment. He wanted to tell her that he loved her, that the thought of fatherhood thrilled and frightened him, that she was more to him than all the world, more even than Stonebridges.

All he said was, 'Are you sure?'

'No,' said Marinda, 'but Sue thinks it must be.'

For nearly a month she had been clasping her secret

close to her, secure in the knowledge that the telling of it gave her an indescribable power over her husband. She had planned to wait until there was no doubt and then to tell him gently. Perhaps one Sunday morning, as they lay late in bed, with the claims of the day relaxed. Now some perverse imp had loosed her tongue too soon and one wrong word brought forth another.

'You must see a doctor,' said Edward.

'Oh, there's no hurry, it's a long time yet.'

Looking across the office at her husband she was swept by a feeling of strangeness.

'Do you feel all right?'

Edward emphasized the words so that each one was detached.

'Perfectly, thank you.'

'I shall send you home in a taxi.'

If he had kissed her there would have been no need for taxis, but Miss Pillar knocked on the door, entered, coughed and withdrew.

'Oh, Miss Pillar,' he called, 'ask Gordon to get a taxi for Mrs Stonebridge.' He signed a letter she brought him and then, when the taxi arrived, he escorted Marinda to it, his eyes so full of anxiety that he looked peevish. He laid his hand for a moment on her knee, as if to drag her back to the comfort of his heart.

Her eyes were veiled with perversity. She knew she was torturing him and gave a half-shamed smile.

'Marinda, please.'

'Edward – I – come home early.'

But her words were lost as the taxi grunted forward. Edward walked slowly back to the office to find Tom Sprake waiting for him accusingly, his hands playing with the new phial.

'I think you're quite wrong about wanting this flatter,' he said. 'It will take up more room in the boxes. The girls aren't used to packing it and then there's the question of cubic space.' He went on delivering his objections, his words roughened by his Yorkshire accent. Edward's mind was working on two themes. Marinda was going to have a child and the shape of the phial must be flat. Marinda had said so.

'You see,' Sprake was saying, 'it's an important step. Stonebridges – and the shape of the bottle. The public have to get used to it, to like it, to demand it. It must be recognized. We must make up our minds.'

'It must be flatter,' demanded Edward in a voice which proclaimed that his word could overrule that of his manager. 'Slightly flat,' he modified, then, with emphasis, taking the phial from Sprake's hand, 'but flatter.'

He wondered if Marinda had arrived home.

'We must have the telephone put in,' he thought, as Sprake dropped the offending phial, with a look of disgusted resignation, into the waste-paper basket.

Chapter 16 — THE SISTERS

In her nomad life in other people's houses, Sue had acquired a trick of making everywhere they lived immediately theirs. First, she banished all the ornaments, and into the warmest and lightest part of the room she moved a table. Ink and blotting-paper were bought before she thought of groceries; this was Mark's domain. Hers lay in an unobtrusive corner. If she was lucky there might be a sofa of sorts, if not she appeared to be camping with a chair for her always tired body, and a rest for her aching legs contrived from a hassock or a box. Within touching distance was Duffy's trunkful of toys. He had been drilled into a quiet child and was content to sit near her, playing with his trains or farm, absorbing unsuitable details of conversation through his pointed and slightly cocked ears.

On one wall Mark would hang one of Challis Peter's vivid horses flying over improbable fields, and on the other the untroubled features of James and Susannah Fairfield, wrenched from the drawing-room at Foxholes, watched all that went on from the small black frames which held their miniatures on either side of the fireplace. At irregular intervals there would be preparations for, or the remains of, snacks, cups of coffee, whiskies-and-soda, and as fast as she cleared it away the cigarette ash reappeared in the open bowels of the red china pig which her father had once brought her home from Marchampton Hop Fair.

Where Sue and Mark lived became a place of smoke and tension, unexpectedly gay one day, befogged with depression the next. It was unlike anything Marinda had ever known, more alien even to Foxholes than Ealing, than Stonebridges Ltd, for in Ealing she had her housekeeping which she enjoyed, and at Stonebridges she took a squire-like interest in Edward's workers. But in the atmosphere of the studio, lent to Mark and Sue at Primrose Hill, Marinda's spirit could escape into a world where it revived. At first she had resisted visiting her sister and then, when it could no longer be delayed, she found that she had worried herself unnecessarily about Mark's feeling for her. He was immersed in the new libretto and had no time to be amiable to anyone. Sue was not well, and as Marinda's body grew awkward and heavy with her child, she felt more at ease at Primrose Hill than she did in her own drawing-room with Edward's hurt, tender eyes upon her. She felt burdened and irritable and her moods, she knew, were a puzzle and a worry to him.

'It's just as if I am possessed of a fiend,' she explained to Sue as they sat on either side of the studio fireplace with their feet on a box, which served at the same time as a bridge for Duffy's railway system. 'Were you like that?'

'I? Oh no. How could I be? I'm married to a much more difficult man.'

Sue lay back, her face thin against a dingy velvet cushion, and thought of her own pregnancies in strange towns with plenty of warm but inconsiderate friends.

'Mark says it's a perfectly natural thing and people make too much fuss,' she said.

'But that's exactly what I keep telling Edward, only he follows me round on tiptoe with footstools and apologizes for banging doors. I feel as if everything he says is really in a whisper. I might have some fatal illness, and it makes me very bad-tempered.'

'So I notice.'

'Do you? Is it as obvious as all that? Mother gave me a lecture when she came to stay.'

'Well she might. You get an angelic husband and suddenly, just because you're going to have a baby, you treat him like a dog.'

'I don't mean to. But he's such a dear. He really asks for it. You know what I mean?'

'I can't imagine. Mark is so different.'

Sue said this almost proudly. It was as if she took a masochistic joy in being trampled on by Mark, for there was no doubt he treated Sue very badly. He insulted her so skilfully in front of his clever friends that she did not always notice. For her health and comfort he had no regard at all, and if he had any money it melted away in bars. In America he had learnt to like a mixture called a cocktail, which made Sue a regular caller at the fishmonger's for ice. With his friends, and he had many, men and women, he made up for his rudeness and temper by flashes of charm and gaiety and unexpected, even overwhelming, kindness, but to Sue, so far as one could see, he was either merely ungracious or roughly impolite.

Edward thought he was insufferable and refused to be taken in by his moments of good humour. Edward's brain was as quick as Mark's, though it worked on different lines, and he did not choose to be mocked, however wittily. Mark could not call his brother-in-law boring, for this was not true, but he thought him cautious and conventional, and managed to make his opinion insulting. The fact that Edward refused to lend him money, but surreptitiously gave it to Sue, maddened him the more.

'Is Edward coming to fetch you?' asked Sue, as Duffy wove his trains silently around their chairs.

'No, he is working pretty hard just now and I didn't tell him I was coming. I must be in when he comes home.'

Marinda sighed and rose.

'You see I mean to be a model wife, and somewhere between Primrose Hill and Ealing I turn into a shrew.'

'Oh no.'

'Yes, I do, a nagging shrew, that's what Mother said I was.'

Sue laughed uncomfortably. On her mother's visit they had spent long hours discussing Marinda's shortcomings, and Marinda knew by Sue's bright, guilty eyes that this was so. She sent Duffy into Sue's bedroom for her hat and coat.

'It's perfectly true – a nagging shrew, that's what I am.'

'I expect it's only the baby.'

'Won't it be lovely when this year is over? I shall have my baby and be sweet and sunny again.' She took her hat from Duffy and gave him a kiss and a sweet from a flat tin in her bag.

'And Mark's opera will be finished.' Sue always ignored Webbe's music as if it were merely an adjunct to Mark's poetry.

'And Stonebridges' new bottles will be on the market, so we'll all be happy.'

'Mark thinks he'll do something for the League of Nations if he can, when he has finished this.'

The League of Nations now became in Sue's eye something entirely Mark's.

'Edward says it's a lot of nonsense, but I have a feeling it ought to work.'

'I don't know anything about it,' said Sue happily, rising slowly from her cushions to avoid coughing, but failing. 'It's only smoking,' she explained, as she sat down again, her face streaked with exhausted lines.

'I'm going to have my hair bobbed,' she said breathlessly.

'What?' cried Marinda, her attention completely distracted from her sister's cough.

'Yes, it isn't very long even now, it's so curly. And Glynn's wife had hers done last week and looks quite different.'

'What will Mark say?'

'He said it might stop me looking like a small, tired cat,' said Sue, twisting Mark's implied criticism into a compliment. 'Why don't you cut off yours?'

She watched her sister stuff her knot of hair into her black velour hat, pulling it out of shape so that her head looked like a boat's hull. Marinda considered this astounding proposal.

'Edward would have a fit,' she said. She sank her round chin into a small sable stole which Edward had bought her for Christmas and drew on her gloves, considering herself with short hair.

'I thought Mark would be home by this to see you to the

station,' said Sue.

Mark had gone to lunch with American friends and had promised faithfully to be back by three.

'And I can't come myself because it is Duff's bedtime.'

Duffy demurred by pulling a face and becoming suddenly audible and visible, instead of a creeping little shadow.

'Oh yes, it is, my man,' said his mother, holding his wriggling body close. She made great struggles that the irregularity of their life should not touch Duffy. He ate and went to bed strictly to rule.

'I like a walk.'

Marinda smelt the night and wrinkled her nose. The dark hid her awkward figure and she forgot it and stepped briskly down the slope towards Albert Road. Then she turned abruptly and decided to walk to Baker Street. It would do her good and she stretched her legs with a country stride. Her feet were in patent leather shoes with comfortable moderate heels. They were tied, not with laces, but with petersham ribbon an inch wide, which added, it was then thought, a final touch of elegance to her narrow foot.

Although she wanted children she was unprepared for her first. In vague ignorance she thought two or three years without the tie of children would be agreeable, and now, just as she was becoming useful to Edward and interested in Stonebridges, this unknown being was clipping her wings. She was incredibly well. All the veiled horrors hinted to her by well-meaning mothers, morning sickness, cramp, irrational fears, found no home in her healthy, normal body. Her face became rounder, her delicate colouring deepened, and she had moments of mature beauty, but she was for some reason not exactly unhappy, but restless, dissatisfied. Edward's grave kindness irritated her and she became easily vexed. Her voice acquired a sharp edge to it. Unwonted temper rose and engulfed her, and she found she had spoken many things which she could not unsay. Her spirit knew that it had depths and heights which her life made it impossible to reach, and without understanding herself she had many moments of acute resentment.

A man passed her and she heard him stop and turn on his heel. The pavement was deserted, but on the corner turning into Baker Street her eye noted with comfort the figure of a policeman. A voice behind her said, 'It is you, isn't it, Marinda?'

Marinda gave a relieved sigh and laughed. She turned and faced Mark. He took the few steps which brought him to her side, the street lamp turning his face into a bony shadow. There was the alert awareness of a fox in his eyes.

'What are you doing here?' he asked.

'Walking to Baker Street.'

'Not alone? You ought to get a taxi.'

He looked round at the empty street. Across the end the traffic flashed by.

'No, I like the walk. I never walk enough in town.'

It had taken Marinda nearly two years to say 'town' instead of London, but now the short, less romantic word, rolled glibly off her tongue.

'I'll come with you,' said Mark, taking a step forward. He carried a stout ash stick with which he hit the kerb.

'No, don't. Sue has been expecting you since tea-time. Go home, Mark.'

'Sue doesn't really expect me. By now she knows I won't come when I say. I can't be "home to tea",' he said petulantly, putting the words into inverted commas with his voice.

'Well then, if you can't, don't say so.'

'I shall walk with you to Baker Street. It's not ten minutes away, and I can take a taxi back. Then I shall be no later than if I had not met you.'

The irritable jerks smoothed out of his voice and he became calm and persuasive. 'You can lecture me all the way. You think I don't treat Sue well.'

'You treat her very badly and you know it.'

'Glynn throws plates at his wife.'

'He once threw a plate at Sandra. She told me about it,' corrected Marinda, 'and he was terribly sorry, and they had it riveted to remind them.'

'Oh well, it makes a better story my way, and I sympathize. I could throw plates at all women.'

'Don't throw them at my sister, that's all.'

'And "be home in time for tea",' he mocked, but he sounded a little penitent.

'Perhaps not penitent, but sad,' thought Marinda. She changed the subject. '*The Harvesters* – how is it getting on?'

'Oh, I dunno.' Mark took off his hat, ruffled his hair and put his hat on again.

'I feel it could be so good if it would only get out of what I am pleased to call my brain, but the words are nothing in an opera –'

'What's the music like?'

'Bits of it are very fine, I think. Very fine indeed.'

He gave a deep sigh.

'The whole thing has a high, sweet quality like Andrew's voice. Remember?'

Marinda stared at the hands of Baker Street clock pointing to three minutes to six and away in the sky was Andrew's voice, flute-like in eternity.

'We've been at it for six months nearly. I think Philip Edson will produce it next summer. Of course, Webbe has a name, but he has never done an opera before in England. It may fail, it may fail very easily. But there's one bit – after the storm dies down – where the words I have done are right, I know they are. It's a short solo for the tenor. You know the sort of thing, ordinary really, but there's something more to it. And it's not only the music. It's the words, and the words are mine.'

Mark turned his head to look into her face with his sudden, disarming smile. There were lines of cruelty and arrogance in his face and when he smiled they disappeared.

'Sue is very proud of you,' said Marinda, adding, 'and so am I.'

'Are you? Honestly, are you?'

She nodded.

'I value that.' He was serious again. 'Sue isn't proud of me. She likes the success when there is any and she likes the money when there is any of that. And those are two things no artist should consider. Why, before I started this she asked me what I'd get out of it. Think of it!'

He emphasized his disgust by stopping dead in the middle of the pavement and speaking loudly. Marinda thought that Mark managed to make himself just as conspicuous in London as he had done at Farley.

'I've often wondered,' he went on, 'how two sisters could be so different. She has the most pronounced faults of the provincial. I suppose that she has imbibed the less endearing qualities of your awful Aunt Emma.'

'If Sue is provincial, so am I,' said Marinda with some heat. 'And there's nothing so wrong with it either. If you stopped half the people in this street you'd find they had their roots in the country.'

'That isn't in the least what I mean. Not in the least. Marinda, there's something almost – pastoral – about you – of the earth.'

He so obviously meant this strange statement as a compliment, that she considered it.

'I think I know what you mean, but it's no use criticizing me or my relations. I can't decently agree with you, at least about my relations. What you think of me is not important.'

The station was ready to swallow her amongst the crowds rushing for their trains.

'Don't come a step further.' She held out her hand. 'Go home to Sue.'

'Thank you for understanding me,' said Mark.

'I don't understand you. I merely listen.'

He laughed and waved his hat as she hurried down the steps to keep pace with the senseless haste of those around her. Suddenly she was conscious of the heaviness of her body and the burden which, while she was with Mark, had seemed scarcely to exist. She put her hand on to the rail to steady herself, but she was too late. Five steps from the bottom she looked at the clock with a short sigh of dismay. Her foot caught in the untied elegant petersham bow and she fell rigid and resisting on to the platform. She was aware of a sharp pain in her side, but she found herself helped to her feet by a stout woman and a small man.

'Hurt, ducks?' said the woman.

Marinda shook her head. 'Not really, thank you. I'll be all right in a minute.'

Nothing hurt at all any more. She just felt sick. Everything hummed loudly in her head as if she were alone in a tunnel. Clutching wildly at the small man, she fainted.

Chapter 17 — THE INVALID

Carey Gray stood at the front door of number seventeen, Allington Road, and bade a formal farewell to Sister Smith, who had been in the house for the past six weeks nursing Marinda back to health after her disastrous miscarriage.

'Mrs Stonebridge will be quite all right if she takes care and, of course, she must exert herself a certain amount. She is likely to be depressed for a time.'

Carey tapped her foot impatiently.

'I will see she behaves,' she said. 'It was lucky I could come.'

'Yes, of course. She no longer needs expert care.'

Nurse Smith pulled on her gloves and the taxi-driver took her suitcase, banged the door and honked; a genteel gloved hand gave a semi-regal salute and Carey shut the door.

Carey, the new nurse, ran up the stairs to the invalid, yelling: 'She's gone! She's gone! Let's celebrate.'

Marinda, lying on the bed in a dressing-gown, smiled.

'I saw the taxi. Oh, Carey, isn't it heaven? Where's Nellie? Can't we have tea early?'

'Nellie is busy smashing the best glasses for joy.

'Nellie,' she called over the banisters. 'Tea is required, Nellie.'

'And chocolate biscuits,' demanded Marinda. 'Are there any?'

Carey amended the order and the water gurgled in the pipes, informing the house that Nellie was filling the kettle.

'I shall dress and come down to dinner.'

'I don't see why not. She said you had to exert yourself.'

'Like Mrs Dombey.'

'Just so, but you must come back to bed directly afterwards.'

'We'll see. Oh, Carey, whatever possessed Edward to make us have that fearful woman for six whole weeks?'

'Because you've been very ill and she was a good nurse.'

'But she could easily have gone a week ago when you came. Edward is such a fusser.'

'He's quite desperately fond of you,' said Carey quietly, preparing a place on the table for the tea-tray.

Marinda studied her face in a hand-mirror and did not answer. 'What a fright I look!' she said at last.

From her high bed, bought on her honeymoon, at Maples, a handsome miracle of slats and corners for dust to lurk, she could see out on to the road where some children were coming home from school. They lunged about, banging each other with their satchels. A nursemaid with a perambulator, whom Marinda recognized as coming from the corner house, urged them ineffectively on. Their vigorous young voices rose in argument and the awakened baby wailed a protest.

Marinda had never been enthusiastic about the child she was expecting, but her spirit rebelled against its death. Something quite uncontrollable within her filled her with misery and a sense of abiding loss. All the children she might yet conceive could not console her. As the high voices died away she turned her head into her pillow and hoped that Carey would not notice her quiet, useless tears.

Carey moved about the room with heavy-footed cheerfulness and the postman's knock with all its pleasurable anticipation and Nellie with the tea-tray made Marinda at last search for her handkerchief and ask for her brush and comb.

She tore open a letter bearing her mother's large spidery writing.

'Mother says she's so very sorry she couldn't come to look after me, but Father is better and if I like to go and stay I can. Oh, and she sends her love and thinks you are wonderful.'

'Shall I pour out?' was all Carey said. She had a certain clear opinion of herself, which was modest yet gave her confidence, so that neither compliments nor criticism moved her.

'Why don't you go down for a week or two? You hardly ever go –'

'I expect we shall at Easter. But I can't bear the thought of that horrible man at Foxholes.'

'He isn't horrible and he has improved it tremendously. You know he has. He has done all the things you wanted to do and you must admit it needed a few improvements.'

'I don't. It was perfect, and if it had to be altered I didn't want him to do it.'

'If it hadn't been sold I suppose you would never have married Edward.'

'Oh, I don't know.' Marinda stretched her arms above her head. 'I was terribly sorry for him, poor darling. He is so good to me, I ought to adore him.'

'But you don't,' said Carey severely, making inroads into the chocolate biscuits with decisive bites.

Marinda looked at her friend with eyes that had a hint of fright in them. 'Perhaps I don't,' she said defiantly.

'I don't think men are up to much on the whole,' announced Carey loftily. 'The way Father went on was enough to put anyone off the species, but Edward is the best one I ever met.'

'I know,' agreed Marinda, 'but a good man is no easier to – adore than a bad one. Do you know, I'm sick of people telling me how good Edward is. What has that got to do with it, or them either?'

'Sorry,' said Carey. 'I suppose it's none of my business. By the way,' she went on abruptly, 'my father is dead – three months ago.'

'Oh!' Marinda looked blank. Did one say one was sorry? The idea of losing her own parents was always enough to chill her thoughts, but this was different.

'His brother, my Uncle Samuel, sent for Mother. It seems the reign of the governess was over and he was all alone in some fearful rooms in Leeds.'

'And your mother went?'

'Yes, by herself. She said I'd better not go with her because I'd make a row. I wouldn't have, though. Deathbeds are no place for rows. He had diabetes and there was no one to keep him in order with his diet. Men are so stupid.'

Carey poured out the second cups and proceeded with the story of her father's death.

'Mother stayed for nearly a week. She wanted to bring him down to Farley, but he died. She wasn't even with him. He seemed much better, so she went down to the library at the corner to get him a book he wanted and while she was away he just died.'

'All alone?' asked Marinda. The story now seemed to her unbearably sad.

'Yes,' answered Carey, adding callously, 'probably just as well.' She stirred her cup with the vigour she brought to her smallest actions. 'You see, if Mother had brought him to Farley, I couldn't have borne it.' She gave a half laugh. 'I'll tell you who was absolutely horrified. Your Aunt Emma. She was at your mother's when I went down to say Mother was bringing Father back. I thought I'd better tell them and, you know, they were shocked, especially Mrs South. She never liked knowing anyone who was divorced, but she was even more horror-struck at the thought of Mother and Father being together again.'

'Just like Aunt Emma,' said Marinda.

How far away Farley seemed! She looked across the road at the unknown 'Mrs Greengate' opening her front door and thought of the width of her own horizons. Not even the doctor's daily visit or the appearance of the nurse had caused any obvious curiosity on the part of her neighbours. How small and self-important were the doings of Farley, but how dear and comforting. She found to her intense dismay that her eyes were filling with tears again. She, who had been so proud that she never cried, was being daily overwhelmed with a kind of uncontrollable woe. This must be what people called depression.

She blew her nose.

Carey looked at her suspiciously.

'Mrs Dombey,' she said sharply.

Marinda's bow-shaped mouth went up at the corners and the contradictory tears ran down her cheeks. She took a gulp of tea.

'Oh, Carey, bless you, Carey,' she said, with a crack in her voice.

'Have a biscuit,' answered Carey briskly, ignoring any hint of affection. 'Then we'll have you up by the time Edward comes home.'

The night before Carey left they were all quite gay.

'It's rather indecent of you to be so cheerful at my

departure,' said Carey, lifting the glass of claret which Edward had opened for the occasion and drinking Marinda's health. Mr Sprake, who had returned from the office with Edward and had created a small crisis by having to be asked to dinner, unbent under the warming influence of the claret and said that he for one was very sorry.

'How can you be sad, Mr Sprake?' parried Carey, her cheeks redder, her eyes brighter than usual. 'You hardly know me. Now if Edward and Marinda showed a faint trace of sorrow I'd be gratified.'

Edward and Marinda both assured her that they would really miss her and Carey, knowing this was true, dropped the subject and turned her attention to Mr Sprake. A Yorkshireman, with hardly concealed scorn of all things southern, he found in Carey's honest good sense and frankness something of the attraction of the girls of his home town, but although he regretted that he might never see her again he was not unduly perturbed. Women were not important to him and he could wait. 'Time enough,' he thought to himself, as Edward refilled his glass.

Without Carey the house seemed twice the size. The curtains rattled along on their poles like echoing chains. The spare-room blankets lay neatly folded on the bed and Carey's sponge bag, which she had forgotten, was packed up and ready for the post.

Edward came out of his dressing-room to share Marinda's bed for the first time since her miscarriage, and as she sat brushing her hair the thought crossed her mind that she regretted no longer having her bed to herself. Edward's face looked at her above hers in the mirror, and she saw with sudden compunction that there was nervousness in his eyes, which was brought there by her uncertain temper. As she lay at last by his side she swore to herself that she would try to be less irritable. She hardly knew or understood the person she had become, but when she felt his arms take her to him she shrank within them as if she could make herself into some small thing he would not notice. His sensitive nerves were repelled suddenly and he released her so that they both lay for a long time conscious of each other, side by side. separated and sleepless.

At the most unpropitious moment in the day, half-way through breakfast, they both spoke of one of the many things which lay in their minds.

'I want to help you again in the office,' said Marinda. 'When can I begin?'

'It only did you harm before,' argued Edward, who was convinced that in some vague way the all-powerfulness of Stonebridges Ltd had brought about the loss of their child.

Marinda sighed, not sadly or helplessly, but with the maddening sigh of those who would rather say, 'Lord preserve me from dealing with a half-wit.'

'It had nothing to do with it. Nothing.'

In her mind she laid the blame for the loss of her child on the shoulders of Mark. If she had not been thinking of Mark she would not have fallen down the stairs. In fact, if she could banish Mark from her thoughts altogether, as she longed to do and as she tried to do, she knew she would be a happier woman.

'Let me work again, Edward,' she said with propitiation in her voice, 'just a little. I do want to, I – I get so depressed.'

Edward looked helplessly at her over the *Morning Post*. He disagreed with her, but he could not enforce his will. It was one of the many small battles he had with his wife which he lost. He looked at her with exasperated affection. She was so young, yet so determined, so inflexible yet so resilient, and he gave in.

'Next week then?' she persisted.

'Yes, I'll see about it. By the way, I shall be a bit late tonight. I'm going to see Bates.'

'Going to the doctor? Whatever for? Not about me?'

'No, no, no,' he smiled, folded his paper and rolled his table-napkin. 'I was just talking to him about this scar and he said he'd see about an operation. They do wonders with scars now. It's nothing much, you know. Plastic surgery they call it. Just takes time, and that I can never afford, but I must.'

'Why "must"? I thought the scars were gradually going. I hardly notice them.'

'Don't you? I thought – I wondered –'

He went to the fireplace and looked at himself in the

mirror. Over his shoulder he said, 'I thought perhaps it made you dislike me – that you might find it – well – revolting.'

'I . . . Oh, Edward! How could you think such a thing? The scars were there when I married you and I tell you I don't notice them.'

'They aren't the reason for your loving me less?'

'Of course not, and I don't – love you less.'

'I think you do.'

He turned and put his hands on her shoulders as she sat at the table drawing back her head against his waistcoat and his father's watch-chain. 'I think you do love me less,' he repeated, bending over her hair, and she did not answer, but reached up to stroke his face, lingering gently over the scars. She felt him relax and knew that she had lightened his heart by a lie. She remembered suddenly how he had given her her first lesson in not hurting people's feelings all those years ago at Aunt Emma's.

Chapter 18 — THE FALSE SPRING

Edward sat forward in his chair at right angles to the surgeon's desk. Leaning back in his swivel chair the doctor tapped his left hand with his fountain-pen. The air in the room was purged by a discreet disinfectant.

'Well, of course it can be done,' he said.

'You say it's not dangerous, but I want time to leave everything in order.'

'No, it's not dangerous as a rule. I must warn you that it is very tedious and painful and, well – quite frankly – do you think it is worth it? Your scars are not so bad as many I have seen.'

'I have made up my mind,' said Edward. His sensitive mouth shut in a thin line, destroying the lines of kindness which he showed in repose. The curves of Edward's mouth lightened the seriousness of his jaw, but at this moment his expression was hardened determination.

At home Marinda echoed the specialist's words. All day she had wrestled with the black dog in her spirit and now, sitting at his feet by the fire after dinner, she realized almost with a shock that Edward loved her more deeply than she had thought possible, more deeply than she deserved.

'Don't do these things for me, darling,' she said. 'I hate operations. You might –' She could not say 'die', but she stroked his hand and contemplated suddenly, with something akin to desolation, a life without him.

'I shan't die, love,' uttering the word her tongue refused. 'Don't worry. But it will be trying, ugly, don't come and see me until it is all over.'

'Edward, how absurd! Of course I shall come and see you. I don't care what you look like. I have the right. Dearest, I must come. Who is to eat your grapes and tell you about Stonebridges?'

He laughed. 'Old Sprake will do that.'

'And so shall I.'

He did not protest, partly because he knew it was useless, and partly because he was touched and happy at her changed manner. He stroked her hair softly. It had retained the fine silkiness of her childhood and since she had, greatly daring, cut it off, she looked like a pre-Raphaelite pageboy. In his single-minded passion for Marinda, Edward, for all his forty-two years, had small experience of women and those episodes of his life when his body had betrayed him filled him now with regret and revulsion. He knew less than most men of the ways of women and the ways of love, but his unselfishness and a sort of steady guilelessness about him gave his love-making a gentleness and a perfection of which he was ignorant. He kissed the soft line where Marinda's neck met her chin and then let his lips slide gently on to her mouth. She relaxed and felt her heart quicken with a feeling which had long been dormant between them. Lying contented in his arms, she was happier than she had been for many months. She did not know why. She did not ask herself the reason. She was only thankful that at last it was so.

All the next day content and happiness pervaded her. The grubby plane trees in the road were beginning to show courageous buds. Nellie started to hint ominously of spring cleaning and having the sweep and Edward put on his light overcoat and asked when Easter fell this year. Even without the premature and by no means stable warmth (because in a month's time it was to snow) it was unmistakably spring.

'Let's go away for a few days, Easter, say?' said Edward.

'Oh let's! Where? Not to Farley. Somewhere on our own, or would it cost a lot?'

Edward was always slightly mysterious about money, and since Marinda had not been seeing the accounts she knew little of their finances except that the figures were up; every month they crept a little higher.

'The country's digestion must be in a shocking state,' he laughed. 'I can afford to take you anywhere – in England,' he added quickly, lest Marinda should suggest China or the road to Samarkand, or even a visit to Mark and Sue, who had suddenly packed up and gone to Italy. He found that he enjoyed life more when they were both at a distance.

Confronted, with only certain restrictions, by a good corner of the world, Marinda could not think of anywhere but Brighton, which she hated.

'There must be a place,' she said seriously, as if England were an uninhabited waste and to find somewhere to spend Easter an almost impossible task.

'Think about it,' said Edward, and Marinda did. She also thought about whether to send Nellie home on board wages or to leave her behind with Mrs Winchmore to do the spring cleaning. She thought about the possibility of one of the new cloche hats and perhaps another frock. She thought of stopping the milk and the papers, but an inspiration for their unexpected holiday eluded her.

The Wednesday before Easter found them in the 10.30 for Exeter, where they were to change for Longbridge. Here they were to be met by Mr Joyce and his taxi and by tea-time they should be at the Lion Inn, Bothycombe. The whole thing had been planned to the last detail by Sprake. Edward had come to rely on the stocky little Yorkshireman to such an extent that he was not only trusting Stonebridges Ltd to his care, but he was also relying on his judgement as to the qualities of the Lion Inn.

Marinda was dubious, but she was so glad to be going away, so enraptured with her new state of content and her cloche hat and the spring that she was prepared to go anywhere.

'Sprake says the food is very good and the views are wonderful. It ought to be warmer down there too, if it doesn't pour all the time.'

'I have a feeling that Sprake thinks anything which hasn't actually got a gasometer in it is a view,' laughed Marinda.

'He told me that he had earmarked the place for his honeymoon, so it can't be too bad.'

The carriage was empty but for themselves, so they spread magazines on the seat and Marinda found her knitting. She contrived to make the carriage their private castle for the moment. Edward thought of his own honeymoon and looked at her no less fondly. In the past three years she had grown a little fatter and it suited her. She had a look of demure maturity, as her purposeful fingers moved the knitting needles.

'I shouldn't have thought,' said Marinda, frowning slightly over the gibberish of her knitting pattern, 'that Sprake had much ideas about honeymoons either. He'd probably take his wife, if he ever finds one, for a day trip to Blackpool.'

'I shall be fed up if we really have come on a fool's errand,' said Edward, ignoring the speculations about Sprake's possible matrimony. 'I did want this week to be – well – I'd like it to be perfect.'

'You don't want much, do you?'

'I want it for you.'

Marinda looked at her husband with a feeling of shame, of humility that he should be so kind, so understanding, and she so undeserving.

'I've always wanted everything to be perfect for you,' he went on, and she put down her knitting and laid her hand across his. 'And it hasn't been. Sometimes I've wondered if you were happy.'

'I am happy, Edward.'

'Are you? Swear it.'

'I swear I am.'

It was unbelievably, miraculously true. Some blessing had come to her soul, some balm to her spirit. A few years later, people might have thought her sense of well-being was due to glands, hormones, fixations, sublimations. Perhaps it was, but as Marinda watched the downs of Berkshire lose themselves in the lush valleys of the west and the rounded hills of Devon, she knew she had never before known happiness.

All her life Marinda was to remember the week at Bothycombe. It lay impressed in her mind as one of the few flawless things. The inn, an ancient haunt of smugglers, lay on a tongue of land at the edge of a small cove, looking across the estuary of the Bothy To the right were rocks and breakers and the roar of the open sea, to the left woods ran down to the shore. For a whole week it did not rain. The locals, unused to such a state of affairs, looked uneasy, and hinted dispiritedly about 'paying for it later', but Edward and Marinda thought of nothing that was not in the perfect present.

They imprisoned each moment in happiness. They walked and fished, and one day, tempted by the alluring blueness of the sea, they bathed, naked and alone in the next cove, in water that was too cold for comfort, but silky and invigorating. They rowed across the mouth of the estuary and saw as they pulled away from the shore that the hills running down to the sea were transfigured by the bluebells. The farther away they rowed the bluer became the hills, like joys of childhood remembered in old age.

On the last evening, Marinda looked out on the scented night and saw a small cloud covering the moon.

'I wish I could stay here for ever,' she said.

Edward walked round the room collecting his things to pack. He thought, with a feeling of success, that at last he understood his wife. At last he had found the magic formula of making her happy, but how he had done it and what the alchemy was he could not tell.

'Did you see my shoehorn, darling?' he asked.

'In the cupboard, I think. I'll pack for you, if you leave it.'

But he persisted carefully in his packing, wrapping his

boots, for he never wore shoes, in newspaper with the carefulness which Marinda often found so irritating. But tonight, soothed and softened by complete happiness, if such a state there is, she merely turned and smiled. He dropped the boots and came to watch the dark sea below their windows, jolting, with soft rhythm, the boats tied up under the jetty.

Marinda felt his arm grow rigid across her shoulders, and she thought with sudden yearning of children yet to be born.

Not three weeks later snow fell in late half-hearted flurries. At number seventeen, Allington Road, the blinds were drawn, and at the neighbouring houses the blinds also tactfully hid unseemly life within. There was a silence in the street which echoed the slow knocking of the horses' hoofs as the hearse turned the corner. The air was drenched with the scent of lilies.

It was the day of the funeral of Edward Stonebridge.

Book Four

Chapter 19 — THE HOLIDAY

In 1929 Marinda had been widowed for six years. The edge of the shock and horror of the spring, when Edward had unexpectedly died before the operation on his face could be attempted, had been blunted, but even now Marinda could not think of his death without bitterness and remorse. It was for her that he had wished the scars to be removed. Had it not been for her, the unsuspected splinter of shrapnel dislodged by the preliminary operation would not have killed him. At least not then, though the surgeon had consoled her by saying it might have happened at any time. But he had died then, when they had just discovered the perfection of happiness, and to Marinda it seemed a blow too cruel to be borne. She never considered that the new-found content before his death might not have been lasting. That most useless, next to jealousy, and that most defeating of emotions, remorse, remorse for the wasted years, pursued her waking moments and stole hours from her sleep.

The Yeadons had carried her off to Putney, and Sprake, good kind Sprake, with Nellie and Carey (who came as soon as she could), performed miracles in that horrific week, which had seemed all undertakers and mourning and relations. With a slowness that progress was almost imperceptible she emerged, older, thinner, haunted even in moments of brittle laughter by a terror that all happiness was a prelude to misery.

Stonebridges Ltd had saved her, On the morning after Edward's funeral, when she had called at the office to see Sprake about the state of her income, she had sat without thinking in Edward's chair. And except for eating and sleeping, and later, for business journeys, she had scarcely left it. After years of living as its slave she realized that it had taken her thoughts and given her an interest, saving her from a remorseful collapse which people were beginning to call 'nervous breakdown'. For three years she had had no holiday.

Of course the credit for her success was due to Sprake. In pity for her he had put aside his dislike of women and had gradually come to admire the mixture of intelligence and charm with which she used to deal with difficult customers or situations.

Marinda took her hat from the stand where Edward used to hang his bowler. The hat, a vase of flowers and a mirror were the only signs of the room's feminine owner. She signed the letters and rang a bell for the faithful Miss Pillar, who had survived a certain amount of *Sturm und Drang* and was now a piece of the furniture.

'Nothing more, Miss Pillar?'

'No, Mrs Stonebridge. There are those two acknowledgements to go to Everton's, but I can deal with them. I hope you enjoy your holiday. You certainly deserve one after this long time.'

'Yes,' agreed Marinda, 'but a holiday seems harder to organize than a business. This one is Mr Sprake's doing. It was a command.'

She looked in the mirror at her wide eyes and her mouth which had forgotten how to laugh. She was always pale by the evening and she drooped a little with fatigue. Studying her face dispassionately and with a careful backward glance at the door, she took some rouge, which she had bought for the first time in the lunch hour, out of her bag and applied it with nervous, unskilful fingers. The first pink tinge to her cheeks gave a new sparkle to her eyes and she felt suddenly gay, almost young.

'Good night,' she said as she went through the outer office and heard a chorus of voices hoping she would enjoy her holiday. Sprake saw her to the door and closed it after her.

Since Edward's death two men had wanted to marry her and she had refused them both. One supplied the cartons for her products and the other dealt with her advertising. She had also received other offers of an amorous but less honourable nature. There was something, had she known, about her widowhood and her resolution and her gentle requests for advice which men found appealing. At first she was appalled at their advances. Then she began to realize that men are seldom the pillars of morality she had supposed and she began to feel full of wisdom and experience. It never occurred to her to accept any of the proposals, honourable or otherwise, but she did realize that the man she had married had been unusually honest in all his dealings. In business, in love, Edward, she knew, had been single-minded. In the despair at the thought of the time she had wasted before she realized this, she worked harder than ever.

At Ealing the house waited for her, with the smells of Nellie's cooking floating indiscreetly from the kitchen, where the door was apt to be left open. Marinda turned the key and saw Carey's handbag on the hall table. From the drawing-room came the sound of *Sheep gently graze.*

'Hullo,' said Carey. 'The notes stick. Doesn't anyone ever play it?'

'Hardly ever. What time did you get here?'

'After tea.'

Marinda and Carey never kissed and seldom shook hands. There was an unspoken revulsion in both of them for all signs of affection between women but they were tied together by an abiding faithfulness. Marinda, who met many people, had few other friends and none who competed with Carey.

'Your mother sent you heaps of directions. Love to Sue and Mark.'

'But we aren't going to see them.'

'Yes, I know, but your mother seems to think that Germany and Austria are like Farley and Marchampton. She thinks we are terribly rash to go at all.'

'Perhaps she is right.'

'Now don't start backing out. I've tried for years to make you go really right away and you just can't back out when I've bought the tickets and got the passports and the money and spent hours at Cooks. Why, Marinda, I'd sue you.'

'You enjoyed it. Show you a map and you're half-way there.'

Carey closed the piano.

'Well, at least I see as much of the world as I can, while I can.'

Through the death of her father Carey had surprisingly inherited a small income, and, as her mother now lived with a sister, she was determined to enjoy her sudden freedom. Her cheeks were as red as ever, powder them as she might, and she always looked as if she were freshly washed with soap and water. She wore her dark hair in a plaited knot at the nape of her neck, and amongst so many bobbed heads she looked older than her contemporaries. Her body was strong and well-made, but with no more grace or elegance than she had as a girl. She was always interested in Marinda's clothes, but careless and lazy about her own and apt to buy dresses in the wrong shade of blue which did not quite fit.

The two young women were going to Dresden the next morning. The holiday was a conspiracy on the part of Sprake, the Fairfields, Aunt Emma, now fat and widowed, and Carey's mother and Nellie, who all agreed that Marinda Must Go Away.

Marinda had not seen Mark since the year of Edward's death. Sue had spent a summer at Farley, where Belle had tried unsuccessfully to put some flesh on her bones and stop her from smoking, for Belle and Emma both agreed that Sue's cough was due to excessive smoking. Duffy was a tall, withdrawn child with a slightly foreign accent, for since the inflation Mark and Sue had found they could live more cheaply in Germany than anywhere else, and they had not returned to England. In the spring of 1929 they had moved on to Vienna. The name of Mark Studland was now respected by the more selective literary critics, but until he wrote *The Rainbow* few people read his works or knew much about him. Two years before he had written a travel book, light and, so the critics said, slightly inaccurate, with moments of bitter humour and unexpected gaiety. It was widely read, especially in America, and the success gave a lift to his spirit. He found that he was still a poet and during that summer and autumn he worked spasmodically, with alternate moods of elation and despair, at a new collection of poems.

'Vienna is really only a step away from Dresden,' said

Carey, as they changed at Leipzig and saw the long-distance trains, with their enticing destination boards, steam out of the vast station. 'Don't you want to see Mark and Sue?'

'No,' said Marinda shortly. 'I saw Sue last summer, and I don't care if I never see Mark again.'

Carey looked at Marinda curiously. The porter in his clean blue coat lifted the strap which held their luggage and led the way into the airless smell of Turkish cigarettes and dust which always tickled Carey's nose and made her want to go at once to Istanbul. A young German in the far corner of the carriage listened carefully to what they had to say, for he was eagerly learning English. He looked at their Anglo-Saxon figures without pleasure. The dark one was too tall and the fair one was too thin, but he liked the curve of her chin as she tilted her head and talked so swiftly that he could not follow. Instead he sat back and let his eyes rove over her long legs and the slightly perceptible curves under her light coat, and thought that there was an elegance about her *doch*.

'I never told you about Mark, did I?' said Marinda, looking over her shoulder at the German and deciding, with the ease of all the English, that he was deaf and dumb. However, she lowered her voice as she went on. 'You know, years ago, I was in love with Mark, before Sue, when we were all young. Do you remember?'

Their youth swam before them, hop-scented and green.

'You couldn't have been, not Mark.'

'But I was. You know what a fool one can be at that age.'

Carey nodded. Marinda was watching the landscape with its surprising houses and advertisements for unknown commodities. *'Pelikan Tinte'*. What could it mean?

She looked back at Carey. 'And then, you know, after he married Sue, I knew he still liked me – more than he should have done, and I was such an idiot. Well, I suppose I sort of hankered after him. Silly, wasn't it?'

'Crazy,' said Carey.

'And wrong too. But ever since Edward died I think I have hated Mark, loathed him!'

She emphasized the word and the German in the corner

wondered what it meant and how it was spelt.

'I could have been much happier with Edward if it hadn't been for him. Sometimes I used to wish that Mark would die so that I would never have to see him again.'

'And in the end it was Edward who died,' said Carey softly.

'And the cruel part, the part I can't forgive Mark, though it wasn't his fault, it was mine, but the senseless part was that Edward and I could have been perfectly happy all the time, just as happy as we were at the end. Thank God we were happy then.'

'And all this you blame on Mark.'

'Yes.'

'You blame Mark for existing.'

'No, I blame Mark for marrying Sue and not marrying me.'

'But surely,' said Carey, 'you don't imagine you'd have liked being married to Mark? I've often wondered how Sue can stand him with his conceits and his moods. He'd have driven you demented in six months.'

'No, he wouldn't. I think I should have understood him.'

Carey made a face of disgust.

'Mark doesn't need understanding. He needs a strait-jacket. My dear, you don't know what that sort of man does to you. He's like my father. One day Sue will leave him. She'll have to.' She hesitated. 'Well, no, she probably won't. She'd have done that already if she'd been going to. Sue is much better for him than you would have been.'

Marinda uncrossed her knees restlessly and leaned forward.

'It would be quite useless for anyone as sensitive as you are to marry an insensitive person like Mark,' continued Carey. 'Oh yes, I know he's a writer – a poet – so I suppose one can't really say he's insensitive, and maybe he doesn't know he is cruel and unkind, but if he did he wouldn't care. I'll grant you this, he can't really help it, but he should never have married anybody.'

'That's what he said to me once.'

'Well, at least he has the decency to admit it. But don't delude yourself into thinking you'd have known happiness of the kind that Edward gave you, because you were happy with him, weren't you?'

'Yes, at the end, only at the end. And I can't forgive Mark for that. It was all his fault.'

'It was his fault for existing,' said Carey again. 'But I understand now why you don't want to see him. You don't loathe him at all. You're afraid of him.'

Marinda looked into Carey's bright bird-like eyes which missed so little.

'Yes,' she said slowly, 'maybe you're right.' Opening *The Good Companions* so that Carey should realize she had said all she was prepared to say about Mark, she added, 'I don't want to see him again.'

'It's almost as good as Oxford, isn't it?' said Carey.

'I've never been to Oxford,' answered Marinda, thinking: 'I've never been anywhere. Why didn't someone tell me there were such things to be seen?'

They were standing on the cobblestones looking at the Hofkirche and the Opera House. The copper roofs, green with time, looked exotic against all the grey stone and the sky. They walked on until they came to the bridge over the Elbe with the forests and orchards on the heights beyond.

'The guidebook says there's a beautiful walk up through those woods to a place called the Keppmuehle. It's a mill.'

'Let's go this afternoon.'

'We shan't be back in time for the opera. We could go tomorrow.'

'It says it must be seen in spring when the blossom is out.'

'Like Farley,' said Marinda. All her life she was to use Marchshire as a standard. Every hill was measured in her mind against the Marchampton Beacon.

They stayed in a small hotel beyond the station at the top of the town. It was for some reason the part where the English congregated, and some of Carey's friends of the previous summer, when she had come with her mother to visit Pen's grave, had called to see her. Human anachronisms mostly, governesses who had become too German for England and were now too English for Germany. An artist couple who had known her mother, and the daughter of a cousin who was learning German. Before the war the colony had been large, with its own church and place in the community, and now those who could bring themselves to forget the German crimes of war were lured back by the beauty and dignity of the town, until they forgot that wars could be. They could not foresee yet another war which would leave no remnant of Dresden's loveliness in a heap of blackened ruins.

'A note for you,' said the hall porter. He had learnt his English in an internment camp in the Isle of Man and liked to practise it.

He handed Carey the note and their key.

'Oh, Marinda, it's for you,' said Carey, who had opened it without noticing the name. 'It's from Mark, of all people.'

Marinda took the sheet of paper with a sudden wave of unaccountable emotion. Like all the letters Mark ever wrote it was brief.

'Dearest Marinda, you will be seeing me. I am in Dresden for a few days. Mark.'

'I shall be out,' said Marinda, crumpling the note and looking away from Carey.

'As you like. It's easy enough to arrange. We shall be at the opera tonight, and tomorrow we can go up to the Keppmuehle. He doesn't even say where he's staying, so it will be easy to escape.'

They walked across the hall, which was long and narrow, to the lift.

'It won't be at all easy to escape,' said a voice, as Mark lazily unfolded himself from a chair at their elbow.

He was completely unembarrassed, and the only hint he gave of having heard their unflattering arrangements was in a certain gleam of his sherry-coloured eyes and a twist to the corner of his mouth.

'Please come out with me tonight.'

'We are going to the opera.'

'So am I. I can see you in the foyer in the interval and we can have supper afterwards on the terrace at the Bellevue.'

Marinda looked helplessly at Carey, but Carey stood stolid, waiting for instructions.

'Oh well, yes, thank you, Mark. Is Sue all right?'

'I don't know,' said Mark. 'She's been up in the Tyrol all the summer.'

'Yes, I know, but surely –'

'I haven't seen her. I had work to do in Vienna. Webbe was there. You know as much about her as I do. She writes to you, doesn't she?'

'Not very often.'

'No,' laughed Mark easily. 'Sue handles a pen as if it were a dangerous explosive.'

'You are not much better.'

'I? I write all day – not letters, of course.'

He walked with them to the door of the lift.

'Where are you staying?' asked Carey.

Marinda stepped into the lift and stood for a moment with her back to him, looking at herself in the mirror and seeing, without vanity, her wide brow and cap of gold dusted hair. She heard Mark's voice over her shoulder as she turned to say 'Goodbye'.

'I am staying in this hotel,' he said, looking into the clear depths of her eyes, adding, as he watched the effect of his words, 'I always do.'

Chapter 20 — STRANGE COUNTRY

The sharp scent of pine needles enveloped the week that Mark spent in Dresden, so that, until the end of her life, its perfume could bring back to Marinda some of the gaiety and high spirits, unpredictable, unexpected, which caught them. It was so long since she had felt the release of fun and laughter that she looked back on the past years and the shadow of Stonebridges Ltd as if it was a cage from which she had suddenly escaped. This is what life would have been, she thought, if Andrew and Pen had not been killed, if Edward had not died: the thoughtless laughter of brothers, the family jokes, the easy protection.

'I'm glad Mark came now,' she said to Carey, 'because I've begun to like him, which I never did before, and I've stopped loving him and I've stopped hating him. It's just a safe, happy sort of relationship.'

Carey twisted her knot of hair and stabbed it viciously with hairpins.

'I must say he has been decent enough this week, and there are lots of things you can't do easily here if you are a woman, like dining on the terrace at Bellevue, only –' she paused and fixed the knot with an air of finality which dared it to come down, and said, 'I feel he really ought to be spending the week with Sue.'

Marinda's face sobered.

'Yes, of course, so he ought.'

She was reading an English paper three days old. The happenings of the world were a long way off, and this week was snatched from reality. From here the items of news looked different and out of perspective. Mark talked of a man called Hitler, but few people in England knew he existed. He was a loud voice of no importance.

'I'll tell Mark he must go back and see Sue,' thought Marinda, and then felt suddenly that, if he went, half the magic of Dresden would go with him. No, that was ridiculous. She shook herself mentally and folded up the paper to read in the train.

Mark was taking them to spend three days at an inn in the Erzgebirge.

'You can see right into Bohemia,' he said, as they made themselves comfortable on the hard seats of a third-class carriage. 'Then you can realize it isn't Bohemia, but a state of mind, a state of freedom, beauty –'

He waved his pipe expansively, enjoying his own words.

Carey pricked him with the pin she so often used to deflate him.

'The average Bohemian peasant is old and hideous, and the towns are ugly and provincial.'

'And no one is ever free,' added Marinda.

'How sad that sounds,' said Mark, looking serious. 'Like the beginning of a dirge.' He looked out of the window and was lost to them. Marinda wondered what was in his mind. She wished she could follow the tricks and turns words made to him, but as she could not, she had the wit to remain silent. Carey knitted an inch on the jumper she was making for her mother. A German in the corner peered benevolently at them through rimless glasses, bowed and asked if he might shut the window. The train panted slowly round the bend and up the steep gradients, ringing a bell with an air of nonchalance. It echoed through the mountains with monotonous melody, until it became part of a dream.

Marinda fell asleep.

They had two hours' gentle climbing until they came to the inn. Quite near, just over the next hill, lay the dark forests of the new country, Czecho-Slovakia. It was hot and they were grateful for the shade of the pines. Marinda had not walked so far for years. She threw her mind back over the chasm of her widowhood to that magic week at Bothycombe, not since then. Nothing now reminded her of it but a trick of memory. She was surrounded by alien trees and strange contours of the land; she was in a foreign country with Mark. The air was fresh and spiced with pine. At the corner of her shoulder-blade an unused muscle rebelled and dragged at the unaccustomed weight of the rucksack containing her luggage. '*'n Tag,*' murmured a peasant woman who passed them carrying a truss of hay. Marinda answered her in her newly learnt German and felt utterly divorced from her former self, light-hearted and strange, belonging to no one.

Mark trudged silently ahead. They were beyond the forest now and on the fruit-tree-lined road. He came out of a deep reverie. 'All right?' he asked with the crack in his voice which gave a spurious tenderness to all he said.

'It's lovely, isn't it?' said Marinda, stopping a moment. 'So still and fruitful.'

'I've been thinking on and off for the past hour,' said Mark as he paused. Carey stopped to tie her shoe and Marinda thought: 'Now I shall know how his mind works. I shall be with him when he puts one word on another to describe this moment.'

Carey straightened her back and Mark gave her rucksack a friendly hoist.

'For the past hour,' he repeated solemnly, 'I have been thinking of *Rehfleisch mit Preiselbeerensauce*.'

'What's that?'

'Venison and cranberry sauce,' translated Carey.

'It's marvellous at this Gasthaus. I believe they bury the venison for weeks and then, when it's just about to give you ptomaine, at exactly the right moment my friend the Wirt laces it with speck and roasts it.'

As Marinda was busy switching her mind from a loftier plane to the contemplation of *Geröstetem Rehfleisch* so that her gastric juices were gently stimulated, she found that Mark was pointing out the wooden building ahead of them and repeating softly, as if to himself:

'"Is there anybody there?" said the Traveller,
Knocking on the moonlit door;
And his horse in the silence champed the grasses
Of the forest's ferny floor.'

He kept her mind taut trying to keep up with his constant change of mood. It was exhilarating at one moment, exhausting at another.

There was a piano at the Gasthaus, and in the evening, replete with the expected venison, Mark started to play flippant tunes of Viennese operettas, which he sang in a clear light baritone. They drank the heavy, too sweet wine of the valley and hummed an accompaniment. A forester with a green hat, shorts and a paunch which spoke of beer, added a hearty tenor. There was a Czech guard from the frontier post and the fat daughter of the innkeeper. The bottles emptied; the forester produced a zither and still Mark played. There was something of the gypsy in the music; *Komm Zigane, Komm Zigane* sang the unofficial choir. The room was thick with tobacco smoke, and Carey was arguing patiently in her careful German about the touchy question of the *Kolonien*. Marinda leant over the piano and watched Mark's hair fall endearingly out of place. He played a final chord, looked up at her and blew her a kiss. She returned the chaste salute with the piano between them. The Czech guard was making progress with the innkeeper's daughter.

'Perhaps he likes the buxom type,' thought Marinda.

Nothing seemed to matter much and her head ached. Mark rose from the piano. She could see that his pupils were large and dark. His glass had been refilled with great frequency by the Wirt.

'Goodness!' thought Marinda, as the room swam a little. 'We've all had quite enough to drink.'

She walked carefully to the door, said 'Good night' and went to bed. The fresh mountain air blew out the curtains like flags of truce. From below again came the tinkling of the piano and the beguiling notes of the zither. The cows mooed gently in the byre next door and when Carey came up Marinda was fast asleep.

Carey sat on the bed and rested her foot on a painted chair. With a wash-hand-stand and two hooks it completed the furnishings of the room, for which they paid the equivalent of half a crown a day with full board.

'It's no good,' she said, 'I can't walk a yard with it, at least not today.'

It had been arranged that Mark should shepherd them over the frontier, walking with them down into the valley to a small spa called, up to 1918, Bad Goldfeld, but now an unpronounceable collection of consonants, and returning by train. There was something enticing at the thought of passing the German and Czech frontier posts and journeying for a country walk into a strange land, and Marinda was disappointed at the thought of giving up the idea, for the next day they were due back in Dresden in order to be home by the end of the month, as arranged.

'But you and Mark can go. After all the fuss about getting those permits, it would be stupid to give up the idea.'

'We can't leave you here by yourself.'

'Why not? I've got plenty to read. I shall hop out into the sun and enjoy myself enormously while you and Mark are staggering up hill and down dale and thinking you're having a wonderful time.'

The pleasures of walking produced less enthusiasm in Carey as she grew older and heavier.

'But it was to be something so special, going over the frontier,' said Marinda.

'I'm not as romantic as you are, my dear. It's exactly the same – same people, same countryside. You can't change people by drawing a line on a map. I wonder sometimes what trouble lies in store for us through it. Old Lloyd George can't have known much geography. Why, the landlord has been telling me that a few miles away the whole village has to cross the frontier to get to its own well.'

Carey was off on one of her favourite hobby-horses, the anomalies of the Treaty of Versailles, and for the first time Marinda was beginning to understand the viewpoint of peoples who were without an island's protection of the sea. She looked out of the window at the pine-covered hills, dark against the sky and the small pastures blue with harebells. To the left was the frontier post, a white pole across the road, vivid against the dark background. Beyond, she felt sure, was something exciting and different, whatever Carey might say.

'I do rather want to go,' she admitted at last.

'Well, go, go with my blessing.'

Carey stuck a plaster over her offending blister and pushed her foot into a bedroom slipper. 'I shall enjoy myself every bit as much as you do, I assure you, and now you've got your emotions sorted out, you hardly need me as a chaperon.'

Marinda laughed, for the day before it had rained and Mark had apparently awakened in a bad mood. He had argued and contradicted until Carey and Marinda had been driven to their room in search of peace.

'I hope he is in a better temper today.'

'I told you he's impossible, except in very small doses,' said Carey with the happy triumph of one who has been proved right. 'I should think Sue must be thankful to be rid of him for a bit.'

'I dare say.'

'*Schinken,*' said Mark, disembowelling the rolls from his rucksack. '*Schinken* again and *Blutwurst*.'

'Translate, please,' asked Marinda. 'Ham and what?'

'Bloody sausage, one might say. Not bad if you don't mind garlic.'

'How queer he is,' thought Marinda, rubbing her back against the pile of logs which was their resting-place and looking down the ravine at a small lake, black with the shadow of the forest. 'He's a poet and all he can talk of is sausage and garlic.' Into her thoughts intruded his caressing voice:

'We are not sure of sorrow;
And joy was never sure;
Today will die tomorrow,
Time stoops to no man's lure;
And love, grown faint and fretful,
Sighs, and with eyes forgetful
Weeps that no loves endure . . .'

'It's Swinburne, isn't it?' asked Marinda.

'Yes. I wonder how far I shall get before I die. I'm nearly forty, so I suppose I shall now begin to decline –'

'Oh no.'

'But I shall, I fear. I ought to have done so much more.'

'We could all say that.'

'Yes, but I've been – hampered.'

Marinda knew he was thinking of Sue, and she remembered Carey's words.

'Sue does many things for you no other woman would.'

He looked surprised. He was used to feeling that marrying Sue was a mistake for which he was paying dearly, and forgetting that Sue must also have made a poor bargain.

'Few women could put up with you,' said Marinda.

He felt in every pocket for his pipe before answering.

'You could have done,' he said, filling his pipe with concentration.

'It's possible.'

It was the first time for many years that Marinda had spoken to Mark of personal things, and it was also one of the few occasions in her life when she had been alone with him. She realized that having Mark to herself had always been disturbing and it was disturbing now. There was no sound in the forest but the occasional rustle as some small creature moved unseen. There was no bird song, no human noise but their own voices, deadened by the pines.

'You know, don't you,' said Mark, 'that Sue and I are – well, you might as well call it "separated"?'

'No, I hadn't realized it. Sue's letters never tell us much, and lately she has been worse than ever.'

'Well, that's how it is, and of course it's my fault. I don't deny it.'

'Poor Sue,' said Marinda softly. She had a swift vision of what Sue, the kittenlike girl, had become. 'I expect she didn't want to tell us.'

'She won't divorce me.'

Marinda thought of her parents' horror at the idea of a divorce, of their total lack of comprehension of the forces which would drive Sue to such a course.

'Why should she?'

'She has cause enough,' said Mark briefly. 'I'm not faithful either in body' – he paused and looked at her – 'or in mind.'

Marinda felt a stir of conscience. She did not trust Mark. She did not love him either, she hoped, and yet she knew that he had the power to make her want him more than anyone in the world. She rose hastily and shook the crumbs from her skirt.

'Come on,' she said. 'It's getting awfully hot and we want to get to Czeny for lunch, don't we?'

'Suppose so.'

He took his dismissal with outward meekness. He was so seldom repulsed by women that when he was, he merely decided that now was not the moment and changed his tactics. It never occurred to him that he would not be able to arouse in a woman the degree of response which he happened to want.

He pointed out the descent that lay ahead of them. Through the gradual opening in the forest they saw the ruins of the monastery and the red roofs of Czeny. It was a watering-place with some small pretence at fashion. The women, German, Czech, and Austrian with an occasional Italian, were conscious of their chic, light dresses. The men's suits were a little too tight, a shade too well-pressed, their shirts were very white, their collars very stiff. There was an occasional uniform, bright with epaulettes and facings.

'I feel bedraggled,' said Marinda, dropping her rucksack and looking at her dusty shoes.

Water splashed prodigally from a fountain and from the bandstand came the strains of Lehar, efficiently executed.

The notices on the board outside the hotel were in Czech, a language which looks in print as obscure as Sanscrit. As Marinda tidied her hair and washed her hands she felt as if she had strayed into some comic opera, and at any moment the chorus would appear out of the wings and do a song and dance. Her linen dress looked deceptively cool, for she was a woman who was easily exhausted by heat, while remaining outwardly pale and unaffected. She had only just begun to use lipstick and still felt, as she watched her face brighten in the mirror, that she was being dashing and abandoned. The fringe, which she had never forsaken from childhood, and her straight silky hair gave her even features a serious expression, and an elusive attraction which fell short of beauty.

Outside, in the shade of an acacia tree, Mark had ordered two tankards of lager beer.

'But I don't like beer,' protested Marinda.

'Try it.'

Marinda still found that she did not like it, but that it quenched her thirst in the most life-giving manner.

'If Arne were here he'd want to paint you,' said Mark. 'Sometimes, you know, you're quite beautiful.'

He looked at her as if now might be one of the times. Few women can resist a compliment, and Marinda was not one of them. Yet, as she felt Mark's eyes examining her, she flushed and picked up the map.

'I want to see where we are.'

Their heads were close together as they traced their route on the map. The country they were now in was marked in a different colour. It was as if, thought Marinda, they had stepped over the boundaries of time and space. Foxholes and Stonebridges and all the anchors of her restricted life simply were not. Even poor Carey and her blister, a few miles beyond the forest, was in another country.

'Let's not go back,' said Mark suddenly. 'Let's go down the Danube to Vienna and Budapest. We can see all the mistakes the politicians have made out of the blood of war. At Predeal we can walk through Transylvania and by autumn we'd be at the Black Sea, at Balcic. It's an adorable little place, with a sort of Turkish feeling.'

He spoke as if he were mapping out a serious itinerary

with her for the next few months. The names of the places, Linz, Sinaia, Constanza, dropped off his tongue like a magic incantation.

'Stop being idiotic,' said Marinda suddenly. 'Why, I haven't so much as a toothbrush.'

'If I buy you a toothbrush, will you come?'

Marinda laughed to show that she knew it was a joke, but something at the back of her mind told her that Mark was half serious. If she said 'Yes' she might find herself spending Christmas on the Black Sea shore, improbable though it sounded.

'I mean it,' insisted Mark.

'You're so crazy, I believe you do.'

'I could buy you a toothbrush, you know.'

'Oh, Mark, you make it all sound so plausible. You take the madness out of things and make them seem quite normal. If you asked me such a question at home' – she had a swift vision of the red brick precision of Allington Road, Ealing, and the timeless conventions of Foxholes – 'of course I should say "No". I should hold up my hands in horror. But here I seem to have lost my senses or something, because I can't say "No" with any force.'

'Then say "Yes".'

The band at the other end of the square began to play *Zwei Maerchenaugen* with treacly seduction. It became background music to her voice as she went on. 'It must be "No". Any other answer would be crazy. Oh, Mark, I do believe if Sue were anyone but my sister I'd say "Yes". It's horrible of us. Haven't you a conscience?'

'You know that I haven't.'

'Any sense of responsibility? There's Duffy.'

'Sue has had Duff, body and soul always. I support them, God help me.'

Marinda thought of all the help which Sue had not been too proud to accept from her family. Edward had always shown generosity to Sue, and Marinda had continued it.

'I just don't love her any more. Doesn't that make a difference? Or are you afraid of what people will say?'

'Only Mother and Father. I couldn't do that to them.'

'Even if I get a divorce?'

'No, that would make it worse. Be sensible, Mark. We

can never be anything to each other.'

She well knew that barriers of relationship, of temperament and upbringing were a wide ocean between them, quite apart from such minor considerations as Stonebridges, and the fact that she had only a rucksack at Rehberg and the rest of her luggage at Dresden, and yet as she sat opposite him under the acacia tree, and watched the sun flicker through its leaves and brighten the red lights in his hair, she was filled with a feeling she dared not analyse. No man had stirred her emotions since Edward's death, until now, and she was caught by a trick of the senses, an illusion of youth and of things past and long forgotten. The band played a final chord and turned over the leaves of the music for the next item with a rustle of expectancy. With a flourish the waiter whisked off their empty glasses. She felt Mark take her foot between his and keep it, as if he would hold her, however hard she might try to escape. He put his hand tightly on her wrist.

'You should have been mine,' he said. 'I will not let you go. However little it is, I must have it.'

The refusals, which her eyes belied, increased his urgent persuasions. They invaded every hour of that day they spent together. Against the black ruins of the monastery, which was the avowed object of the expedition, he explained, quietly plausible, how easy it would be – a meeting in Paris in the spring – a few weeks in London or Scotland. Had she ever been to Skye? She had only to give up that idiotic job of hers, make excuses, slip away.

How easy he made it sound! He lived a life where such relationships were in fact easier than at Ealing or Foxholes, but, even so, stirred by this unwanted passion, Marinda saw many difficulties which he ignored; the small deceptions, the inward unrest which she called her conscience. Yet she knew that if Sue had not been her sister, but some unknown misunderstood wraith who had lost Mark, she could have followed him to the end of the world.

She said nothing of this as she listened to Mark all that hot afternoon. His voice had an absurd inflection which gave gaiety to even his serious dissertations on the path of Attila the Hun, the Thirty Years War, political boundaries, and what fattened the Teutonic torso. Suddenly he would leave it all and disarm her with a look and say quite calmly: 'I adore you, Marinda. I want you.'

There was a nicely arranged viewpoint which seemed to overlook Europe. Somewhere in the misty distance was the Danube and its seductive cities. Behind them, blocked by forest and mountains, was Germany, France, the sea. Somewhere indeed was England and Foxholes. But it was not here, disarmed by the beauty, that she finally listened to Mark. It was on the station, where a certain Bohemian dirt and disorder had replaced the old Teutonic cleanliness. The train was late. They sat on their rucksacks and waited, surrounded by notices in Czech which, if they had only understood, implored them not to spit. A train thundered past on its way to Prague.

'We ought to be going in that direction,' said Mark.

'Oh, Mark, don't. Please leave me alone. How could we?' She thought of Carey and her restraining blister. 'And there's Carey, and all my things left at Dresden.' The small concrete difficulties in such a course of action presented themselves clearly to her. The clock ticked on. The short dusk deepened to a luminous darkness. At the other end of the small station the would-be travellers were crowding by the restaurant. Mark put his arm protectively round Marinda. It was comforting and disturbing. Suddenly he turned and kissed her, tilting her head back, hurting her. Slowly he released her.

'I wish I'd never set eyes on you,' he said.

From the edge of the mountain came the warning bell of the train. They rose in silence and Mark dragged the rucksacks behind him. With a queer feeling of exhilaration and despair Marinda made a resolve. 'Where will you be in October?' she asked, and while he made eager, excited plans she listened, helpless, amazed at herself, and frightened. She knew with a strange feeling of fatality that they had to belong to each other, that they were two of a kind and at the same time she knew they would never be happy.

Chapter 21 — THE RETURN

The sea had been swept by one of the swift summer gales and Marinda was not a good sailor. It was Sunday night and she sat on a seat at Victoria looking at the orderly crowds and the familiar sights, and feeling that she had been struck by some madness.

'The Graf Zeppelin has flown round the world,' said Carey briskly, giving a quick glance to the newspaper. 'I'm always glad to be back. When you get to Victoria it's just as if you take a sponge and wipe your holiday off a slate.'

'Yes,' said Marinda, moving stray foreign money from her handbag to her pocket. There was a Czech coin which she was keeping for luck. It was cold and she was tired. Seasickness had brought her to the depth which makes all travellers, thus afflicted, equal at a low level.

'Are you all right?' asked Carey.

'Of course, only tired. I've got to go to the office tomorrow.'

'Must you?'

'Oh yes, there's a lot to be thought of just now.'

Carey said goodbye at Victoria for she was spending the following week with friends in Buckinghamshire. Sitting alone in the taxi, Marinda tried to bring her mind back to the affairs of Stonebridges. She had been considering the step for some time and Mark had now made her mind up for her and persuaded her to give it up. She knew that her parents would be delighted, even though they were ignorant of the reason behind it.

There was a great deal to be done, interviews with Sprake, lawyers, accountants. She wanted to be rid of it all. Her future income would be less, but sufficient for a single woman, though she could not be sure of her financial position. She did not care. She was sick of Stonebridges, sick of work, sick of her house and of herself. In October she saw it all ending, saw herself starting off on something wonderful and different.

*

All that week Sprake's voice talking about valuations and debentures seemed to be in another language. His brother from Leeds was lending him the money to buy a half-share in Stonebridges, and he wanted to be sure that it was being well invested. He was a larger edition of Tom, with a habit of banging one fist on the other and calling money 'brass'. He announced superfluously at intervals that he was a plain man. Tom was alternately proud and ashamed of him, but even the ties of brotherhood would not let him drive a hard bargain with Marinda. Negotiations quivered on the edge of success and when it was finally settled with some advantage to her, he was surprised that she received the news with so little enthusiasm.

'You know, you've always really disapproved of my being here, and now you'll have it all your own way,' was all she said.

It was her last week at the office. The virginia creeper, which she had planted at an angle of the factory wall, was turning red. September had come.

Tom Sprake had never been given to compliments. 'I won't deny you've done a good job, though I never thought you would.'

The roughness of his vowels made everything he said sound crisp and gruff. 'But I'll be sorry when you've gone.' He held out his hand. 'An' I'll always do anything I can for ye.'

'Yes, Sprake, I know. It makes me feel safe.'

'Aye, ye'll be safe enough.'

She turned the key in the lock of her desk and took it off the gold key ring. 'I must remember to give you this with the other keys.'

'Safe,' Sprake had said. But she was not safe. With Mark there would never be safety.

In the end the farewells to Stonebridges were hasty, for her father wrote that her mother was not well and they would be glad if she could come and stay. Belle was not really ill, Henry hastened to explain, but she needed a rest.

The way the letter was worded gave Marinda a feeling of guilt. She did not want to go back to live with her mother and yet she hated to know that she was not well, and at moments she tormented herself with the worry of what life would be like when her mother's cushion of love was no longer there as a refuge. There was so much to be done and she must leave it all. She had not found anywhere else to live and as yet she had done nothing about selling her house at Ealing. By October, she thought despairingly, everything must be settled and ready. All the odd corners of her life must be tidied up and packed away for Mark. She was so certain of the inevitability of what she was going to do that she did not conflict her mind with worry or regret, only just before dawn (and now for the first time in her life she slept badly) she was suddenly worried that she might be found out. It was most important, she thought desperately, turning her pillow and watching her pink curtains warm the room with a bogus glow, that no one should know. She deluded herself that this was in order not to cause her parents and Sue pain, but it was also because she could not accept with any comfort the role of Mark's mistress.

'If I go to Farley on Thursday, you might as well shut the house up and come down on the Saturday. Then you can give my mother a hand. The new maid doesn't seem to be very satisfactory.'

Nellie had grown from the mature child into a young woman with a capable figure and a round, pleasant face. She had, although Marinda knew nothing of it, weathered an unhappy love affair with the ex-window-cleaner, but she was used to freedom and comforts which marriage was unlikely to give her and seemed happy enough as a spinster, tyrannizing over Marinda and running the house as if it were her own. There were certain niceties of service which she would only perform on special occasions, and her cooking was unimaginative, but she was aggressively honest and battled with the London dirt cheerfully. Marinda alternately thanked God for her after her week-end off or dashed thankfully to the office to escape from her. Now she realized that Nellie was another person from whom all knowledge of Mark must be hidden. She was giving up Stonebridges, giving up her house, and now she saw clearly that she might have to give up a good servant for the convenience of Mark.

'I never thought that girl from Wexton would be any

good,' asserted Nellie. 'They are a dirty lot over the hills.' A decade in London had not removed certain prejudices from her country mind. 'But we ought to be back by October, for the autumn cleaning.'

'Oh yes, we must be back by October.'

Nothing must prevent her return.

'I may go away for a week or two then,' she added.

She, who had hardly left Ealing for years, now found it difficult to account for absences.

'Again?' said Nellie, looking at her face, fattened and elongated, mirrored in the silver teapot.

'There's nothing odd about that, I hope. I dare say I shall go away a good bit now and then.'

Marinda was nettled to find that she must make explanations and excuses to Nellie. 'You can stay on at Farley, if you like.'

'If the house is to be sold I'd rather come back and get on with the cleaning. It will be October before you know.'

By early September the fields of her home county were enclosed by the soft shelter of the hop vines. It was so long since Marinda had lived in the country that she had forgotten the excitement of hop picking. After the war its character had changed slightly, it was more of a money-making concern, less of a picnic, but everything was altered for it, the children's school holidays, Harvest Festival at the church and the Jumble Sale in aid of the new Parish Hall.

Marinda walked through the shade of the unpicked vines on her daily walk. Carey was still away and after the first week of interested welcome from everyone, from the post-mistress to Robert Shipley, she became restless. Her mother was not ill enough to hand over the reins to her daughter and not well enough to do half that she insisted on doing. Marinda was alternately touched and infuriated to be treated as if she were a slightly imbecile adolescent. It was, she discovered, one thing to do a hard day's work and another to be sent off on a succession of errands, to the garden for a bunch of mint, to the village for a forgotten loaf, upstairs for a handkerchief. By tea-time she found she had done nothing and was completely exhausted. She had not even the comfort of feeling that she really was helping her mother, who, after a few days, appeared equally exhausted from treating her daughter as a visitor. Her father, obviously glad to see her, was so thin and fragile that Marinda could not look at him without anxiety. She could not envisage one parent without the other. She had never considered whether they were or were not happy. They were her parents, safe, united, a prop to her life which must be inevitably removed by ruthless time.

'Sue doesn't say how she is,' complained Belle, holding Sue's letter at arm's length, because she did not want to ask Marinda to fetch her glasses and the mere thought of climbing the stairs tired her, even if she could be certain she knew they were there.

'I expect she is all right,' said Marinda, whose mind slid away from all thoughts of Sue.

'Didn't Mark tell you much about her when you saw him?'

'You knew she wasn't well in the summer and he sent her up to the Tyrol.'

That would make her mother think of Mark as a loving husband.

'I hope it did her good. She never says,' repeated Belle helplessly. 'Somehow I can't picture her so far away. Why won't Mark live in England? I should have thought the sort of work he does could be done here as well as anywhere else.'

'Sue hates the winter here now, so you'll have to wait until spring. Perhaps she will come then.'

'Yes,' said Belle, folding up the letter. She turned to Henry. 'Write and tell her she must come in the spring. It seems so strange to have one's only grandchild a sort of foreigner. I thought he was going to grow up like Andrew, but –'

She did not finish the sentence and Marinda knew that she was contemplating Andrew's yellow curls and imperious voice; Andrew singing somewhere with celestial choirs. Neither of her daughters compensated Belle for the loss of her son.

'Age shall not weary, nor the years condemn,' thought Marinda.

*

Robert Shipley braked severely at the crossroads, having recognized Marinda's blue dress.

'Can I give you a lift?'

'Well, I was really out for a walk,' Marinda hesitated. It would be pleasant to speak to someone of her own age. 'Thanks awfully, maybe I've walked far enough.'

He moved his dog into the back and, apologizing for the smell of fertilizer, waited until she had settled herself into his shabby car.

'The door must be banged,' he said.

Marinda banged it loudly but ineffectively, and he leant over and fixed it with a practised hand.

'We don't often see you in Farley.'

'No, I don't often have the chance to get off the chain like this.'

'And yet I can't imagine you running that show of yours. It seems such an odd thing.'

'Well, I'm giving it up. Didn't Mother tell you?'

'I hadn't heard. I don't see many people, you know. Still a bit of a foreigner. Perhaps you will be down here more?'

'Possibly. I'm looking for a flat in London, but of course I shall be free.'

Freedom, what sort of a thing was it?

'How is the farm going?'

He pulled up at the gate. 'Come in and see. You know better than most what farms are. I don't make a fortune, but on the other hand I don't starve and I don't think I shall as long as I can work. I've had to give up some of my grand ideas, worse luck. They swallowed up the spare capital without giving enough results and I don't know enough about hops. But I'm learning, Jeff says. I've still got your Jeff, you know. The hops look well this year, don't you think?'

He parked the car and they went through the gate into the hopyard. Marinda had not forgotten how hops should look and she examined them with a critical eye. Robert picked a flower and rubbed it between his fingers, giving her the crushed aromatic petals in his palm to smell. 'Last year we were plagued with red spider.'

Swiftly it brought back her childhood: Foxholes, shrill laughter across the river. The scent tickled her nostrils and she was silent for a moment.

'When I am old,' she thought, 'and when Mark is over and gone, I shall come back here to live.'

She could not deceive herself that her relations with Mark could have any feeling of permanence. It was just something fatal and it would begin in October.

'Come in and have a sherry,' Robert was saying.

'It's much too early,' protested Marinda. 'I've only just had tea.'

'Well, just come in then. I don't often meet anyone in these parts whom I enjoy seeing. It takes a time to make friends, you know.' He laughed to show how little he minded. 'No one ever forgave me for putting strawberries in the bottom yard.'

'But I see you've got hops there again now.'

'Yes,' he answered, as he showed her into his study and took a decanter of sherry and two glasses from a corner cupboard. 'I learnt. Mind you,' he went on, sticking up his square chin as if he were willing to fight, 'I still think they were wrong. I understand soft fruits and I don't understand hops, but Jeff was determined I should fail and of course I did. He breathed on the strawberries and they withered away. He prayed for late frosts and blight and we had both. There was always a shortage of pickers, and the only year we did well Jeff personally arranged a glut and a falling market. I think he was in league with a witch.'

He poured her out a sherry and laughed. He had a deep cheerful laugh which was infectious.

'So you see,' he went on, 'it wasn't really my fault.'

'Nothing is in farming. That's what's so comforting about it. It's the best way of losing money that I know.'

'You didn't want your father to sell to me?'

'No, I hated the idea.' She lifted her glass and looked at him over it. 'I still do.'

'But you don't hate me, I hope?'

'Not consciously any more. I don't go around poisoning the cattle or anything. You needn't worry.'

She smiled and Robert, who knew that she must be near his own age, thought how absurdly young she looked.

'You see,' said Marinda, 'you committed the unforgivable sin in the country. You improved things. I quite realize you've made the house charming. We might have got as far as putting water and electric light in, in fact we were always meaning to one day, always "one day", but I should never have thought of half your improvements. Look at this room.'

He looked obediently round.

It had been the gun-room-cum-office where Edward had first shown her how to manage the farm accounts. From that far-off beginning had sprung all her success at Stonebridges. The dark peeling paper had gone and the roll-top bureau, bulging with tattered copies of the *Farmers' Weekly*, was replaced by a mahogany knee-hole desk, on which stood a typewriter, a pipe-rack and a photograph of a horse. Row upon row of books enlivened the whole of one wall. The chairs were covered in cherry-coloured linen. It was so cheerfully masculine that the blue and white Spode on the mantelpiece looked as if it might have been put there by a feminine hand.

'I'm quite proud of this,' he said. 'I put up the shelves myself and nearly set fire to the place burning off that dark paint.'

'You didn't do it yourself?'

'I do most of the jobs. I fancy myself as a carpenter. You must see my workshop. I've made a grand one in the end barn. Oh, I forgot. You don't like my alterations.'

'I'm prepared to forgive them all but one –'

'I know. It's the wistaria.' A worried look clouded his eyes. 'But honestly, it died a natural death in the frost. I thought I might replace it with a magnolia. Do you think that would be all right, or shall I get another wistaria?'

'You might be defending yourself for murder. No, it's not the wistaria. It's the squeak.'

He looked puzzled.

'The gate – it always squeaked and now it doesn't.'

Relief relaxed his features.

'Oh yes. I oiled it. Was that wrong?'

'Horribly wrong. It has always squeaked and I can forgive you anything but that.' She rose, smiling.

'I don't know how one makes gates squeak.'

She walked into the shining hall.

'I suppose you wouldn't like to come over to the Gymkhana at Merrel with me on the fourteenth?' he asked.

'I'm terribly sorry. I'd have loved to, but I'm going back at the end of the month.'

'So soon?'

'Yes, I have to be there in October.'

Her life after October stretched before her as something perilous and blissful. She had ceased to worry about the ethics of what she was going to do. It had to be. But now the thought smote her again that she must not be found out. She began to lie volubly and recklessly and she was unused to lying. Robert gave no sign of disbelieving her, but escorted her to the car.

'I'll walk back. I'd sooner, honestly. I can go over the field, can't I?'

'Of course, if you'd rather.'

'I love the view up the river.'

He shook hands with her with unexpected ceremony and opened the gate.

'I'll see about the squeak,' he said as it silently closed.

Mark had written so few letters to his wife's parents that Belle did not immediately recognize his writing on the double-sized envelope with the Austrian stamps. She was in the kitchen, superintending the making of the plum jam and apple jelly, which meant that she was doing most of the weighing of sugar and sorting of the fruit herself. 'That girl from Wexton', as Nellie scornfully called her, stood by looking vague and bewildered, or making sudden dashes in the wrong direction for something her mistress required. Marinda, filled with an irritation of which she was ashamed, had gone for a walk to see an old school friend at Merrel, and Henry was in Marchampton. It was seldom he missed a chance of meeting his old friends on market day at the 'Black Swan' in West Gate.

Belle at last left Edna with many and complicated instructions, which were rightly interpreted as 'never stop stirring'. She seized the spoon and began to obey instructions vigorously.

There was no sound in the house but the ticking of the clocks, a faint intermittent clatter of Edna's activities in the kitchen, and the gentle snoring of Rab as he lay sleeping in the sunshine. Belle made her usual ineffective search for her glasses and finally held Mark's spidery Cambridge hand at a distance with her head on one side. The clocks ticked on. Rab stirred and put his paw on her knee. She dropped the letter with a little cry. In her plump face the colour flamed suddenly and then left her cheeks grey and stricken. She picked up the letter to re-read Mark's bald words:

I am very grieved to tell you that poor Sue died yesterday. She had a haemorrhage on Sunday, but no one had considered it to be worse than usual, or I would, of course, have gone to her. I am afraid she must for a long time have been more seriously ill than she gave one to understand, and she had not the resistance to withstand this. She is to be buried on Saturday in the little cemetery of St Martin. It is on the mountain-side and is apparently what she wished. Duffy is with friends. I hardly think I shall return to England for some time. There is much to cause one sorrow and regret . . .

The paper rustled in her hand and tears blurred her eyes. When Marinda came in by the back door she was met by Edna and the hot sweet smell of plum jam.

'The mistress said "stir", and stir I have this long time. My wrist fair aches,' said Edna, leaning on the spoon.

Marinda dropped her hat in the hall and opened the drawing-room door. She was so used to her mother at the gate spluttering out whatever news there was and the silence filled her with foreboding. She did not know what those few quiet minutes had made her fear, but when she saw her mother in the chair, quietly stroking Rab, she could have cried out with relief. Then Belle rose heavily, as always, and Marinda saw her stricken face.

'Mother darling, darling! What is it?'

She put her arms round her mother, who seemed to have evaporated and shrunk. Her cheek was damp with tears.

'There's a letter from Mark,' she said. 'Oh, Marinda –'

Marinda gave a shiver and held her mother more tightly. Surely Mark had not written to say that he and Sue were separated, that he loved her sister, that he –. The whole vista of complications flew before her eyes. On the floor she could see the letter upside down, half back in its folds. She pushed her mother gently into her chair, holding her hand tightly.

'I must make her realize,' she thought, 'that it's something outside me that loves Mark, something . . .' With her free hand she picked up the letter and read it with emotions that varied from line to line. She was relieved, and then a feeling of revulsion engulfed her at her relief. It was as if she had killed her own sister. Sue's thin face and the pertness of her nose, the inconsequence of her curls and the thoughtless tinkle of her laughter, seemed more alive to her now than at any time since Mark's marriage.

'You'd better have some brandy, or something, hadn't you, dear?' she said gently at last. 'Does Edna know where it is?'

'It's in your father's cupboard, and he has the key with him.'

The familiar feeling of impatience at her mother's domestic arrangements did not arise. 'Poor darling,' she thought compassionately. 'She makes everything more difficult.'

'Well, sal volatile, where's that? You've had a shock. You must have something.'

'I'd like some tea,' said her mother faintly.

Marinda opened the door and was met by the pungent smell of burning jam. All her life the acrid smell of burnt sugar brought back Sue's death to her, swiftly, in the midst of happiness.

'Oh dear, oh dear me, the jam,' said Belle. But she did not move, for she was suddenly an old woman, tired and no longer quite as capable as she thought she was. She had lived a long time and had lost five children and a dearly loved son-in-law. She sat stroking Rab and thinking of them all as they had been when they were young at Foxholes, and it was not Sue who lay uppermost in her mind, but Andrew.

Chapter 22 — VISITOR FROM FARLEY

The autumn of 1929 was a bad time for selling houses, the agent told Marinda. She felt desperately like replying that it was a bad time for anything. The leaves of the plane tree in the garden had fallen and lay dank and sour on the path. October, which was to have brought Mark, had come and gone and already the shops were bright with Christmas tinsel. Perhaps at Christmas Mark would write. Surely he could not let Christmas go by without a word. Yet, though she looked eagerly through the post on the tray in the hall, she was always relieved when there was no foreign stamp among them. She had lost the first feeling of horror, when she was haunted by an insane feeling that she and Mark had been the cause of Sue's death. Sometimes she was not sure that she wanted to see him – at least not just yet.

She looked forward to the week-end when Carey was coming for a few days. Now that she had no work to take her time and interest the house seemed not only empty but a nuisance.

'Anyone been over the house?'

Nellie shook her head.

A gentleman telephoned, but hadn't left his name, which meant, thought Marinda, that as usual Nellie had forgotten to ask.

'Probably someone about the house,' she thought. 'Or Mark! Could it have been?'

'I do wish you'd remember to take names, Nellie. It might have been important.'

Nellie set her head high and Marinda knew she had offended her. The telephone began to ring at her elbow and Nellie closed the door with a degree of restrained force that was not quite a slam.

A male voice asked for Mrs Stonebridge and said it was Robert Shipley.

'I'm in London for a few days and I wonder if we could meet. You said I might ring you up if I came, didn't you?'

'I'm delighted to hear you. Won't you come to dinner?'

'Well, I wondered whether you'd dine with me somewhere and go to a show, or are you engaged for the evening?'

His voice sounded confused and anxious.

'No. I'd like to come very much. Have you seen Mother and Father lately?'

'They seem fairly all right. I saw them on Sunday.'

'You have been so kind.'

'Oh, nothing.'

'But you have.'

She thought gratefully of all he had done for them at Sue's death, from producing brandy to wiring the British Consul; of his casual friendly visits, of his resilient cheerfulness. Her heart warmed at the thought of seeing him again.

'Where shall I meet you?'

'I'm staying at Brown's Hotel. There won't be time to fetch you, I'm afraid. What would you like to see?'

She had never realized that Robert Shipley was handsome. His old but well-cut dinner-jacket became him, and as he came forward to meet her she thought ridiculously, 'How clean he looks.'

He had a vague male impression that she was wearing something black with frills round her feet, half hidden in the softness of a velvet cloak. Across her shining cap of hair was a black ribbon which put her looks apart from fashion, and he thought he had seen nothing so charming since he came to town.

He pulled a chair for her in the dim respectability of Brown's and ordered two Martinis.

'What on earth brings you so far from Foxholes?'

'I'm buying some sheep.'

'Not in London, surely?'

'No, down in Kent. London is just on the way. As a matter of fact I come up when I can, and go to a concert and do a play. I'm a Cockney, really. But my mother's people came from Sussex and I always wanted to be a farmer. I was really very lucky because it was "doctor's orders" for me when the war ended. So my parents gave me all the help possible, and you'll agree I was lucky to find Foxholes. Yes,' he went on musingly, 'I was damned lucky.'

He smiled at Marinda and ordered two more Martinis.

There was something unquenchable about him. Whatever happened to him, thought Marinda, he would make the best of it and count himself 'lucky'. She wondered why he had never married.

The next day, as they sat before her drawing-room fire, eating Nellie's slightly too solid plum cake, he told her. The tunes from *Bittersweet* were still running in her head and something in Robert's cheerful company and the supper at Valentine's had lifted her out of the misery of the last few months.

The purchase of his sheep had not appeared to be an unduly urgent matter and he had accepted her invitation to tea with noticeable speed. Over it they exchanged selected portions of their past histories and Marinda was suddenly tempted to tell him about Mark, but she bit her tongue on the words and listened to his deep agreeable voice.

'I got engaged in the war,' he was saying. 'We all did. It was part of the madness. Fortunately before I could get leave to marry her she threw me over for a gallant captain with two thousand a year.' His grin took the bite out of his words. 'It was a bit of luck in the end, because she was the kind of girl who'd never have lived out of sight of street lamps. We hadn't a thing in common and I often wonder what on earth we talked about. I suppose the answer is that we didn't. Love is such a thing of the senses.' He gave a deep sigh. 'Of course, I was heartbroken at the time.'

'I don't believe it.'

'But I was. I do assure you. I became a woman-hater. Look at me.'

He leaned back comfortably in Edward's chair and invited her gaze. She looked across the hearth and considered his brown, healthy skin and the piercing blueness of his eyes. The shoe on his artificial leg, unwrinkled and new-looking, and a scarcely perceptible limp were all that one could see of his war scars. He could dance, he could ride and even play tennis with such hopeful energy that pity was quenched.

'I didn't realize you were a woman-hater.'

'Ah! But I don't hate you.'

Suddenly he was serious. The light atmosphere changed. He looked away from her into the fire and spoke slowly. 'I've always thought you were rather wonderful,' he said quietly. 'I mean, the way you ran the farm, and I know how well you did that. The first six months I was there I used to be sick of Jeff talking about the way Miss Marinda did this and that. And then your life here. You're successful in so many ways.'

'I don't feel in the least successful, and it wasn't such a violent change as you imagine. My husband, Edward, he always helped me so much at Foxholes. He was the first person to put profit and loss into my head. I don't believe any Fairfield had ever thought of farming except as a way of life. And then my interest here was gradual after all; even after Edward – died – I only took to it as a sort of drug. And now I miss it.'

'Yes, I suppose so. Have you any plans?'

Marinda thought what a solace, what a blessed solace it might be to tell him about Mark, to explain to him that she seemed to be living in some hideous half-life until she saw Mark again and that the future balanced dangerously on what Mark might do or say. It seemed somehow as if Sue, by dying, had not set them free, but had left them in some bondage of the spirit which made marriage an indecent procedure. Confronted with the possibility of Mark as a husband, she was not sure that she wanted him. This conflict, which was nowadays the exhausting accompaniment to any thought about her future, cleared a little as she talked to Robert.

'I'm selling this house, if I can find anyone who will buy it, and I'm taking a flat, at least that was the idea.'

'You hadn't thought of coming back to Farley?'

'Well, I had, but now Mother and Father talk of going to live with my Aunt Emma in Marchampton. They seem to think they may like it. I can't imagine why. My plans depend on so many things.'

They depended on Mark. He could, by the crack in his voice, entice her to Paris, make her laugh, make her cry, write a sonnet to her eyebrow and effectively remove her sense of duty.

She gave a little shiver. Carey had been right. She was afraid of Mark.

'I can't help hoping you'll come back to Farley,' said Robert. He hesitated, as if he were searching his mind for words, stroking the arm of his chair with his long, square-tipped fingers. At last he said, 'I think we could be friends.'

'Yes, I think we could.'

Marinda had in her life received many unexpected declarations of love, and she thought she was experienced enough to recognize the signs, but she was unprepared for Robert's next words.

'More than friends,' he said, and looked at her with a question in his eyes. Then he said gravely, with his restless hands suddenly still, his eyes steady with resolve, 'Could you marry me, do you think?'

Marinda shook her head and tried to smile. The bright look left his face and he felt in his pocket for his cigarette-case.

'I – shouldn't have asked,' he said.

Marinda stretched out her hand, and he crushed it so tightly it became nothing in his fingers.

'Oh, Robert, if I only could say "Yes" – if only I could.'

'Was it cruel of me to ask? I don't want to make you sad.'

Marinda stared at him and slowly it dawned on her that he was thinking of Edward, and she realized that Edward, for all his calm influence and the sudden realization of his passion before he died, had never filled her thoughts as Mark did. It was Mark who now prevented her from marrying Robert Shipley.

She was again oppressed by a compelling desire to tell him.

'It sounds a hard thing to say, Robert, but it isn't Edward. You know, after a while one doesn't exactly forget, but one can remember without it hurting. It's –'

'It's not someone else?'

Marinda held her breath.

'Yes.'

'Ah,' said Robert, releasing her hand and leaning back

in his chair. 'I was afraid of that.'

'I'm terribly sorry. I wish to heaven it weren't so.'

'I hope you will be very happy.'

He rose to go, and although Marinda felt she was losing a dear friend she made no effort to keep him.

'I don't think I shall ever be happy,' she said.

'I'm sorry.'

'Don't be sorry. I am a fool, and everything is my own fault. I just don't learn.'

'Do any of us?'

At the door he looked at her again. 'Don't forget I'd do anything for you, anything, any time.'

He spoke slowly, emphasizing the words.

She nodded, finding herself very near to tears.

'Remember that.'

'I will.'

He walked squarely down the steps to the short path, with only the merest trace of a limp. At the gate he turned and waved, and she realized that his usual wide smile was not there and she shut the door feeling that she had been to a funeral. She imagined him in ten years' time telling some other woman how lucky he was, and she found the thought depressing.

Chapter 23 — THE LAST DAY

'It doesn't seem possible that I've been over a year selling this benighted house,' said Marinda to Carey in November, 1930, 'but I simply had to get as good a price for it as I could. My shares aren't doing so well at Stonebridges. It's this awful slump. The figures have never been so low. I am sorry for Sprake. He has had to sack a lot of people. I'm sure I could never have done that. Edward used to say if I had my way I'd employ nobody but those with widowed mothers and ten children. I certainly couldn't sack a man in cold blood. Have you seen the queues at the Labour Exchanges?'

'They say it will get worse. It's only just beginning.'

'The people who have bought this house are making it

into flats. I might have thought of that myself. They want to be in by December, a god-forsaken time to choose, and even now I haven't found a flat.'

'I don't believe you are really looking. There are heaps of flats.'

'You don't know anything about it.'

'Well, as a matter of fact, I do.' Carey turned round suddenly on the piano stool and said, 'I am going to be married.'

'What!'

'Don't sound so astonished. It isn't polite!'

'But you've never said a word about it.'

'One doesn't have to, you know, and I rather felt you'd been sort of far away lately, looking for flats and selling the house and so on. And anyway, I've suffered so much from human outpourings myself I – well, I don't know how it happened.'

'But who on earth to?'

'I wish you wouldn't sound so utterly disbelieving,' said Carey, laughing. 'It's Hal Merryweather. I met him six months ago and he proposed on Gloucester Road Underground Station last Monday morning.'

'Nobody could expect to be accepted on a Monday morning.'

'He was lucky, then. I accepted with alacrity though I must say I was pretty surprised myself. It's rather disarming to be loved.'

Marinda had often tried mild matchmaking for Carey. There were times, if she took trouble with her clothes, when she might be considered good-looking, even handsome, but she was unaware of it, and if this had not been so she would not have cared. She had no knack of attracting men, who were often disconcerted by the look in her bright brown eyes, which saw through all artifice.

'Oh, Carey, I hope you'll be awfully happy. I'm terribly glad, really I am, only sort of surprised.'

'Well you may be – so am I – but there it is.'

She faced Marinda with her hands folded in her lap.

'It just shows what fools women are,' she said. 'I can see myself being perfectly stupid about Hal. Can you imagine it? Marinda, I'm melting, I'm softening, particularly my brain.'

'When are you getting married?'

'Don't ask me. Let me get used to being engaged first.'

She whirled the stool round and began to play the Wedding March, Tum tum te TUM. Tum tum te TUM. 'Lor' love a duck, Marinda, but I am happy.'

'You must bring him to dinner.'

She tried to get used to the idea of Carey married to anyone at all, most of all to this unknown Hal Merryweather. He was a barrister, Carey told her, lived in the Temple, was rather plain, quite clever, people said. He was toying with the idea of standing for the Conservatives at the next election.

'No, I'd forgotten. You can't bring him to dinner while we are in this state,' said Marinda. 'Nellie is determined to have everything cleaned and garnished and by next week we shan't have a carpet or curtain in the place. If I haven't got a flat by then I shall shove it all into Harrods' Store and go down to Mother's for Christmas.'

'I can't think why you don't go back and live there. Not necessarily with your people, but get a cottage somewhere near. You've never really become a Londoner.'

Marinda thought lovingly of a small dream house in Marchshire, with a garden and a white gate and sun catching the windows. She couldn't explain that the reason she had to live in London was Mark. She couldn't go back to Farley if she married Mark, and certainly not if he became her lover. She had to have somewhere where her affairs could be anonymous and lost, some hidden perch of her own where she could persuade herself that what she did was her own business.

In her desk was a letter from Robert.

Dear Marinda (he wrote),

I hope you won't mind hearing from me, but I thought of you the other day – not that I don't do that often – but the other day I heard that those two cottages at the back of the church in Farley St George are likely to be vacant in the spring. Old Miss Leggit has died and the sister won't live next door by herself. It could be knocked into one and would make a rather charming house. I quite itch to have a hand in it. I only mention this because your mother said that you hadn't found a flat and she hoped perhaps you might come back to Farley. If you do, I should be awfully glad, and I solemnly promise that I will never be a nuisance if I can help it. I hope all goes well with you.

Yours as always,

Robert.

P.S. The camellia is planted.

She said nothing of this to Carey, because in her bag was a letter from Mark.

Marinda dearest (wrote Mark),

I am coming back to Europe in the Bremen, *and as soon as I have settled some tiresome business in Germany I shall come to London and might stay a week or a month. I don't know. We must have some time together. Duff is settled at last with my brother. He felt his mother's death very much. My nerves behave badly and make work difficult. Did you see 'Winter Sun' in the Standard Review? Not bad, I thought. Wish I knew. Write to me c/o G.P.O. Hamburg.*

Yours, my dear love,

Mark.

As yet she had made no reply to either.

From the moment the house was sold life mysteriously left it. It seemed to reject her, thought Marinda, as she tore up letters at her desk on the last day of November. Too late, she realized the folly of not leaving at least one room where she might be comfortable, but Nellie had so arranged it that the house was a carpetless waste. Chairs, bereft of their light chintzes, showed unexpectedly dreary underclothes, and the bare windows leered uncomfortably. On the carpetless floors, footsteps echoed through the house. Carey had promised to support her on the day, but Carey in love proved undependable, and for the moment she was lost to Marinda.

It seemed as if all the thwarted affection of two hitherto unloved creatures had spilled out and was now making them faintly ridiculous. Their behaviour in public made Marinda blush for them. Hal's hands seemed always to be touching Carey, as if they were magnetized. His desire for her leapt out of his eyes almost indecently, and Carey, the sensible Carey, revelled in it. Her happiness gave her a kind of bloom and dulled her conversation. Marinda was glad to see her friend in such a state of bliss, but she missed the rational biting comments of the old Carey, and for the first time in her life she envied her.

Nellie had put a ban on coal fires after her orgy of scrubbing, and Marinda sat back on her heels by the electric fire and re-read Mark's letter, trying to find in it some note of certainty. She let the affectionate ending repeat itself in her mind. She was 'his dear love'.

She could not bring herself to tear up Mark's letter and now she turned to her desk to write to Robert. She longed to accept his offer of the cottage at Farley St George, but she was held back by the possibility of seeing Mark.

Dear Robert (she wrote),

It was awfully kind of you to think of the cottage for me, and I am sorry I have been so long in making up my mind. It sounds very enticing, but I think . . .

She paused, and wondered what indeed it was that she thought.

I think a flat in London will be more convenient for my plans.

She had no plans. She was rudderless, probably homeless, and her income was nearly halved. All this she had done for Mark.

Thank you very much indeed for your kindness,
Yours most sincerely,
Marinda Stonebridge.

P.S. I hope the camellia thrives.

Stamping the letter, she gave it to Nellie, who had come in with the tea.

'Leave it in the hall with the others,' said Marinda. 'I will go out to the post with it later on. I should like some air.'

'There's a fog coming down,' said Nellie gloomily, hanging a dust-sheet over the windows to protect them from the eyes of the passer-by. The waste-paper basket filled as Marinda felt that she was tearing up all evidence that she had lived at all. On her desk burned one table lamp, and she sat illumined by its light, while the rest of the sheeted room was lost in the shadows.

Then, outlined, in the doorway, there was a stranger.

'I've just caught you,' said Mark. 'I hoped I would.'

She stood up uncertainly, ready to be taken into his arms, but the width of the room was between them. The night was cold, and the electric fire warmed, but did not cheer the air.

'Oh, Mark –' she wanted to say. 'How wonderful to see you,' but she could not. It was no longer true.

She pushed the sofa into the orbit of the fire and looked at him. A nerve in her neck fluttered with the irregular beats of her heart. She was conscious of all the inadequacies of the room, the thin layer of dust on the mantelshelf, the slum-like appearance of the windows, and the rattle of their feet on the boards as they moved nearer to each other. She was not a woman who was habitually untidy, but today she had shrugged herself into an old, unbecoming jersey, with a button missing and a small hole beginning in the elbow. An embarrassed frown creased her eyebrows together, although she knew that to Mark surroundings were, on occasions, matters of supreme unimportance. He could be more put out by a picture he did not like than furniture made of packing-cases.

He now sank back on the dust-sheeted sofa as if it were a throne, and held out both his hands to Marinda.

'When did you come?' she asked.

'Last week, Thursday, no Tuesday. Time goes so quickly.'

So he had been in London nearly a week and she had not known. He had not even telephoned.

'Where are you staying?'

'With the Webbes.'

'And Duff?'

'Oh, Duff. Well, at last he seems all right again. I had trouble with him for a long time – after –'

He paused as if he couldn't pronounce Sue's name.

'He was very fond of Sue,' said Marinda.

'She made a fool of him.'

'Did she? I thought she brought him up pretty well – considering.'

'Considering what?' Mark grinned. He looked like a fox with a sense of humour. He answered for her. 'Considering what a shocking creature I am, isn't that it?'

Marinda's lips curved upwards into her endearing smile.

'You aren't a good father,' she said.

'I'm not a good anything.'

'But Duff?'

'He's with Polly and Bill. They've got two kids of their own, younger than Duffy, a boy and a girl. They spend all summer at the sea and have a heavenly time, and in the winter they are just outside New York. He will go to an American High School where no one minds his foreignness, and then to College. You know he'd have hated it here. God knows I hated it, and Duff hasn't my tough hide.'

'I shouldn't have thought that poets had tough hides,' she mocked him gently. 'Don't they have to be sensitive?'

'Of course they do. And I am, aren't I? Darling Marinda, aren't I?'

'Oh, I don't know. What do I know about you, anyway?'

'Almost everything. That's what makes me nervous of you. You see through the top layer, and I find I can't deceive you.'

She leant back against the desk playing with a pencil.

'Don't stay miles away as if you were interviewing me for a job,' he said, patting the dust-sheet by his side, and she walked over to the sofa and sat beside him, erect with one thin arm folded over the other, one finger playing with the hole in her jersey.

'I'd like to deceive you, but I can't,' he went on.

She realized that she had altered her whole life for him and he had not asked one word about herself or her parents or her plans. She began to interrupt him to tell him about her search for a flat, but before her lips were closed on the words he repeated, 'I wish I could deceive you, Marinda.'

'Why? I don't want to be deceived any more than anyone else. What a silly expression anyway, between friends.'

He took her hands again and doubled the fingers gently and then crushed them together, kissed the tips and put them back in her lap as if he were giving her a present.

'I should never have made you happy,' he said with sudden decision, as if his mind had travelled a long way since his last words.

'People don't always want happiness.'

'Rubbish, of course they do, and they ought to have it. You ought to have it – I ought to have it –'

He paused and there was a moment of such stillness that Marinda found herself listening to the tinny vibrations of the electric fire and the beating of her own heart. Her meetings with Mark, she reflected, were simply small isolated blocks of time. Her life and his in between these meetings seemed to have no relation to the present. He never spoke of it and he was apparently uninterested in her, except for this present distilled moment. There was so much she wanted to tell him about her parents, about Carey, about herself, and it came to her suddenly that she desperately needed someone with a sympathetic heart which would receive her worries, large and small, and Mark was not that person.

'You haven't heard the news about me, then?' he said.

'No. Oh, Mark, not *The Fishers*? Have you finished it?'

'I shall, in good time. Don't hurry me.' His voice grated with irritation.

He opened his wallet and she thought he was about to produce a press-cutting. With a faint smile he looked at a square of cardboard before handing it to her. It was a photograph and at first glance it seemed to her that it must be a last unrecognizable snapshot of Sue, until she realized that Sue had died a tired, ill woman, bordering on middle age, and this was a young girl. She had the same tilted nose as Sue, the same short curls, but she had a squarer chin, higher cheekbones, which gave her an air of determination that had never belonged to Sue.

'She's German, but her mother is American.'

Marinda continued to look at the photograph, not

daring to look up in case her face should reveal the feelings which chased round her brain and took the strength from her body.

'I'm going to marry her,' said Mark, stretching out his hand for the photograph.

'Are you?' said Marinda, holding it out to him. Their fingers touched as he took it, and suddenly it meant nothing. Mark meant nothing. She was rid of him. She was free from his enchantment.

'Aren't I a fool?' he said, laughing a little. 'I could have you and I tie myself up again to someone who is too young to understand me.'

Carey's words came back to Marinda, 'Mark doesn't need understanding, he needs a strait-jacket.'

'Why should you suppose you could have had me?' she said, her voice proud with resentment.

'If only you'd stayed with me last year – if Sue hadn't died just then.'

She got up: 'If – if – if. Heavens! I'm sorrier now for Sue than I ever was, and I'm sorry for – what's she called?'

She nodded violently in the direction of the photograph still in his hands.

'Helga,' he answered.

'Well, I am sorry for Helga, and you can tell her so.'

'She adores me.'

'I am glad to hear it. I thought you found being adored strangling, suffocating, you used to say.'

He stopped laughing. 'Good lord, Marinda, you're right. I don't now, but I shall do. I know it's going to happen, and yet I am powerless. It's like being mesmerized.'

'Carey always said people never learn, that they make the same mistakes over and over again. Did you know she is being married?'

'No, really?' He was surprised but uninterested. Only his own affairs concerned him, the working of *his* mind, the needs of *his* body and then, a long way off, like midgets on a stage, the affairs of the rest of the world.

'I'm such a fool I don't deserve to be happy. I've missed two chances of marrying you, darling.'

'I don't suppose I would have looked at you,' said Marinda untruthfully. Her thoughts were dulled by a great weariness. The years had deepened the lines by Mark's mouth. She noticed for the first time the thinness of his upper lip and that his smile was outlined with faint cruelty.

'Of course you'd have looked at me. I'd have made you. No, I couldn't. You're the one person I can never force. I've no control over you. If I could have kept you in Czeny . . . Remember?'

She remembered with a dart of pain a composite picture of sun and sharp shadows and the pungent smell of the pine trees.

'We were both a little mad then,' she said.

'I am much happier when I am a little mad.'

The clock began to whirr with the preliminary excitement of striking six.

'I'll ring for the sherry,' said Marinda.

She seldom rang a bell and was relieved when Nellie answered it with due decorum. While they were waiting for it they talked in different voices of harmless things. Mark enquired politely of her parents. Marinda was able to tell him about her search for a flat. He made murmurs of interest which did not deceive her, and she was appalled at her own idiocy in trying to arrange her life to fit in with his.

'When do you go?'

'Tomorrow. I am going back to Farley.' Suddenly she found herself adding: 'I am going to live there. I belong there.'

The upheaval now seemed useless. The glasses chinked as Nellie arranged them on a small table.

'You pour it out,' she said. 'I hope it's a decent one. I've begun to know a bad sherry, but I cannot always recognize a good one.'

'You have learnt a great many things since you left Foxholes.'

'Yes. Not all of them either necessary or useful.'

She lifted her glass and drank gratefully and her body warmed and her heart revived. Mark leaned back and she thought with horror, 'He'll stay for hours.' She longed for him to go so that she could lie down somewhere alone in the dark to stop her head throbbing.

'It's quite good, this sherry,' said Mark. He sipped it enquiringly as if he were not sure why it should be good. Marinda handed him the cigarette-box and took one herself.

'I thought you didn't smoke.'

'I hardly ever do, only in moments of stress.'

'Is this one?'

She avoided the question. 'I've had a hard day,' she said and blinked. The pain in one side of her head seemed scarcely bearable, as if a nail were being driven slowly into her brain.

'I never noticed your eyes were green,' said Mark, and Marinda realized that all she had been saying about the business of putting the furniture into store had gone by unheard.

'They aren't green – they're a sort of grey-brown.'

'But they are green,' he insisted.

'Oh, that's only because I'm wearing green.' She looked deprecatingly at her old clothes, which she had worn to help Nellie clear out the attic, and wished she had bothered herself to change. 'It's the reflection. They can be any colour.' She fixed her cool gaze upon him. Now there was no emotion left for him except the beginnings of dislike.

'The only changeable thing in you,' he said, and continued to look at her with his sherry glass at arm's length in an attitude that was lazy, but not without grace.

'When are you getting married?'

It did not hurt her to ask. She merely wanted to know.

'Soon, in the New Year. Write and tell your people for me, there's a dear. They ought to know, I suppose. We've already had an engagement party which was worse than marriage. Germans believe in tying you down so that you can't escape.'

'You're like a man we had in the factory who was a prisoner of war, and once he told me he had an odd feeling of longing to go back.'

'You mean, I walk back into the same cage? And you will still be outside sending me files in a loaf of bread.'

'Don't flatter yourself.'

She could see he did not believe her. In his conceit he thought that whenever he wanted her she would be there.

And now she knew that this was not so.

She found she was not listening to him. For the first time his caressing voice meant nothing to her. She did not hate him as she had done when Edward died. She did not love him as she had as a girl. At Czeny she had been disturbed by her own physical desires and for the past year she had been tormented by uncertainty, and what she supposed was her conscience. Now indifference laid its steady hand upon her. She was able to criticize, she was able to laugh. It was like bathing in a cold sea.

He said goodbye at last, kissing her cheek gently, unconscious of any change in her, while she made conventional wishes for his happiness and asked him for Duff's address. Turning up his coat collar, and giving a little shiver, he walked down the steps into the fog. It swallowed him, even before his footsteps were dulled and he became a wraith.

Her unposted letter to Robert lay beside the evening paper on the hall table, and into her mind flashed a series of pictures, the skyline of the March Hills, the willows dipping their branches in the river, the new camellia Robert had planted. They seemed to merge into one, which was simply Foxholes. The vision was gilded by time and distance and longing, so that improbable sunlight bathed it. Slowly, with relief, she tore the letter across and then across again.

She picked up the evening paper, and read the headlines without assimilating them. 'Gale in the . . .' Her headache made the words swim a little. She hugged herself inside her jersey and shivered, wishing she could surrender to this malaise and spend a day in bed. But the work of tomorrow was already starting its preliminary exercises in her overtired brain, a more exhausting process than the day itself.

Everywhere in the house was the smell of the fog. She dropped the paper and went in search of aspirin, each step on the stairs turning a knife in her head. Sitting on the edge of her bed, gulping water and aspirin, she reviewed the last two hours solemnly, as if they had happened to someone else. In the mirror she saw herself reflected, and she watched the image of her features grimace as she began to cry.

FICTION

GENERAL		
☐ **Stand on It**	Stroker Ace	95p
☐ **Chains**	Justin Adams	£1.25
☐ **The Master Mechanic**	I. G. Broat	£1.50
☐ **Wyndward Passion**	Norman Daniels	£1.35
☐ **Abingdon's**	Michael French	£1.25
☐ **The Moviola Man**	Bill and Colleen Mahan	£1.25
☐ **Running Scared**	Gregory Mcdonald	85p
☐ **Gossip**	Marc Olden	£1.25
☐ **The Sounds of Silence**	Judith Richards	£1.00
☐ **Summer Lightning**	Judith Richards	£1.00
☐ **The Hamptons**	Charles Rigdon	£1.35
☐ **The Affair of Nina B.**	Simmel	95p
☐ **The Berlin Connection**	Simmel	£1.50
☐ **The Cain Conspiracy**	Simmel	£1.20
☐ **Double Agent—Triple Cross**	Simmel	£1.35
☐ **Celestial Navigation**	Anne Tyler	£1.00
☐ **Earthly Possessions**	Anne Tyler	95p
☐ **Searching for Caleb**	Anne Tyler	£1.00
WESTERN BLADE SERIES		
☐ **No. 1 The Indian Incident**	Matt Chisholm	75p
☐ **No. 2 The Tucson Conspiracy**	Matt Chisholm	75p
☐ **No. 3 The Laredo Assignment**	Matt Chisholm	75p
☐ **No. 4 The Pecos Manhunt**	Matt Chisholm	75p
☐ **No. 5 The Colorado Virgins**	Matt Chisholm	85p
☐ **No. 6 The Mexican Proposition**	Matt Chisholm	75p
☐ **No. 7 The Arizona Climax**	Matt Chisholm	85p
☐ **No. 8 The Nevada Mustang**	Matt Chisholm	85p
WAR		
☐ **Jenny's War**	Jack Stoneley	£1.25
☐ **The Killing-Ground**	Elleston Trevor	£1.10
NAVAL HISTORICAL		
☐ **The Sea of the Dragon**	R. T. Aundrews	95p
☐ **Ty-Shan Bay**	R. T. Aundrews	95p
☐ **HMS Bounty**	John Maxwell	£1.00
☐ **The Baltic Convoy**	Showell Styles	95p
☐ **Mr. Fitton's Commission**	Showell Styles	85p
FILM/TV TIE-IN		
☐ **American Gigolo**	Timothy Harris	95p
☐ **Meteor**	E. H. North and F. Coen	95p
☐ **Driver**	Clyde B. Phillips	80p

NAME ....

ADDRESS ....

....

Write to Hamlyn Paperbacks Cash Sales, PO Box 11, Falmouth, Cornwall TR10 9EN.

Please indicate order and enclose remittance to the value of the cover price plus:

U.K.: 30p for the first book, 15p for the second book and 12p for each additional book ordered to a maximum charge of £1.29.

B.F.P.O. & EIRE: 30p for the first book, 15p for the second book plus 12p per copy for the next 7 books, thereafter 6p per book.

OVERSEAS: 50p for the first book plus 15p per copy for each additional book.

Whilst every effort is made to keep prices low it is sometimes necessary to increase cover prices and also postage and packing rates at short notice. Hamlyn Paperbacks reserve the right to show new retail prices on covers which may differ from those previously advertised in the text or elsewhere.